© Copyright by Aja

MW00413115

Dear Reader:

I hope you will enjoy the third installment of the *Dark Ones* saga on the following pages (Book #4 in Pure/ Dark Series). You will soon see that much more is yet to come.

Every story has many points of view, many different interpretations and versions of the truth. So what about the perspective from the Pure Ones' POV? If you're curious, check out the story that started it all, *Pure Healing*.

Email me at megami771@yahoo.com to find out more. And follow me on https://www.facebook.com/AjaJamesAuthor and https://aja-james.blog/. I will have free chapters and other goodies on Book #5 Pure Rapture, available for pre-order.

And also check out Book 2, *Dark Longing*, and Book 3, *Dark Desires*.

I love hearing from you!

Enjoy!

Aja James

Glossary of Terms

Blood-Contract: Contract by which a human Consents to surrender his/her blood (and sometimes soul) to a vampire for a promise in return that the vampire must fulfill. The vampire has the choice to accept or reject the Contract. Upon acceptance, he/she must fulfill the bargain or risk retribution from the unfulfilled human soul in the form of a curse. See also Consent.

Blooded Mate: the chosen partner for each Dark One. Once the Bond is formed between two Dark Ones, it cannot be broken unless a third party has prior claim of blood or flesh. The third party can elicit a Challenge to one of the Bonded Dark Ones to obtain rights to the other. The Challenge is fought to the death. Save in the case of a successful Challenge, the Bond cannot be broken except through death. Blooded Mates do not need to take the blood and souls of others to survive. However, they must take blood and sex from each other on a regular basis, else they will weaken and eventually go mad and/or die.

The Chosen: six royal guards of the New York-based Vampire Queen, Jade Cicada.

Consent: a human's willing agreement to surrender his/her blood (and sometimes soul) to a vampire.

Dark Goddess: supernatural being who is credited with the creation of the Dark Ones. She is a deity to which Dark Ones pray. It is unclear how or whether she is related to the Pure Ones' Goddess. See also The Goddess.

Dark Laws: One, thou shalt protect the Universal Balance to which all souls contribute. Two, thou shalt maintain the secrecy of the Race. Three, thou shalt not take an innocent's blood, life, or soul without Consent.

Dark One: supernatural being who prefers to live in the night and who gathers energy and prolongs his/her life by feeding off the blood, and sometimes souls, of others. Dark Ones are born, not made. Sometimes confused with the term *vampire*.

Decline: condition in which or process of a Pure-Ones' life force depleting after he/she Falls in love but does not receive equal love in return. The Pure One weakens and his/her body slowly, painfully breaks down over the course of thirty days, leading ultimately to death unless his/her love is returned in equal measure.

The Elite: six royal personal guards of the Pure Queen.

Eternal Mate: the destined partner to a given Pure soul. Each soul only has one mate across time, across various incarnations of life. Quotation from the Zodiac Scrolls describing the bond: "His body is the Nourishment of life. Her energy is the Sustenance of soul."

Gift: supernatural power bestowed upon Pure Ones by the Goddess. Usually an enhanced physical or mental ability such as telekinesis, superhuman strength and telepathy.

The Goddess: supernatural being who is credited with the creation of the Pure Ones. She is a deity to which Pure Ones devote themselves. She protects the Universal Balance.

The Great War: circa 2190 B.C., the Pure Ones who had been enslaved by the Dark Ones rebelled against their oppressors en masse. At the end of countless years of bloodshed, the Pure Ones ultimately regained their freedom, and the Dark Ones' empire lay in ruins with the members of the Royal Hive scattered to the ends of the earth.

Nourishment: the strength that Mated Dark Ones take from each other's blood and body through sexual intercourse. Once Mated, they will no longer need others' blood to survive, only that from each other. Sexual intercourse is required to make the Nourishment sustaining.

Pure One: supernatural being who is eternally youthful, typically endowed with heightened senses or powers called the Gift. In possession of a pure soul and blessed with more than one chance at life by the Goddess, chosen as one of Her immortal race that defends the Universal Balance.

Shield: referred to as the base of the Royal Zodiac, wherever it may be. Not necessarily a physical location.

True Blood: a vampire born of Dark parents. See also Dark One.

Vampire: supernatural being who prefers to live in the night and who gathers energy and prolongs his/her life by feeding off the blood, and sometimes souls, of others. Contrary to prevalent beliefs (see Book 1: *Pure Healing*), vampires are both made and born. Some vampires are Pure Ones who have chosen Darkness rather than death after they break the Cardinal Rule. Some are humans turned by other vampires. Some are True Bloods that are born of a vampire mother or father, more accurately called Dark Ones.

Prologue

Hi again. It's me, Sophia.

It's been a while since you heard from me, I know, you're probably wondering where I've been...

Or not.

I mean, I'll be the first to admit that I'm the least interesting amongst all of the beautiful, fascinating, kick-ass Pure and Dark Ones (or as my pint-sized protégée Benji would say "Elves and Vampires") in my immediate circle.

And me being me, an ordinary human college student playing at being Queen of the Pure Ones, well, I'm not terribly interesting in the grand scheme of things.

After all, I've only lived a measly nineteen years, not a whole lot of living when compared to the hundreds and thousands that my Pure and Dark friends have experienced.

I just finished up my sophomore year at Harvard (still have no idea how I got in, but thankfully, no one has filed any petition to kick me out yet) and about to start my summer internship at the MET in NYC.

I'll be helping to curate their long-anticipated exhibit on ancient Persia. Unlike previous exhibits, this one will focus more on the daily life of Persian men, women and children rather than artifacts from war.

I love getting inside peeks to how people in ancient history lived, the clothes they wore, the books they read, the food they ate, their daily rituals and nightly prayers.

Sometimes I feel like I've lived these lives despite my measly nineteen human years. And when I look in the mirror, I don't always recognize the person that looks back at me.

One small interesting fact is that I have a Pure soul. The soul of a long-lost Pure Queen.

Which is why I was sought out and put upon the figurative throne at the age of seven. And the Dozen expects me to have my Awakening sometime in the near future because of what the Pure Seer, Eveline Marceau, divined from the Zodiac Prophesies.

So I guess that means I *have* lived a few (or many, as the case may be) past lives. Because humans with Pure souls are generally Pure Ones who have died and are reborn.

Pretty dizzying stuff, right?

I try not to dwell on it. I'm focusing on surviving the last of my teenage years. I'm only a stone's throw away from my twenties. Feels like I ought to suck it up and embrace my womanhood, take on more responsibility, act more mature, and maybe stop playing hours at the latest fighting games and empire building stuff online.

Maybe finally get a boyfriend or at least finagle a first kiss.

Okay, okay, I know what you're thinking. How lame is this girl, who's never been kissed! Never mind the whole hymen-still-intact thing.

It's not totally my fault, let's be clear.

First, it's kind of difficult to meet anyone and strike up an acquaintance when one always has a slew of bodyguards at one's side.

Matter of fact, I'm here in NYC "escorted" by three of the most powerful ancient warriors—Inanna the Light-Bringer, Gabriel her Blooded Mate (and one of the fiercest fighters in Akkad from his previous life), and Inanna's father Tal, who's *the* legendary General harkening back to the time of the Great War millennia ago when he led Pure Ones to victory against their Dark suppressors and changed the course of history.

Side note, Tal is *extremely* attractive for a male of his vintage. I'm rather in awe of him.

Second, I have to be really careful on the dating front, because Pure Ones who have sex with anyone other than their Eternal Mate will die a slow, excruciating death within thirty days.

Or, if given the choice, become Dark Ones who must live off of others' blood to survive. It's wired into the DNA. Probably the cost for remaining eternally youthful.

If it were up to me, I'd probably just take the sex and the average human lifespan, if the tales Aella, my best and only girlfriend who also happens to be an Elite warrior, tells me are true, and all the romance novels I read with the scorching sex scenes are to be believed.

And yeah, I'm still human, so the Cardinal Rule might not apply to me, but you never know.

What if I have my Awakening and don't know it (highly unlikely but who's to say)? What if my DNA already carries the code for self-destruction just waiting to be triggered by The One? Or rather, the 3.8 billion or so of Not-Ones?

And thirdly, perhaps most pertinent, I just haven't met anyone I'd take that risk for.

Well, maybe I have, but since he's been AWOL for over a year now, I've determined to put him from my conscious mind.

My dreams, on the other hand... he features more often than I'd like to admit in those.

But enough about me. I started this conversation to update you on what's happening more broadly.

You'll recall we battled (and won) against a devious vampire foe a couple of years ago—still don't know whether it was a he or a she, that strange, evil, yet hauntingly beautiful creature—at great cost to our own. We are still searching for replacements to complete the Dozen.

Progress has been made on the baby front though, as a means of repopulation, what with Isolde, Ayelet and Tristan's daughter, Benji, Inanna and Gabriel's adopted son, and now Kane (pronounced Kah-nay), Ryu and Ava's son.

I'm sure continuing the line of eternal races wasn't what prompted the making of these babies (queue the eye rolling), but nevertheless, perhaps one day, one or all of them will choose to take on critical roles for their Kind, just as their parents have before them.

As you may have guessed, we forged a temporary alliance with the New England Vampire Queen, Jade Cicada, and her Chosen warriors. Together, we investigated and successfully shut down an insidious fight club network that spawned right here in New York and executed the vampire traitor who led its expansion.

But in both cases, our ultimate nemesis—or nemeses—remain at large, and we continue our hunt for them.

Meanwhile, just because we settled things down in NY doesn't mean fight clubs have lost traction elsewhere in the world. Following that trail has led us to a mysterious entity called Medusa. We're relatively certain it's a female, and she's probably the mastermind behind all of the recent chaos and destruction.

Leading the hunt for Medusa as charged by the Dark Queen is the vampire Chosen warrior Devlin Sinclair.

I don't know much about him, to be honest with you. But I've heard he has pretty wicked, impressive *skills*. Not quite sure what Aella meant when she put the wink-wink-nudge-nudge emphasis on that word when she talked about the Hunter.

But I guess we'll soon find out.

Chapter One

How did a two-hundred-thirty-year-old vampire find himself on a blind date with a human female cyber genius?

A remote part of Devlin Sinclair's mind pondered this question with immense curiosity and astonishment while the rest of him focused on the task at hand.

"That seat is taken."

The Hunter of the Dark Ones flashed his most engaging and disarming of grins, nearly blinding the occupants of the nearby tables at Raoul's with its brilliance.

At the very least mesmerizing guests of the female variety.

"*Mith*, am I right?" he called the woman seated before him by her encrypted chat room handle, knowing full well that her name was actually Grace Elizabeth Darling. Twenty-nine years old, single, and wanted by several government agencies for her cyber hacking skills since the age of twelve.

She tipped her head slightly to one side and gave him a slow, meticulous, dispassionate appraisal from head to toe.

As if he were the restaurant's special menu for the evening, and she found every item on the list less than appetizing.

"You're not *Azor Ahai*," she stated with absolute certainty.

Devlin mentally rolled his eyes and stifled a sigh.

No, he was not the Prince Who Was Promised, according to George R.R. Martin's magnum opus *A Song of Ice and Fire*.

He wasn't even the man who used the name as his online handle in the chat room where he occasionally traded conversational volleys with Grace.

No, Devlin Sinclair, Marquess of Hartington in his human life, was the royal henchman to the New England vampire queen, Jade Cicada.

Devlin had, in the past few months, painstakingly insinuated himself into the role of Grace Darling's chat room flirtation so that he could track the elusive cyber genius down in the flesh.

"I am," Devlin said presently, blinking his eyes with innocence and injecting a slightly wounded look into his countenance at her immediate rejection of his identity.

She stared unblinkingly back at him, her expression unsmiling and devoid of any emotion.

"I expected you to be balding and pudgy, and maybe a foot shorter," she said.

"There are no pictures of me anywhere, I made sure of that," Devlin pointed out, though he knew that the real man *was* in fact as she described.

He'd chosen to get closer to her through this particular identity precisely because the man suffered from extreme paranoia and took care never to leave traces of himself. Who better to impersonate than a ghost on the Net and an invisible man in real life?

That, and the fact that he engaged in far more conversations and commanded more minutes of Grace's time than anyone else in cyber space, where she lived for fourteen out of her sixteen waking hours each day, ostensibly as the work-from-home Enterprise Architect at the hottest new tech startup Zenn.

It was a stroke of pure luck that Grace herself initiated this face-to-face meeting just as Devlin almost gave up on tracing her, though his own digital abilities were substantial.

But not as good as hers.

"I hacked some satellite images and filtered the distortion. I got one of you walking through Central Park while eating a Big Mac a couple of weeks ago."

There was no accusation or apology in her voice. She simply stated a fact and waited for him to refute or confirm.

Huh.

Devlin had to admire her resourcefulness, but he was not surprised. He would have expected no less given her skills.

"I must have had some sun glinting off my hair that day, which you mistook for the bald spot, and I was bundled in a heavy coat, which probably made me look a bit...fluffier," he suggested smoothly.

"It was nighttime."

"How forgetful of me," he corrected with another flash of teeth, but she didn't seem the least bit distracted by their brilliant whiteness.

"It was the light from the street lamps, not the sun."

She made no reply.

Instead, she unhurriedly took her napkin from her lap, put it back on the table, pushed her chair back, slung a small backpack onto one shoulder and got up to leave.

Devlin thought fast.

"How is Miu-Miu?"

She paused and looked up at him, her expression still a neutral mask.

"And Antony and Cleopatra?"

Devlin quickly glanced at his watch, quickly because he didn't trust her not to disappear in a puff of smoke if he took his eyes off her for even a millisecond.

"You don't need to go home to feed them for another few hours. Let's sit down and have our dinner, shall we? I, for one, am famished."

She stood there regarding him with that fathomless dark stare, and Devlin would have given half his considerable fortune to know what she was thinking.

He read people very easily; it was one of his many natural gifts. But this woman was a Sphinx as far as he was concerned.

Perhaps because in order for a human book to be read, there had to be emotional signatures, but in Grace's case, there was only cold logic. Encrypted cold logic.

Seeing that she was hesitant enough to at least remain stationary rather than dash out the door and disappear without a trace, Devlin pushed his luck further by walking around her and pulling out her chair again.

"Please do take a seat. This is your favorite restaurant, isn't it? It took some doing to get a reservation. I would hate to waste it."

He held his position for several seconds, one hand on the arm of her chair, one hand ever so lightly settling on her shoulder to guide her into the chair, while she considered her options.

But really, any choice she thought she had was an illusion.

Now that Devlin had seen her in the flesh, she would only escape him if he allowed it.

The Hunter never lost his prey.

*** *** *** ***

It was the barely-there touch on her shoulder that decided Grace.

She would stay for a meal with the impostor *Azor Ahai* and take him home with her afterwards.

If the rash of sparks that his glancing touch generated was any indication, sex with him would be nigh incinerating, and she was in a state of utmost arousal this night.

Grace sat down and waited for the stranger to likewise settle in the seat across from her.

Her arousal wasn't due to *him*, though aesthetically speaking, he was a priceless work of art:

Golden-honey waves of hair streaked with sunlight, perfectly symmetrical and evenly spaced features, dark blonde brows arching elegantly over heavily lashed bright blue eyes, the type of blue that sapphires envied.

A blade of a nose that drew attention to sculpted cheek bones and the fundamentally masculine hollows beneath, a wide, full mouth that looked like it smiled a lot, bracketed by faint grooves that hinted at dimples.

There were adjectives that most people might use to describe such a face. Handsome was too bland. Beautiful did not do justice to his overwhelming *maleness*. Gorgeous suggested something showy, not quite authentic.

This man knew full well the impact his looks had on others, and used it to further his own goals—like finagling a dinner with Grace even though he must know that she didn't buy his impersonation. But he didn't dwell on his magnificence (was that the right adjective?); he didn't invite attention.

He used it like a shield. A mirror to deflect attempts to see beyond the exterior. A mask that hid the man inside.

Grace's adjective for him was: intriguing.

And as she was hardly ever intrigued by anything, she decided to see how this would play out.

But equally, she simply wanted to jump his bones. Because his touch set her afire.

It was the closest she'd ever felt to a human being apart from her aunt Maria, who had raised her since she lost both her parents seventeen years ago.

But not the same kind of closeness.

Grace tried to differentiate the two feelings in her mind.

She wasn't good at identifying feelings much less categorizing them. Her psychiatrist was amazed she could identify feelings at all given her unique case of Asperger's, though putting a name to her "condition" wasn't quite accurate—scientists hadn't found the explanation yet for the faulty wiring in her brain.

Perhaps even in her DNA.

She tapped into her very limited emotional bank now and decided that the closeness she felt toward her aunt was soft and warm and safe.

Whereas the closeness she felt toward the male seated across the table from her was sharp and volcanic and extremely dangerous.

But she was intrigued.

His touch seemed to switch on a part of her that had always been dormant, and this alien part of herself pulled Grace into his orbit like steel flints to a Neodymium super magnet.

In an inner voice she'd never heard before, that part of her shouted *Take him! Lock him up somewhere and throw away the key! He's the answer to all of life's questions.* Your *life.* Your *questions. And the holy grail of puzzles that you will never solve but take endless pleasure in trying.*

Hmm. Maybe her arousal *was* infinitesimally due to him.

More to the point, it was that time of the month for her.

Every month, her hormones surged for a couple of days. Every six months, it lasted more than a few days, a two-week period during which she was especially aroused. She supposed every woman had her own cycles, and this was hers. Which was why she chose a sex partner every six months since she first discovered intercourse with the opposite sex at the age of twenty.

She was already isolated from the world because of her "condition." She couldn't relate to or interact with others like normal people. But during this time, when the planets aligned in her own peculiar solar system, she felt *alive*. She felt fundamentally female.

And she needed a male to fill and fulfill her.

So for the couple of months leading into her sexual crisis, she hunted one down and dragged him home to feed her inner beast.

She intended to *devour* this particular male.

As she speared him with her unblinking stare, he finished ordering for both of them, handed their menus to a flustered waitress who couldn't stop grinning at him like a teeth whitening commercial, and looked back at her.

He blinked rapidly at the intensity of her gaze, as if trying to snap himself out of hypnosis.

Yes, magnificent one, her inner harlot coaxed, *succumb to my will and obey all my commands. These next two weeks with me will be the best you've ever had.*

Grace was not boastful. Not even to herself. She pored over and studied every line and footnote of sex instruction manuals she could get her hands on, online and off.

Especially the tantric sex manuals. When her mind fixated on something, she was nothing if not thorough. And she'd practiced quite diligently on willing partners over the years that she felt her skill in this area had just about reached perfection.

This male was strong.

Though he was taken aback or perplexed by her unwavering gaze, he hadn't yet melted into a puddle under the hot rays of her stare. He neither tugged at his collar nor bobbed his Adam's apple in nervous swallows. He simply sat there and looked steadily back at her.

Perhaps he was intrigued by her as well.

"I hope you like my choice for you," he said, "You didn't respond when I asked what you want to order, so I took the liberty of ordering for us both. I seem to recall that you like seafood, especially of the shellfish variety."

She didn't comment, too busy sifting through the pieces of the puzzle that was this male.

One, he was definitely *not* her blind date. But he pretended to be.

Why?

Two, he obviously had special skills or special friends to be able to hack into the ultra-secure, exclusive chat room only cyber geeks of a certain caliber could get into, *and* he hacked the identity of a hacker.

Who was he?

Three, had she been chatting online with him all along or with the real *Azor Ahai*? Well, not the real one. There was no such thing. But the man who used the handle.

It was disturbing to think that she'd shared intimate bits of herself with an imposter. Slightly more disturbing than sharing with a complete stranger online in an anonymous chat room, anyway.

Four, he was quite ridiculously attractive, not just in looks but in the confidence with which he carried himself, the aura of raw power about him, the primal sexuality that all but magnetized the particles around his person like an energy field.

Even Grace, who usually experienced the world within a mental bubble of her own making that muffled most sounds and sensations, could feel his pull, like gravity.

Why was he going on a blind date with anyone, least of all her?

Five, where *did* his accent come from? He spoke in fluent American English, but with a crisp enunciation, grammar and vocabulary that seemed misplaced in the twenty-first century. The preciseness with which he spoke suggested that he either picked up the American accent later in life or learned English as an auxiliary language.

"A bit of wine?"

He didn't wait for her reply—wise, since she hadn't said a word since they sat down—and poured some into her goblet.

Grace wasn't a fan of alcohol. It ate at her control like mild acid. She disliked anything that disturbed her perfect management of everything around her, especially her own person. But some small sips of wine on a night like this, when she was practically vibrating with sexual tension, wouldn't go amiss.

Weird. She was starting to think like the way the stranger spoke. Like she was an actor in a Jane Austen movie.

"Where are you from?"

Grace blurted the question out loud, too curious to stop herself. She realized after the fact that she'd interrupted him mid-sentence.

He paused ever so briefly before answering, "Born and raised in England. But I've lived a number of years here in the States."

That explained his accent. Half of one question answered. Still didn't explain why he sounded so... anachronistic.

"Who are you?"

He opened his mouth to speak, but then she added, "Who are you really?"

He took some time before answering, cutting his medium-rare ribeye with an elegance that Grace had never witnessed before.

She watched, riveted, as he put the perfectly proportioned bite into his mouth and chewed silently with the same immaculate sophistication.

Her gaze fixated on his sensuous lips and sharp, angular jaw as it flexed in ways that made her thighs clench under the table. When his smooth, pale throat undulated in a swallow, her core shuddered in response.

Oh, she definitely chose him because of *him*. A realization that was new and alarming for Grace.

"My name is Devlin Sinclair," he finally answered. "And you?"

Grace regarded him closely. She could always tell when people lied. She herself lied with no hindrance, though she seldom saw the need to. She could beat any lie-detector test. All you had to do was truly believe in what you say. Most psychopaths and sociopaths had the same ability.

No wonder the FBI took her into custody.

"Grace Darling."

He smiled a little, crinkling the corners of his bright blue eyes.

"Lovely name," he murmured, and she felt the compliment ripple over her skin like a gentle caress.

He paused in his methodical demolishment of his steak to regard her, as if just realizing something puzzling.

"Why aren't you eating?" he asked. "The food here is quite good, as you should know, since you come here at least twice a month."

Ah, so he'd done his own reconnaissance on her. Grace didn't recall telling him about this habit.

"I'm not hungry," she replied.

He dabbed his mouth gently with his napkin and took a sip of wine.

"Have I ordered the wrong items?" he inquired solicitously. "We can go somewhere else if you like. I—"

"For food."

Her interjection was so abrupt that he gave her his full attention.

"Pardon?"

"I'm not hungry for food."

"What would you like to—" he started the question, but she interrupted again.

"I want to go home."

*** *** *** ***

The "date" was not going well, to put it mildly.

Devlin considered the female conundrum before him.

He couldn't get her to hold any semblance of a conversation. Not even to engage in pointless small talk. She was so awkward and abrupt. He'd never met anyone like her in all his life, which was really saying something.

And now he was about to lose all the months of meticulous planning and infiltration he'd done to find her, engage her attention, build some semblance of a *relationship*.

He couldn't afford to lose her now. He had to think of something fast.

"Surely there is something I can offer you before I escort you home," he coaxed with another melting smile. "Some pastries and coffee or a walk through the park? The night is still so young, and I have been waiting so long to meet—"

"I want to go home," she repeated in the same non-negotiable tone. She put her napkin on the table again.

Devlin switched tracks.

"If you insist. But allow me to escort you." He rose and circled behind her chair, helping her out of it, though she avoided his touch.

She didn't wait for him to put a few bills on the table to pay for their half-eaten—rather, his half-eaten meal for she hadn't touched hers at all— before heading determinedly to the restaurant exit. Devlin lengthened his strides to catch up.

By the time he caught up with her, she'd already hailed a taxi and was getting inside. He ducked inside as well and closed the door just as the cab took off.

What an exceptionally strange woman, Devlin thought, as he huffed a breath after his mad dash out of the restaurant to keep up with her.

He angled himself slightly toward her in the backseat of the cab so that he could observe her in close proximity.

She sat toward the center of the cab and stared straight ahead out the front window, completely ignoring his presence, though the better part of their thighs and knees touched, given the confined space.

While he noted with practiced ease the landmarks and street signs they drove past, the better to retrace their location if he needed to find her again, Devlin focused most of his energy on studying this perplexing human cyber genius.

Surely he could discover some weakness, some way to get closer to her.

He'd managed to keep her interest in the chats, after all, even if all they talked of was code and programming.

Once in a while, they debated the mysteries of the universe, like why the sky was never green or brown, though it reflected every other color of the rainbow; whether there were extraterrestrial beings and worm holes; and whether the events of *Matrix* the movie could ever become reality.

Random, disjointed curiosities that either one of them thought of in the moment.

He'd managed to get her to reveal some personal information too, like the fact that she'd always wanted pets but could never keep anything living alive. He was the one who suggested that she start with something easy like fish. Then graduate to a hamster or similarly docile rodent. All would be contained. In tanks or cages. Manageable.

Next thing he knew, she'd taken his advice and bought two goldfish.

He then encouraged her to name them so she'd feel a stronger sense of responsibility and closeness to them, the better not to forget to feed them and clean their tank. Hence, Antony and Cleopatra got their names, despite the fact they were both male fish. She said she'd been watching an old movie marathon on TV and the names stuck.

Encouraged by the fish surviving past the one month mark, she'd gone out and gotten a chinchilla, passed by a Miu-Miu store on the way home, which inspired her naming of it, and voila—a contained, manageable family of four was formed.

Devlin had felt a vicarious sort of satisfaction himself when she'd proudly shared her new addition.

Surely, he could find a way to get through to her now, when they were squeezed together in the backseat of a bloody cab.

Devlin was just a smidgen frustrated. He'd never tried so hard to gain a female's attention before. All the smiles and smoldering glances and charm he threw at her slid off of Grace Darling like raindrops from a duck's well-oiled feathers.

He couldn't even coax a smile from her.

She refused to engage in conversation. She interrupted just about every train of thought he started. It was as if he was sitting alone at the table talking to a wall that bounced back his conversation starters like racquet ball shots.

The one thing she did do aplenty was stare at him.

Unblinkingly and unnervingly.

He wondered what her thoughts were while she stared. Probably her mind was blank, like her expression. Or perhaps her thoughts were written in code, and only someone of the same as-yet-undiscovered species could decipher them.

Such an odd woman.

And coming from a vampire, this was saying something.

He looked at her now, taking in her nondescript brown hair, knotted into a haphazard bun on the back of her head, her slender, boyish figure, a very slight bosom, and knobby knees.

She was *not* what he'd pictured in his head while chatting remotely with her. Seven of Nine from *Star Trek: Voyager* was what he pictured. Someone with a super-processor for a brain, a robotic personality and the bod of a goddess.

No, the real Grace Darling was definitely not that, at least with regards to the body. The rest of Devlin's imagination fit her to a T.

Her profile wasn't bad—a nice slope to her brow, a straight, pert nose, well-defined but largish lips, and a pointy chin. Her neck was long and graceful, quite deserving of her namesake; her eyebrows prodigiously thick and expansive, nearly meeting together in the center. Her eyes were an unremarkable brown but framed by sooty, long, extravagant lashes that spread around them like spider's legs, or perhaps a centipede's.

Huh.

Devlin wasn't terribly romantic with his portraits tonight, which was a surprise. He could always find attractive things about any woman, no matter her background, race, shape or stature. He was a connoisseur of women, after all. They were one of the three loves of his life.

Right up there with great food and the thrill of hunting.

And yet, his assessment of Grace Darling's physical attributes wasn't altogether complimentary. Though he wouldn't go as far as to say she was *un*attractive.

She was... intriguing.

But just as he started to percolate some inspiration around the ways she intrigued him, she interrupted his thoughts.

"We're here."

Chapter Two

The taxi jolted to a stop and Grace got out without waiting for Devlin to disembark first and open the door for her.

He never understood this aspect of modern women, in particular American women. Were they so independent that they couldn't appreciate gentlemanly behavior? Did they never think that some men simply enjoyed being a gentleman?

After some two hundred years, Devlin would always behave according to the principles and manners that had been ingrained in him since birth. Not because they were habits he couldn't shake off but because they were part of who he was, part of the man he was.

Well, bloodsucker now.

He rapidly scoured his mind for ideas. How could he get this strange, Sphinx-like woman to invite him inside? Surely there was a—

"Come inside," she intoned with nary a trace of emotional inflection. Not excitement, anticipation or nervousness.

But at least she saved him from thinking up an excuse to impose on her.

Devlin was about to thank her for her invitation when he met her eyes.

Her pupils had fully swallowed her irises. Her stare was so intense now that it actually gave him pause.

Just who was the hunter and who, the prey? Her unblinking black eyes reminded him of a cobra hypnotizing a field mouse.

He silently accepted her invitation anyway by following her down the steps of her basement apartment in a posh part of Soho, and then inside her abode once she unlocked and opened the door with efficiency.

He was well over ten times as strong as she and a trained killer besides. He was certainly not the prey in this scenario.

Just as efficiently, she locked the door the moment they were both within the entryway, working a series of four locks and deadbolts in addition to punching in the codes to a state-of-the-art security system. No one was getting into her fortress unless she voluntarily admitted them.

Devlin wondered if the same applied for getting out.

And then she turned to him, her back to the door, as if blocking his nearest exit, adding further fuel to his suspicion.

It occurred to him vaguely that she hadn't turned on any lights. Devlin's eyes quickly adjusted to the darkness. A vampire's vision was almost as keen in the dark as it was in light, sometimes more so if on the hunt. He could see her staring solemnly and fixatedly at him.

She moistened her lips with a small pink tongue. Like a lioness about to dig into a fresh antelope.

Devlin was becoming just a tad alarmed.

"Grace, perhaps we should—"

Again she cut him off, this time by coming to stand immediately before him, her fingers methodically and calmly working on the buttons of his silk Gieves and Hawkes French-Cuff shirt.

"What are you doing?" he asked rather inanely.

Clearly, she was unbuttoning his shirt. Probably why she didn't deign to respond.

When she tugged the tails out of his tailored slacks, he caught her wrists in a loose but firm grasp.

"Grace, we've just met, and while I'm flattered by your..."

Attention? Interest? None of those seemed to be the right words. She hadn't expressed any interest nor given him any special attention all night, short though their time had been.

But she did stare at him. There was that.

"Grace," he tried again, when she deftly twisted free of his grasp and started on his pants zipper, "is removing my clothing a necessary part of being a guest in your home? Is this the Grace Darling version of shucking shoes upon entry?"

He asked the question teasingly, but one never knew with Grace. He'd had enough exchanges with her by now to glean that she had unusual habits, unexpected idiosyncrasies.

Perhaps removing the guest's clothing *was* one of her many rituals, like feeding her goldfish and chinchilla promptly at 10pm every night and eating a banana with a cup of coffee every morning without fail, followed by thirty minutes in the bathroom.

While most people found comfort and calmness in having a recognizable pattern to their days, Grace's patterns were non-negotiable, immutable. If any aspect of her rituals was altered, she could barely struggle through the day.

She seemed to have inordinate trouble with his zipper, though she showed no signs of impatience as one hand gently tugged at the silver tab while the other boldly and unapologetically palmed his male parts, pushing his person away from the fly to help get it open.

Because strangely, his cock was already hard and leaping against the fabric, so swollen in fact that the zipper was unable to descend without risk of snagging his most sensitive flesh as he wasn't in the habit of using underwear.

And he wasn't even attracted to the woman!

Was he?

Devlin grasped her hands again and held them away from his body, this time in a tighter grip, one she couldn't wiggle out of.

"Grace, if this is headed where I think you're intending it to go, I have to tell you now that I'm not the sort of man who has one night stands."

His comrades wouldn't believe it, but Devlin was speaking truth.

Even those closest to him thought he had a different female every night, that his sexual appetite was insatiable and needed variety to take the edge off.

But while he did indeed flirt with and appreciate a wide array of females, and generously shared kisses and caresses as naturally as he breathed, and he did indulge in marathon bed sport whenever he felt the urge with accommodating partners, each woman was a friend, each knew his rules.

And their number over the three or four human lifetimes he'd lived was actually shockingly small.

In fact, he'd only been with one woman in his human life.

Grace finally looked up into his eyes.

"It's not a one night stand," she stated reasonably, "we have two weeks."

He narrowed his eyes, the better to concentrate, because he'd never had so much trouble understanding another living being.

"What do we have for two weeks?"

"Sex," she said in her low, rather sultry voice.

Devlin shivered at the sound of it, at the way she drew out that particular word like a sinful promise.

"We will have sex for two weeks," she elaborated. "Not one night. So it's okay."

He had to ask.

"Why two weeks?"

She looked back down at her hands trapped in his and tugged. He didn't release her. Her words were muffled by her lowered head when she replied.

"That's how long before I feel normal again. It's a chemical thing. Hormones."

She said this matter-of-factly and clearly expected him to accept without question that she was horny and needed regular sex for two weeks to provide relief.

And he happened to be the closest penis.

Wait.

Had she been planning to have a sexual marathon for *two weeks* with a pudgy, balding *Azor Ahai*? And Devlin just happened to be at the right place at the right time and was really a consolation prize?

It would be too lowering if true.

"Grace," he tried again, though he wasn't sure any logic or reasoning would work with her, alien creature that she was, "this is our first date. I'd like to get to know you better before we're intimate."

And honestly, he would have preferred not to mix business with pleasure. He was getting close to her for a purpose—information. And potential leveraging of her skills. But since sex was apparently a bonus thrown in the mix, he was not philosophically opposed to it either. It was just that casual sex had never appealed to him.

Surely that wasn't too much to ask. He knew that humans in the twenty-first century, especially in the world of online dating, didn't think twice about sexual congress with strangers.

To be fair, strangers humped each other during his era as well, just usually within the bounds of marriage or in a designated den of iniquity.

This was careless sex. Like bumping into someone on the street. Or greasy fast food. It might feel good going down, but one felt revolted afterwards.

Devlin had always regarded sex as something very personal. To enjoy it, he must feel some sort of connection or affection for the other party.

She looked back up at him.

"You're not a virgin?" It was a statement posed as a question. As if she was certain he couldn't possibly be untried, but couldn't otherwise puzzle out his hesitation.

"No. That's not—"

"And we haven't just met," she plunged on, "We've chatted for months online. It's longer than most relationships these days. I consider you a friend of sorts."

Disturbingly, Devlin couldn't say he didn't feel the same for her.

True, they spoke of very platonic, superficial things, but occasionally, there was a deeper connection. She often amused him with her short-circuited thought process and unintentional wit.

She stopped trying to get her hands free and instead used his grip on her to pull herself closer to him until they were infinitesimally touching, torso to torso, toe to toe.

"I can make this the most euphoric two weeks you've ever had," she promised in that low, unconsciously sensuous contralto.

Everything went ramrod straight in Devlin's body, catching up with the posture his cock had the foresight to strike first.

"I know six hundred ninety three ways to make a man climax and prolong his pleasure. I've only ever used twenty-seven of those ways on anyone, collectively, not individually—after all, men are easily brought to orgasm—but if you have the stamina, I have the creativity."

Holy...

She didn't speak much all night. That was the longest monologue yet.

But, Good Lord!

When she did speak, she certainly packed a wallop.

She put her lips on the heated skin of his chest, bared by the open shirt.

Not to kiss him. No, she merely grazed her satiny lips back and forth, barely touching, across a concentrated patch of skin. Moistening his epidermis by methodical degrees.

In her bare feet, the top of her head reached just under his chin. Her lips were level with the deep groove that bisected his pectorals. And while her lips played havoc on an erogenous zone Devlin didn't even know he had, she added the tips of her breasts to the sensual assault by pressing the hardened buds to his ribs and lazily stroking them like the strings of a harp.

With her nipples. Through the fabric of the nondescript blouse she still wore, while he was already half undressed.

Devlin was distantly shocked at how turned on he was.

His passions ran high, it was true, but he always had full control of the accelerator and brakes. He'd even been able to fully control the pace of his first time as an idealistic, randy youth of twenty.

It was also his last time as a human.

Now it was as if someone had cut the brake lines of his libido, and pleasure blasted forth like a runaway train. He was an uninitiated adolescent again, discovering his first erection after a night of wet dreams, both awed by the power surge of sexual awakening and horrified by his inability to contain it. He was simply at its mercy.

At *her* mercy.

She tilted her eyes upward as she kept the delicate pressure on three critical points on his torso, the Bermuda triangle of ecstasy he didn't even know he possessed, and murmured:

"How about it, friend? Shall we proceed?"

*** *** *** ***

Yep, he was a strong one, Grace thought to herself.

None of her other sex partners (she would never call them something so inappropriate as *lovers* because that emotion, or any emotion, wasn't required for the act) had ever lasted this long.

Matter of fact, none of them had ever thought to decline her invitation to two weeks of orgy where they benefited as much as she did.

She'd had partners of all sorts, some awkward, some extremely introverted, some with strange fetishes; one was actually a closet sex addict. All carefully chosen, all screened for STDs, all perfectly harmless, she'd made sure of that.

Harmless and easily controlled by her.

Slaves to her every whim once she showed them early on how adept she was at giving pleasure. She never saw them again after the two weeks were over. She didn't want to form any attachments.

Or rather, she wasn't *able* to form any attachments.

But Devlin Sinclair was a whole different ball game. Even though he didn't escort her home expecting to get laid, usually when a man was offered sex with no strings attached, he didn't often decline.

Sinclair apparently did. Or valiantly tried to anyway.

But Grace could see him cracking under her expert assault. It wasn't just her skill that was undoing his restraint, however, it was the man himself.

He was a born sensualist.

From the tips of his wavy dark blonde hair to the ends of his manly heels, Grace was certain his entire body could become one giant erogenous zone. She could tell, because, ironically, she herself was a sensualist. Ironic, because mentally and emotionally, she was cold as stone. But physically, her senses were extremely keen, well attuned to the full spectrum of pleasure and pain.

She could tell, for example, that he was sensitive to sounds. His breathing had deepened when she lowered her voice and added husk to her tone. She could tell that if she nuzzled his nipples with her face, he would feel the caress deep in his scrotum, sending fissures of pleasure into his penis.

As she did so now, she felt his erection leap between their bodies, trying to batter its way out of its confines to freedom.

She looked up and gave him a rare smile.

She felt triumphant that she was able to provoke these reactions from him, that she was able to bring him such exquisite pleasure. And this was only one speck in the infinity of ecstasy he was capable of unleashing. She knew that even now, he was holding himself in check. That he was allowing this to happen. Perhaps only up to a certain point.

She wanted to be the one to drive him wild.

So strange. She'd never felt this way with anyone before.

But when she gazed into his eyes, she got trapped again within the bright blue beams, simply stuck there like a fly flattened on a spider's web.

It had happened many times over the course of the evening. Sometimes she was so mesmerized she couldn't even blink, and more than once she'd had to remind herself to breathe.

Even in the pitch black of her lightless studio apartment his eyes glittered like diamonds. His pupils were dilated and enormous, like two solar eclipses, as he held her immobile with his gaze.

Grace felt herself falling into those twin black pools, into the tumultuous depths of his memories.

She felt like she was drowning. And she didn't care if she did.

"Grace," he murmured her name, as if he felt it too, this indescribable magnetism that held them both enthralled.

They didn't know each other at all. Not really. She'd never wanted to *know* anyone.

To know someone you would have to take interest enough to learn. Learning took patience and dedication and persistence. And in the process you would have to open yourself up to be known in return.

Grace could never find the interest to start this arduous journey, much less complete it.

But suddenly, she discovered that she was interested in this man.

Well, truthfully, she'd been interested in him since she spied him making his way toward her table in the restaurant. She might have even prayed, unconsciously, to some minor deity that this resplendent creature was meant for her, for she never dreamed he would claim to be her chat room connection.

The real *Azor Ahai* was definitely a foot shorter, pudgy and balding.

But after he sat down and started conversing, she knew, *knew*, that he was actually the one she had been chatting with, perhaps starting from the second week of their online acquaintance. His use of words, his subtle dry wit—they were exactly the same.

She'd tried to block out the inexplicable feelings the sight of him aroused, less because of his beauty and more because of *him*. But after he touched her shoulder… that was it. He'd sealed his own doom.

She wasn't lying earlier just to get him to stay with her. She wanted to be his friend, and she wanted his friendship in return.

What did that even mean? It was such a foreign feeling that she inwardly recoiled. She had no confidence that she would be able to learn him. She hated to fail, so she never started anything she couldn't do.

And then she remembered that she could give him pleasure. Perhaps she could start to learn him through shared pleasure.

Two. Whole. Tantric. Weeks. Of it.

Grace finally blinked and broke their gaze. With her sense of purpose restored, she tugged at her hands again, still trapped in his.

This time, he relented, loosening his hold on her enough that she pulled herself free.

With utmost concentration, she worked at his pants zipper again and pulled it down without hurting his swollen, sensitive flesh.

She pushed the tailored slacks down the perfectly round, sculpted muscles of his buttocks where it pooled around his ankles. Next, she pulled his shirt off his shoulders as he shucked his shoes and socks.

He was finally participating rather than trying to stop her. Her heart, an organ that Grace usually forgot was there, gave a little leap of jubilation.

Still fully dressed, she put her palms on his pecs and gently pushed him backwards until the backs of his knees hit the over-sized leather armchair at the foot of her bed.

With another more forceful push, he fell into the chair in a sprawl while she stood facing him between his opened thighs.

She knew he was staring intently at her, trying to catch her eyes again, but she wouldn't let him. She couldn't afford to get stuck in the web of his gaze; she wanted, needed, to concentrate on giving him pleasure.

Because when she heard his breath hitch, felt his skin heat, smelled his musk deepen...*she* felt pleasure.

She was already hot and wet at her core. She could feel her fluids soak through her panties and pants. He didn't even have to touch her—all she had to do was touch him—and she was on the verge of orgasm herself.

This was an unexpected new discovery her methodical mind wanted to explore at length, trying every one of the six hundred and ninety three means of pleasing him. Meanwhile her sensualist body clamored for her to just get on with *one*, so she could find *release*.

Grace slowly straddled his thighs, bracing her hands on the arms of the chair, dragging the slightly scratchy fibers of wool in her blended-cotton slacks along his legs, until her fully clothed crotch met his naked erection.

She undulated just slightly, abrading his sensitive flesh.

His breathing deepened, as if he was trying to control his reactions.

She didn't want him to be in control, so she concentrated on breaking it. She kept her hands on the armrests, and she noticed that he kept his arms and hands at his sides, not holding her, not touching her.

His posture said that he was willing to cede some of his control, to see where she led this.

Grace was thrilled.

But where to start?

His body was too beautiful—there was no other word for it in the end, the English language was simply too limited, and no other modifier would do because his beauty literally overwhelmed her.

Her mental acuity was rapidly receding under the onslaught of raw, pounding lust as she took him in... so many pleasure centers to choose from.

This was going to be the most exciting and rewarding treasure hunt Grace had ever embarked upon, finding all the secrets of his body.

Puzzles and treasure hunts. The two favorite past times from Grace's childhood. Ones in which she'd seldom had the opportunity to indulge as an adult. Combined in the person of Devlin Sinclair.

She was almost giddy with anticipation.

She leaned in close until her mouth hovered beside his right ear. And gently blew continuous puffs of warm breath into it.

His breathing faltered and his large, elegant hands fisted at his sides.

Ah, found another one.

She darted her tongue out and began to lightly lick the delicate whorls of his ear, intermittently dipping the tip of her tongue inside and worrying the soft lobe between her teeth.

He moaned low, the husky, raspy sound pinging against each ridge of her spine like padded mallets striking the bars of a xylophone.

And she climaxed right then and there.

*** *** *** ***

Devlin almost embarrassed himself when Grace's long, voluptuous groan of completion stroked his eardrums.

As it was, his cock jerked against her crotch helplessly while his balls seized painfully with anticipation. He managed to prevent ejaculation, but couldn't do anything about the copious pre-cum that seeped down the length of his aching sex.

"What are you doing to me?" he rasped out when the wave of pleasure-pain from thwarted release ebbed enough for him to form words.

She was still breathing fast from her orgasm when she said, "Finding your secrets."

Well, she was doing a stupendous job of it, he thought to himself. They could hardly be called secrets if she could so easily arouse him to this feverish pitch.

She must be some kind of sex goddess, commanding these unexpected reactions from his body, a body he thought he knew well.

But apparently not.

He never knew a few puffs of air against his eardrums combined with the tip of a tongue could be enough to make him come. He would have too if he hadn't exerted restraint. And he only restrained himself because he wanted this to last for her.

She required an erection for two weeks, after all. It wouldn't do to deflate after a little ear sex.

When he wasn't trying to maintain control, an effort that was superhuman in the current context, he felt a strange sort of amusement.

It would appear that he was indeed the prey this evening, and she, the hunter.

She hadn't seemed interested in him when he first approached her table, but somewhere during their brief half-eaten dinner, she'd decided to bring him back to her lair to feast on the abundance of sexual possibilities between them.

He had no idea this had been her intention, not until she'd started on the first button of his shirt. Even then, he couldn't quite believe what was happening. His mind had frozen even as his body erupted into an inferno.

He was the one hunting *her*.

He'd painstakingly tracked her digital footprints for months. He was certain she held critical information for getting to his ultimate target—the enigmatic Medusa, who had orchestrated all of the chaos and violence the Pure and Dark Ones had been combatting for the past two years.

And if that wasn't enough, he was a *vampire*, a dangerous predator who fed on human blood. Some of his Kind even took souls.

In what universe would he ever be the prey to a small, defenseless, human woman?

Apparently this one.

She had doffed her pants and panties while he contemplated this bizarre reversal of roles.

But all thought vanished when she resumed her position straddling his lap. As her naked, hot, wet core pressed against the root of his erection, Devlin's vampire fangs descended from his gums.

Grace Darling was in for more secrets than she'd ever bargained for.

Chapter Three

Estelle Martin was putting a fresh batch of *palmiers* into the upper part of her double-oven when the bells dangling from the store's front door jingled.

With a smile of anticipation, she wiped her hands on her apron and moved from the back kitchen to the front of her all-things shop, Dark Dreams, as fast as her matronly, mama-bear form would allow.

It had been many months since Inanna, Gabriel and little Benji had come to see her. Their last visit had been all too brief, given that they were currently dividing their time between New York City and Boston. They only stopped by for a few minutes on their way to some other errand.

"I've been waiting—"

She broke off the greeting when she realized that her visitor in the middle of the night was not the ones she was expecting.

Her smile froze for a moment but spread wide again when her guest turned toward her.

It was the handsome, bookish young man who had stopped at her shop some time ago.

She had fed him pastries and tea and given him her favorite comb as a souvenir. They hadn't exchanged many words, but his presence in her shop had been comforting for a woman who spent her life mostly alone.

"Well isn't this a happy surprise," she welcomed warmly. "I didn't know if you'd find your way back to my little shop again."

He gave her a small but genuine smile and let her usher him to a seat at an oval tea table.

"I wasn't sure whether you'd be open at night," he said by way of greeting. "It's not safe, especially in this neighborhood... but I'm glad for my stomach in this particular instance."

He made a show of sniffing the air.

"Is that *palmiers* I smell?"

"What an astute nose you have," she replied. "I just put a batch in the oven. But I have some macarons you might fancy while we wait."

The young man inclined his head, smiling sheepishly now, as if abashed that he was taking advantage of her generosity, expecting to be fed.

Estelle never took money for the treats and refreshments she made, mostly for herself because she had a sweet tooth, and whatever she had left over she donated to the Little Flower Orphanage down the street.

In truth, it would be more fair to say that she baked for the boys and girls at the orphanage and couldn't resist filching a couple of treats for herself before sending the goods over.

And all the thousands of little trinkets she displayed on the floor to ceiling shelves in her shop were not for sale. But occasionally, when she found the right persons to treasure them, she would give some away.

She alone managed the "shop," which generated no revenues whatsoever. It was really just an extension of her home in the back, where a small but modern and efficient kitchen, dining area, bedroom and bathroom were hidden from view.

As to safety... it was never a concern. For Estelle Martin was not what she appeared.

After she brought out a tea tray with both coffee and tea and an assortment of colorful macarons, she settled on the seat opposite the young man and fixed him a plate.

"Now, my dear," she began, "if we're going to make a habit of this, I should like to know your name at least. But if you're too shy to share, I'll simply continue calling you whichever endearment strikes my fancy."

The young man hesitated and took his time stirring a dollop of vanilla cream into his coffee.

So mysterious, Estelle thought. Surely a name wasn't too difficult to share, even if he had to invent one.

As a rule, she never pressed her visitors for personal details. She opened her doors to all kinds of wanderers, travelers and lost souls. But she felt that this young man was too alone. Too lonely. He needed someone who knew him just a little. Even if it was merely his name.

"You can call me Binu," he finally answered.

Estelle almost dropped her tea cup. As it was, the delicate porcelain cup clattered onto its saucer, sloshing some liquid out.

Bīnu.

Did he know what it meant? It couldn't be a coincidence.

As if hearing her thoughts, he said, "It's the Akkadian word for 'son.' I'm a researcher of ancient civilizations and like to collect phrases and words from lost languages. No one's called me 'son,' before, since I'm sadly an orphan, so I thought I'd like to hear it. But asking for the...endearment... outright seemed too presumptuous."

He told her this in a teasing tone, said with a disarming, self-deprecating smile, but she heard the sadness and despair all the same.

She gave him her most glowing grin.

"It's a pleasure to make your acquaintance, Binu," she said. "And I'm Estelle. You can call me Mama Bear if you like. A great many folks do."

"Mama Bear," he murmured, as if testing the words on his tongue.

"Binu, my dear, you mustn't hold back on the macarons. If you don't help me with them I fear I'll add another inch or two to my waist trying to prevent them from going to waste."

He grinned boyishly at her and plopped one into his mouth, closing his eyes to savor the sweetness that was as light as air, instantly melting in the warmth of his mouth.

Estelle watched him eat with pleasure as she sipped her tea.

She loved feeding people. It gave her the sense of accomplishment others might gain from building empires, winning the Nobel Peace Prize, walking on the moon.

It was the way she chose to make her mark in the world. Feeding one lost soul at a time. Providing them a safe haven whenever they should need it.

*** *** *** ***

Grace noticed the subtle change in temperature in the room; a fragrant musk effervesced from Devlin Sinclair's skin.

Darker. Fuller.

It went straight to Grace's bloodstream like a shot of cocaine.

At least she imagined this was the sort of irresistible intoxication to which addicts were enslaved.

She felt enslaved.

Her hands skimmed up his arms to his shoulders, up the strong column of his neck to enfold his face.

It was so dark in her apartment she could barely see what was in front of her. She purposely kept it dark for these sex marathons because her other senses came fully alive when her sight was handicapped. She could better attune herself to each and every reaction in her partner, the better to discover the most efficient ways to make him writhe in pleasure.

And she was better able to use her imagination in the darkness.

She was not a picky woman. Almost any male body would do. Thankfully, none of her partners had smelled bad, were too hairy, had too many fat rolls or sported tiny penises. Cyber geeks, for the most part, were skinny and soft. Too absorbed in their programming obsession to eat well. Too glued to their desks to build any muscle.

She was the orchestrator of both theirs and her own pleasure. She could manipulate even the most premature of ejaculators to hold their stiffness until she granted their release.

And while she conducted her own symphony of sensations, she conjured in her mind whatever ideal male form she wanted. Images of sculpted, perfect marble bodies by the Greeks and Romans. Flashes of paintings by Renaissance masters.

And, yes, a few Giorgio Armani underwear models here and there.

No real man could ever match the ideal of her imagination.

Until Devlin Sinclair. Perhaps he even exceeded it.

She looked into his face now, avoiding his eyes, trying to make out his features with her inquisitive fingers.

Her thumbs roved leisurely over his wide brow, starting from his temples, smoothed across the poetic slants of his eyebrows, down the straight, slightly bumpy bridge of his nose.

Interesting, that tiny bump. So he wasn't all flawless. Somehow that made him even more perfect.

The sensitive pads of her thumbs dragged back up over his eyelids, closing those bright blue beacons of light, and flirted with the thick, long sweeps of eyelashes that fluttered against his high cheekbones.

Back and forth, back and forth, she dragged her thumbs across those delicate bristles, becoming almost mesmerized by the ticklish sensations until he inhaled a tremulous breath.

Ah. Found another secret.

She kept brushing her thumbs along his eyelashes and added slight pressure at the corners of his eyes while she rotated her hips lazily below, grinding gently down on his lap.

His hands moved from his sides to grasp the arms of the chair. She could hear his fingers digging into the sleek leather. It sounded like the cords of his control unraveling.

But beyond that, he still hadn't touched her, as if he couldn't decide how far to let her take this.

By now, her past partners would have already either begged for mercy and/ or grabbed any part of her they could in their frantic pursuit of release.

He did neither.

He simply figuratively dug his heels in and waited for her to continue her exquisite torture.

She gyrated against his hot, hard, quite magnificently proportioned erection while she played havoc with his eyelashes and lids. His body trembled in time with each brush of her thumbs against those lush lashes. Her fluids and his made the drag of her cunny against his cock slick and satiny, sending tiny bolts of electricity all along her swollen labia, and the most delicious buzz against her pearl.

"Come," he commanded in a low, guttural growl. "Again."

Gladly, she obeyed, her body releasing in a quivering torrent against his, her sex convulsing around the root of his staff. The pressure of his hardness made it so *good*.

But not nearly good enough.

When she caught her breath, she opened her eyes and looked into his, unable to help it any more.

"I want you inside me," she stated clearly, almost demandingly.

But also with a question, because she recognized that he was still holding back. She didn't want to take him fully without permission, and she wasn't sure he'd given it. Not explicitly.

She really, *desperately*, wanted him to say yes.

He held her gaze for the longest time. What was he thinking? What did he see in her?

She was starting to lose herself in those solar eclipses again.

So many delicious secrets. It would take lifetimes to discover them all.

Still, he didn't answer.

His breathing was deep and rhythmic, as if he'd run many miles, but still had the stamina to run many more. The rise and fall of his wide, hairless chest she detected out of the corner of her eyes only added to her hypnosis.

"Are you certain?" he finally said. "You don't know who or what I am."

The vibrating timbre of his voice broke through her trance, making her blink.

"Who are you?" she asked, truly curious, impatient to know.

"What are you?"

He was silent again for so long she thought he wouldn't answer.

Then, finally, he parted the seam of his lips, just enough to reveal the sharp tips of what looked like two glistening fangs.

*** *** *** ***

Instead of screaming, fainting, running through the wall, as Devlin fully expected her to do at the sight of the unmistakable fangs he revealed, Grace Darling tilted her head to have a better look.

"How odd," she murmured with a scientific air, lowering her face a bit so that she was eye-level with his mouth, "I'm pretty sure they weren't there a minute ago. Do they extend and retract on command?"

Devlin couldn't help the huff of disbelief that escaped his chest.

She tested one of the tips with her index finger and ran the same finger along the row of front teeth between the two fangs as if comparing the consistency and validating the authenticity of the pointy canines.

"Doesn't feel like inserts," she said in the same wondering tone.

Devlin collected himself enough to respond, "You have some experience with fangs, do you?"

She tipped her head the other way and sat back a bit to peer at his teeth from a distance, as if zooming in and out would help her better assess the situation.

"You can never tell. I know people with a lot of peculiar fetishes."

She shrugged.

"But honestly, who am I to judge? I have a few myself. It's probably abnormal for the average person but it's normal for the persons with the fetishes."

She gazed into his eyes again, with the same unblinking intensity she had been demonstrating at intervals throughout the night.

"You're becoming a fetish for me," she told him as if in a trance, "I want to make you come in a thousand different ways."

Whoomph. Devlin's body promptly erupted into flames.

She said the damnest things. And they had the damnest effect on him.

He drew a deep breath to steady himself. His fingers clawed deeper into the armrests of her chair.

"Are they just for show or do you have a use for them?" she continued to try to unravel the puzzle of his fangs.

Devlin swallowed and replied, "I use them to break the skin and vein of my prey, the better to drink their blood."

Again, she did not have the reaction one would expect.

"Do you suffer from anemia or have an iron deficiency? Why do you need to drink blood? What happens to the people you drink from?"

A bombardment of questions that were unemotional and detachedly curious.

"I—"

She leaned in close again pressed the pad of her index finger hard enough against the tip of one fang to draw blood.

A growl, deep and feral, resonated like the struck strings of a bass guitar in the pitch black apartment.

"Found another secret," she said with not fear but delight, "you have two more pleasure points than the rest of the human population. This just added some exponentials in the ways you can achieve orgasm."

She literally quivered with excitement, and declared in that sultry voice of hers:

"Fascinating."

Finally, Devlin reached for her, putting his hands roughly on her hips, his fingers digging into her flesh.

"This is not a game, Grace," he ground out in a guttural snarl, no longer flippant, no longer amused, "If we continue this… if I give you what you want…I will also take what I want, damn the consequences."

She didn't hesitate in her reply.

"That's fair."

Even with the Consent she just gave him, Devlin held back.

Nothing was going according to his plan. He made sure to be in control of every situation he entered, a lesson he learned the hard way. But for the first time in the hundreds of years since he turned vampire, he was in control of nothing.

Not even his own reactions.

"I want you inside me," she urged again, sensing his doubt.

Shifting her gaze to his fangs, she said, "In every way possible I want you inside me. And I want to be inside you too."

She undulated her hips slightly so that the hot, slick opening of her core was pressed against the plump head of his sex.

Slowly, she sank down upon him just half an inch.

They both groaned at the indescribable sensation. It was *sooo good*. It had never been this good.

Between gasps of pleasure, she looked into his eyes and asked him one last time, "Yes?"

Devlin held her penetrating stare, tightened his grip on her hips and bared his teeth as the last shreds of his control finally snapped.

"*Yes.*"

Chapter Four

"Devlin, you missed the Queen's summons, where have you been?"

Even as wobbly-legged and bone-deep sore as Devlin felt, he still registered the marked displeasure of the Chosen's Commander, Maximus Justus Copernicus.

And just in case he hadn't picked it up, the heavy tail lash against his shins from Maximus' ever-present panther Simca would have alerted him.

But thankfully, the displeasure and pain were diluted through a thick post-coital fog.

About a dozen or more post-coitals worth of fog.

Really, he lost count after the first six or so orgasms. And who could blame him? Most of his climaxes seemed to last hours. At least a few of them probably did.

He had never been this physically *wrung out* in the whole of his existence. He felt like every last drop of semen had been squeezed and sucked and milked out of his body. Every last nerve ending fried to a crisp. Every last bone, muscle and sinew melted into putty.

God, his testicles hurt. His cock hurt. The roots of his hair hurt. His toenails hurt.

But he felt absolutely sublime despite all that. Countless, full-bodied orgasms had that effect on a man.

"Devlin, are you hearing me?"

"Hmm?"

He finally turned in the direction of the distant badgering that reached his ears, whose drums were still ringing from the large amounts of blood that had repeatedly rushed against them. Everything was muffled—the noises, the sights, Devlin's ability to discern.

His brain had turned to cotton candy.

"You look wasted," the Commander judged with a shake of his head. "I'll debrief you later. Go get some sleep."

Happy to oblige, Devlin staggered on unsteady feet down the corridors that led to his private chambers within the Cove, the vampire queen's royal stronghold, hidden in plain sight in Midtown Manhattan.

Once inside, the door automatically and soundlessly slid closed while Devlin flung himself across his gigantic bed.

He let out an abbreviated, humorless laugh, too exhausted for the full version.

If this was what sex with strangers with no emotional attachment was like, he really ought to have started the trend a lot earlier.

Now, he was actually living the sort of life of debauchery his comrades had always given him credit for.

Twelve whole hours of nonstop orgy.

Not even a minute to pause in between ejaculations. Just long enough at 10pm sharp for her to feed her creatures. She just kept going and going, like the Energizer Bunny on steroids.

God!

Wasted was an apt description for his current state of being.

But somehow, through all that, he'd managed the superhuman feat of not giving in to his bloodthirst. Besides that one drop of blood from her pricked index finger, he had not taken advantage of the Consent she'd given.

Perhaps he'd be stronger now and less of a wreck if he had taken her blood. But he didn't trust himself not to take too much.

He wanted Grace Darling with a ferocity that shocked him to the marrow of his bones.

Blame it on the chemistry. Or her sorcery of tantric arts. There was something about her—about the two of them together—that pushed Devlin to his limits.

Then broke right through them.

Strangely, the best sex he'd ever had was not with a woman he cared at all deeply for. It was laughable when contrasted with the first time he'd ever had sex, with a woman he thought he loved.

But as Devlin fell into a deep, dreamless slumber, it was not laughter that bubbled in his throat.

It was the burn of tears...

1810, England.
Summerfield house party, Essex.

"Oh Dev, I love you so."

Long, graceful limbs pulled Devlin close, until his head was cushioned by an ample bosom, arguably the finest in all of England.

Restless fingers sifted through his heavy locks, massaging his scalp, rubbing his temple.

It felt like heaven.

"You need a trim, darling," his lover murmured in her soft, exquisitely feminine voice, "but I loathe to have anything cut these gorgeous waves. Even when your hair is longer than fashionable, you always look divine."

Devlin supposed it was love that made Lavinia speak so highly of his physical attributes, for when he looked in the mirror, he saw the visage of a studious, pale, rather thin erudite who preferred studying lost languages and unraveling mathematical equations to the typical pastimes of young men his age.

To the everlasting shame and disappointment of his father, the Duke of Devonshire.

His brother William, who was only a year and a half younger, fit much more the mold of their ancestors—he was a favorite in all of the gentlemen's clubs, raced phaetons every other Wednesday, could hold his liquor better than most, was an avid hunter and horseman, collected hounds of the best pedigree, and held his own in the boxing ring.

There was no one prouder of William than Devlin himself. But the brotherly love went only one way.

"You are such a wonderful lover," Lavinia continued to praise him. "Though it makes me so jealous to think it, you must have had other women before me. Have you?"

"No," he answered simply.

He'd never understood the urgency and haste with which his male compatriots pursued female sexual companionship from the time they were old enough to understand what a cockstand was for. He was attracted to his fair share of women, but controlling his baser impulses had never been a challenge.

He hadn't planned on saving himself, so to speak, for love or marriage. It just happened that he lost his virginity to the woman he cared for most in the world. What they just shared, he and Lavinia, was an expression of their affection, regard, and attraction for each other. It happened a bit earlier than he would have preferred, but she had been quite insistent and he was planning to marry her after all.

Besides, this might be the last time he saw her for a good long while, and he'd selfishly wanted to create some vivid, passionate memories to comfort him with during the darkest hours ahead.

She was silent for some long moments, idly playing with his hair.

And then, she ventured, "Do you regret getting carried away? Do you think I'm wanton?"

Devlin was well aware she'd set out to seduce him ever since they arrived at the house party in separate groups a week ago, but he was the one who chose to enter her bedroom this night. He allowed her seduction to succeed. He'd desperately wanted to make love with her before he left.

"No, of course not," he answered. "We will, of course, be married. We simply anticipated our vows a bit. You know that I adore you."

She sighed happily. It seemed she had received the answer from him that she'd been fishing for.

"When shall we announce our engagement? I cannot wait to be yours forever."

"At tomorrow's ball if you like," he replied, then hesitated.

Ever attuned to his moods, she noticed his reticence.

"What is it, Dev? What's wrong?"

He shifted until he lay beside her so that he could look directly into her eyes.

"I have already asked and was given your father's permission a few days ago. My father has no objections."

More to the point, his father didn't care who he took for bride as long as she was capable of bearing his sons and came from a noble family of the ton.

She smiled at him encouragingly, reaching out to caress his face.

Devlin took a deep breath before continuing, "But I'm afraid our marriage will have to wait until I come back from the war."

Abruptly, she retracted her touch.

"What?"

Devlin knew that this was a shock to Lavinia. She could not have been happy about it, but he hoped that she would understand why he felt compelled to serve his country.

"I have skills that are highly valued by the government," he tried to explain, "I have been helping on a freelance basis even from school. The Duke refuses to buy a Commission for me—"

"Understandably so," she retorted.

He was heir to one of the oldest Dukedoms in the country, which commanded a staggeringly large fortune and a dozen estates scattered throughout Britain. It was not his place to go off to war.

"And William is much better suited than you," she added.

Devlin shook his head. How was he to make her understand?

"William has no interest in the military. Nor do I want him to put his life at risk..."

"So you will put yours at risk instead?" Her voice was becoming shriller with each passing moment.

He smoothed his hand up and down her arm, trying to calm her, but she twisted out of reach, pulling the bedclothes to her chin, hiding her glorious nakedness.

"I am more prepared for what lies ahead than you know," Devlin told her quietly. "I've been training for this. I'm ready for this."

"What about me?" she demanded of him, her eyes going wide with a sort of wildness and panic. "What am I to do for however long it takes for you to tire of this lark? You cannot expect me to wait a year, or Heaven forbid, even longer, not after what we just did."

He had taken care not to spend within her, but he knew it was not foolproof as a means to prevent conception.

"We can marry by proxy if there is urgent need," he said, "I don't believe there will be, but you mustn't worry. I would never let you down."

"When are you leaving? You talk as if you're going straight away."

Devlin confirmed with a nod. "I depart for London after the ball, and sail for Portugal the day after."

She sat up, swaddled in the sheets and blankets and turned away from him.

"How can you do this to me? To us! What if you never return?"

The further this conversation progressed, the colder Devlin's heart grew. Lavinia was overset, he understood, but her thoughts evolved only around herself. It was as if she didn't care if he lived or died as long as he married her promptly.

His suspicions were confirmed when she turned back to him with a sudden brightness in her eyes.

"We could marry by special license before you leave."

She let go of the coverings and launched her soft, voluptuous self at him, wrapping her arms around his neck and squeezing her impressive breasts against his chest.

"It would be so romantic, Dev, let's just run away to Scotland. I won't feel as lonely when you're gone if I'm your wife. I'll be able to commiserate with all the other officers' wives. You know they have more access to the men abroad than any fiancée ever would."

The last part was true. Perhaps the rest of it too. But her frantic tirade moments before had planted a seed of doubt in Devlin's mind.

He did indeed adore Lavinia.

True, she was sometimes selfish, occasionally manipulative. But he certainly wasn't all virtue himself. Lavinia was also smart, funny, passionate, and had a practical, level head on her shoulders. Her laugh was throaty and unrestrained. Her saucy smiles made him forget how to breathe. Not surprisingly, she was immediately dubbed a Diamond of the First Water and Queen of the Season when she debuted in Society two years before. And she'd been its reigning Queen ever since.

She'd turned down numerous proposals. Devlin knew from all the talk in the clubs. It was difficult to avoid, despite his irregular attendance. She'd been the object of countless wagers, fisticuffs, even a couple of duels.

He might have been a virgin, but he suspected she had not been. Though she seemed uncomfortable when they'd joined at first, he hadn't felt a barrier. Nor was there any blood when he'd pulled out. Untried, he might have been; ignorant, he was not.

It didn't matter to him. He would never ask her about it.

But he wasn't completely certain she loved him.

He'd never been certain throughout the course of their courtship, which had taken the better part of a year. Despite that she told him early on, and repeated consistently since, she loved him fervently, desperately, he never truly felt this love, or perhaps he never accepted her love.

His parents had hated each other. His mother had died in a boating accident with her lover of the moment a year after giving birth to William. His father flaunted mistresses in front of everyone in the household, servants and sons included, since as far back as Devlin could remember.

They both despised him quite completely, for different reasons—his father because Devlin took after his mother's looks, all golden and blue-eyed and pale, his mother because Devlin was his father's son, equivalent of Satan's spawn begotten of her unwilling body.

And perhaps, most of all, because he was an "unnatural boy," as both parents frequently called him. He was quiet, serious, sensitive and bookish. The opposite of his brother William who effortlessly cajoled everyone around him since the moment he was born.

Devlin sometimes wondered in moments of weakness and self-doubt whether he was lovable at all.

Even William, upon whom Devlin doted, seemed only to tolerate his older brother.

He wanted, needed, to believe that Lavinia loved him. But hearing her say it wasn't enough. Perhaps time and distance afforded by his decision to join the war effort was a blessing for their relationship. He needed to know her true feelings, and be certain of his own, before they committed the rest of their lives to each other.

He intended to marry her, however. It was the right thing to do after taking privileges. He would take all responsibility for her. But he hoped a long engagement would help them see each other more clearly, come into their lifelong joining with a better, deeper understanding and appreciation.

He gently set her apart from him so that he could look into her eyes.

"We will be engaged," he said firmly. "I will make sure everything is done right. I fully intend to come back to you. I will be fighting for my country and I will be fighting to protect those most precious to me. Including you. All I ask is that you wait for me. It is what someone who loves me would do."

"What are you implying?" Her voice had gone shrill again, and she pushed away from him a second time. "That I don't love you enough? Is this some kind of awful test? How can you be so cruel! How can you—"

"It's not a test," he replied calmly, "My decision to serve my country at this moment in time is separate from my relationship with you. This is something I have to do, I cannot explain it any better. It doesn't mean I care for you any less. But being apart will help us see things more clearly. Help us be more certain of what we feel, whether we are truly meant to be together... or not."

"How can you say that!" she raged, "After everything we just did! Why are you doing this to me!"

Devlin took hold of her upper arms and held her steady, keeping silent while she continued her diatribe for some more minutes. When she'd finally exhausted herself and stilled, he pressed a kiss to her forehead, to each of her cheeks, her nose, her lips.

"Do you hate me now?" he asked in the same gentle voice. "Shall I not announce our engagement?"

She clasped him tight to her again and nuzzled her face in the crook of his neck.

"You're awful," she pouted. "I don't know why I love you. Of course I wish for our engagement. You must announce it straight away. You had better come back in one piece and marry me soon though. You know I am not a patient person."

Devlin smiled.

"Yes I know. I am asking much of you. But I will come back, I promise. Just please wait for me. Have faith in me."

*** *** *** ***

After four hours of sleep, Grace finally rolled out of bed to start her day.

It helped that she had no office to put in face time, no direct boss to displease with her tardiness. She worked whenever and wherever she wanted, raked in an after-tax income of six figures annually and never suffered the pain of year-end performance reviews.

The perks of being indispensable to her employer.

Mind completely empty of thoughts, she prepared a latte using her Jura Giga Limited Edition Expresso machine, peeled a banana, cut it into precise slices and arranged it in a smile on her breakfast plate.

For the eyes of the happy face, she decided to use two macaroons from the batch her aunt Maria had brought a couple of days ago from a trinket and dessert shop called "Dark Dreams."

Once her coffee was ready, she poured it into a large, cow-shaped cup with a super-glued handle, arranged it at three o'clock vis-à-vis the breakfast plate and sat down to dine.

It was a routine she had to go through every morning to turn on her brain. This morning was no different, despite the most explosive and euphoric sex she'd ever had just a few hours ago. Her mind didn't analyze anything—it was a soothing blank slate.

But her body remembered and relived every touch, every sensation, every sound. She still tingled from head to toe from the aftershocks of bliss. Her nerve endings continued to hum with pleasure and need.

Yes, her body remembered.

It also anticipated. Would he come again tonight?

They hadn't spoken of it, but she'd made clear how long she intended to have him. Her previous partners had been very prompt at following her instructions, thrilled to prolong the orgy-filled encounter.

But Devlin Sinclair was different. She couldn't anticipate him at all.

A muscle ticked near her left eye. Apparently she could have a few thoughts before her brain fully woke up, after all. Disturbing thoughts. Stressful thoughts.

She needed to regain her inner balance.

Grace finished her breakfast, washed the dishes and locked herself in the bathroom for the next half hour to set herself to rights again. By the time she emerged, she'd successfully focused her mind and body on other things.

Calming habits like taking her chinchilla Miu-Miu to the apartment's rooftop terrace, to which only Grace had the key, having reserved it for the duration of her lease.

While the pet rodent sniffed around the potted plants and wicker furniture, enjoying her thirty minutes of liberation from her cage, large and well-stocked though it was, Grace diligently wrote in a red, leather-bound journal, as her psychiatrist had directed her to do.

It was a way to get more in touch with herself, Dr. Weisman had said. By writing down her thoughts and going back over them every day, she might be able to peel the layers of the metaphorical onion back and reveal her *feelings*.

He encouraged her to use adjectives and adverbs, rather than simply nouns and verbs. Rather than state, she should describe, even if her words didn't make logical sense, even if it was just a jumbled stream of consciousness.

Her phone buzzed beside her with a text from her aunt.

I brought groceries, let me in.

Grace punched in a series of codes that automatically unlocked her front door, but stayed on the terrace until the full thirty minutes was up. Her aunt knew her routines well and was never offended by her apparent lack of welcome.

In truth, Grace looked forward to each and every one of Aunt Maria's visits.

When she finally made it downstairs and put Miu-Miu back into her cage, Grace went to stand before her aunt, lining up for her usual hug.

Which she received without a moment's delay. Aunt Maria gave the best hugs. A good five seconds' worth. A lengthy, fragrant squeeze of affection that never failed to warm Grace inside out.

"Grace, honey, what am I going to do with you?" her aunt admonished when she finally released her. "A piece of molded brie, water, bananas and macaroons. That's all you have to eat in the house?"

Grace shrugged. She didn't see any issues with this diet. If she craved anything in particular, she'd get it at a restaurant nearby. There were many good eateries in Soho.

"Well, I brought you ready-made salads, they come with dressing, mandarin oranges, your favorite, a fresh-baked sour dough bread, and some meats and cheeses. You just have to warm it up in the oven or microwave if you want that roasted taste with melted cheese."

Most likely Grace would eat them cold, though her kitchen was outfitted with a high-end induction range and other stainless steel appliances. They still shone like new because she never used them. The refrigerator, sink and coffee machine were the only kitchen installations she used on a regular basis.

"How are you, Aunt Maria? How is work?" Grace asked perfunctorily.

Niceties didn't come naturally to her, and she'd rather take a needle to the eye than make small talk. But this was Aunt Maria, and she wanted to make an extra effort.

Her aunt bustled about in the kitchen, preparing herself and Grace plates of roast beef sandwiches with fruit and salad, as it was almost twelve. She knew that Grace had her lunch promptly at noon.

"We took in another child yesterday," Maria said as she worked, "sweet little thing of maybe four years old. Doesn't seem to know her own name. Parents died in a car crash with no will and no close relatives. She's been shuttled to and fro in the system for weeks already. Probably still shell shocked from her loss and all the confusion ensuing. I'm trying to get her to talk to us, but she hasn't said a word since she arrived."

They sat adjacent to each other at the kitchen counter, Maria taking the end and Grace taking the side. There was a dining table large enough to seat six right next to the counter, but Grace used it more to spread out her work, while the desk in the corner served mainly as a place to put all the flowering plants her aunt gave her over the years.

Grace had long since stopped taking care of the plants, since she apparently had a very brown thumb; Maria came by almost every day, regularly enough to make sure they were given the right amount of love.

"I can come talk to her if you want," Grace offered.

She often volunteered at the orphanage to spend time with the children. She related so much better to them than to adults. And they seemed to understand her and weren't put off by her awkwardness. Given the amount of time she spent there, perhaps it was fairer to say that the children volunteered *their* time to keep Grace company than the reverse.

"That would be nice," Maria answered, taking a big bite of her sandwich and chewing robustly. "Maybe she'll talk to you. You have a way with the children."

Grace used a knife and fork to cut her sandwich into four quarters of triangles before starting on one with measured bites. She chewed each mouthful exactly eight times before swallowing.

"I don't really feel like an adult," she said in between bites.

Except for when she engaged in marathon orgies with the opposite sex.

Maria paused in her eating to regard her niece closely. She was silent for long moments, but Grace took no notice. She interacted with the world around her at her own pace, which led her sometimes to pick up conversational threads that others had long abandoned, or enter into prolonged silences while others waited in vain for her to finish her sentence.

"Grace," Maria began, laying a hand gently on Grace's shoulder. But she didn't finish whatever thought she started on.

Instead, she looked toward the massive California-king bed in the northeast corner of the studio. It was made with military precision, not a wrinkle in sight. But a corner of the coverlet was turned down. Like an invitation to sink into the downy softness again.

Grace always made her bed after breakfast and bathroom, in that order. But the folded corner indicated that she was expecting company later.

Every six months for two weeks like clockwork.

Maria didn't understand it, but despite how her niece felt, she *was* an adult, and it wasn't Maria's place to pry.

When this "habit" first began, Maria had the misfortune of running into Grace's guest on his way out of the apartment. When questioned, Grace had calmly and logically explained what she'd been doing and why she was doing it.

Maria didn't approve, but she also couldn't forbid the daughter of her heart from making human connections any way she could, for she did it so rarely.

Not that Grace ever heeded her aunt in any case. She always did whatever she wanted. On the one hand, you could say she didn't conform to societal norms. On the other hand, Grace Darling was freer than most other human beings who did behave as expected, who lived within boundaries.

But… Maria decided to broach the subject anyway. These emotionless "connections" couldn't make her niece happy. Wouldn't comfort her when one day Maria was gone.

Grace needed someone to lean on in life. Someone to give her tight hugs and feed her good food.

"Are you busy with a guest these two weeks?" Maria asked, trying to sound nonchalant, even though Grace wouldn't pick up on her moods or tone.

"Yes," Grace answered, finishing her last bite of sandwich and moving on to her salad, again, cutting the leaves into organized sections.

Maria nodded. Making conversation with her niece was like pulling teeth.

"What does he look like?"

"He's magnificent."

Maria choked on the sip of water she was just in the process of swallowing, the bold adjective taking her by surprise, even though Grace said it with not a smidgeon of emotion.

"Really? Tell me more," Maria encouraged.

But Grace abruptly left her seat and walked away.

Well, that seemed to be the end of that conversation.

Except, shortly, Grace returned with a red notebook.

She sat back on her counter stool and flipped to a page bookmarked by a string.

"Face: classic, sapphire, bumpy nose, thick lashes. Form: tall, hairless, lean, muscled, angular. Sound: deep, husky, rich, soothing. Smell: clean, crisp, minty, male. Taste: salty, spicy, chocolatey—"

She paused in her recitation to interject, "Just his nipples. He tastes like chocolate there."

"Oh." Maria's blush was steaming up her face.

Grace continued on, "Sexual organs: prodigious, steely, satiny, plum—"

"That's quite enough, dear!" Maria interrupted with a high-pitched squeal. "I get the picture."

Grace closed her journal and set it on the counter, picking up her utensils to finish her salad.

"Do you, ah, do you jot down such details for all of your... your guests?" Maria ventured, after gulping down the rest of her water.

"No. My past partners haven't been memorable. I don't usually think of them the day after. But this was on my mind when it was time to write in my journal. I have three pages of descriptions and would have continued but time was up."

"So this one is special?" Maria leaned in with an optimistic smile.

Grace shrugged.

"It's what I thought of this morning, that's all. Maybe I will think of something else tomorrow."

"Isn't he coming back tonight?" Maria knew her routine well, disapproving or not.

Grace splayed the sections of her orange like a flowering lotus blossom on her plate, before plucking one off its pin and putting it into her mouth.

Maria waited while she chewed. Grace didn't speak while chewing.

After a swallow, she said, "I don't know."

And that was the end of the discussion, Maria thought, but then Grace said something she'd never uttered before, for it presupposed a degree of feeling, a type of emotion—she said:

"I hope so."

Chapter Five

Benjamin D'Angelo could barely stop himself from skipping as he walked, hand in hand between his favorite women, down the street.

On his left was Sophia St. James, the Pure Ones' Queen, but to Benji, she was simply "big sister Sophie." Sophia smiled a lot and laughed a lot and always said the funniest things. She just finished her second year of college and was going to spend all summer staying with Benji and his parents in NYC for an internship at the Met.

On his right was Nana Chastain, Benji's new Mommy, though his father Gabriel called her Inanna for some strange reason. Benji just called her Mommy, and sometimes Mom or Mother when he was feeling particularly mature given that he was already six years old. She's not so new anymore, but Benji always felt the same thrill every time he claimed her for his very own. Nana looked like a golden angel, and she gave the best kisses and hugs.

On Nana's right was Benji's Uncle Tal, though Mommy called him Papa. Benji had learned early on that one's mother's father was one's grandfather. But since Benji wasn't born to Nana, perhaps that rule didn't apply.

Besides, Benji had met grandfathers before, those of his classmates and new friends made at parks and playgrounds, and they looked really *old*. Uncle Tal looked older than Daddy but not *that* old.

It likely helped that Daddy, Mommy and Uncle Tal were all elves and vampires, and vampire-elves. That meant they never grew old. Whereas Sophia and Benji were just humans, though special humans according to Sophia, and they couldn't wait to grow up.

Benji wished Daddy could have come on their outing too, but he had to run some errands like getting their rental stocked and prepared, buying groceries and cooking dinner.

Nana's apartment where they usually stayed when in the City wasn't spacious enough for everyone, so they found a bigger home within walking distance to the Met. And among the five of them, only Daddy knew how to cook and cook well, though Sophia made some mean breakfast dishes, like Benji's favorite French toast with Nutella.

"Where are we going now, Mommy?" Benji asked eagerly.

They had just finished a tour of the Metropolitan Museum of Art—Sophia was going to help curate the Persian exhibit—had a light lunch in the cafeteria there, and took the subway to Brooklyn to rummage through the street fairs.

Benji's stomach growled.

"From the sounds of it, we're going to get an afternoon snack," Inanna answered, hearing her adopted son's hunger pangs despite the boisterous street they were walking down.

"Count me in!" Sophia seconded the notion. "How about some kind of dessert? Like ice-cream or pastries?"

"I know just the place," Inanna said. "It's not far from here."

She turned to Tal, whose arm she held close to her right side.

"Papa? Are you up for it?" she asked quietly, so the others couldn't hear.

Her father had a lot of pride, as any warrior-class Pure male would. Though he'd regained much of his old strength over the past year, his blindness still made him uneasy in strange, new surroundings. The hustle and bustle of the City were even more disorienting than Boston where they'd been staying since they'd liberated him from his centuries-old prison in Japan. She knew he must be exhausted after several hours of being out and about.

New York City was intimidating to most. But to a blind, four-thousand-year-old warrior who had spent most of that time imprisoned and closed off from civilization, the City was Tartarus.

Her father gave a brief nod and squeezed the hand on his arm reassuringly. But the tight clench of his jaw did not escape her. His entire body was strung tight as steel, vibrating with tension.

She'd rather have left him at their temporary home where it was calm and quiet; he could have used the time to familiarize himself with the layout. But she also knew that he didn't want to be treated like he was special because of his disability and history. He didn't want the extra attention or to be handled with kid gloves. So she off-handedly invited him to come out with them on an excursion in the City, and he accepted.

Inanna searched her father's face with a concerned, heart-aching gaze.

He'd come such a long way in such a short time. When they found him, he'd been a barely-breathing skeleton with so many open, festering wounds on his body, the Pure Ones' Royal Healer, Rain Ambrosius, had cursed vehemently in Chinese while shaking her head in amazement that he'd managed to survive thousands of years of torture and captivity.

Once, the Healer had the ability to use her *zhen* to draw out and absorb the pain and poison from wounds, healing sufferers much faster than any medical procedure or drug. But she'd lost her ability when she gave her life and Gift for her Eternal Mate. Now, she was just a Healer like any other, albeit an exceptionally talented one.

This meant that Tal's recovery had been long and arduous. It was a testament to his will and determination and hard-headed stubbornness that he was mostly whole today.

Mostly. Not completely. He and Rain refused to say a word, but Inanna knew that her father was far from well. She worried for him constantly. She couldn't bear to lose him again.

Not ever again.

"It's just around the corner. You'll love it," she said, valiantly making her tone cheerful and putting an enthusiastic bounce in her step for Sophia and Benji's sakes.

No one soothed and calmed like Mama Bear. And her pastries were to die for. Tal would feel so much better after a good long sit-down in her delightful shop "Dark Dreams."

*** *** *** ***

"I'm leaving for the Shield today," Ryu Takamura said after knocking twice on Devlin's tech room door.

Devlin swiveled around to face him, folding his hands casually over his stomach, tilting his chair back and sprawling his legs.

His lips tipped up at one corner.

"Seems you're all abandoning our little group, first Inanna, now you. And let's not forget the traitor who met her deserved fate. It's getting downright boring around here."

Ryu was not fooled by his comrade's careless tone.

"I'll only be in Boston for a few weeks while Ava and the baby get checked out and she works with the Healer on her research. Her parents would never part with Kane longer than that."

Devlin tilted his head to one side. "Does your wife's people know about what you are yet?"

Ryu uncomfortably rubbed the back of his neck, though the word "wife" never failed to put a dopey grin on his face, a rare occurrence for the Ninja.

"We didn't see the need to alarm them yet," he answered, "it's up to Ava when she's ready to tell them. It would have to be soon, though, because as she makes progress on finding a treatment or cure for her father's Parkinson's, she's going to have to involve him and explain where the drug comes from, the powers of her new DNA."

Devlin was silent for a few moments and Ryu grew self-conscious under his friend's intense blue gaze.

"What?" he couldn't resist asking.

Devlin shrugged. "Nothing. Just that love and marriage and a baby carriage seem to suit you," he said simply, sincerely.

The Chosen's Assassin colored, both from shyness and pleasure.

"I don't have a clue what I'm doing," he admitted. "But I'll do whatever it takes to make them happy. I'll spend the next thousand years, Dark Goddess willing, to deserve this."

Devlin rose from his seat and clapped a hand on his comrade's shoulder. Ryu was his closest friend among all of the Chosen. He was the brother Devlin had always wanted, someone fiercely loyal, brave and good.

Unlike his biological brother.

"You've always deserved this life," Devlin told Ryu solemnly. "I don't know a better man to heap with happiness."

"I do," Ryu returned, clapping a hand of his own on Devlin's shoulder on the other side, "You, *kōhai*."

Devlin gave Ryu's shoulder a couple of manly thwacks and pulled back, huffing a falsely light-hearted laugh.

"Not me, *senpai*," he said. "Why would I ever give up all the beautiful feminine bounty in the world for just one in particular?"

"Because you choose her, and she chooses you," the Ninja answered, ever a man of few words, but they always made an impact.

Uncomfortable with the direction of the conversation, Devlin sat back in his chair and swiveled to face the giant screens full of code.

Without looking back, he said, "Have fun in Boston and try not to miss me too much while you're gone."

When he heard Ryu's departure and the soft click of the door, Devlin slumped a bit in his chair and stared at the screens unseeingly.

The Chosen was down from six to just Maximus, Ana and himself. Ryu was technically still part of the team, but he had his own life now and seldom stayed at the Cove. Their Queen seemed to be in no hurry to repopulate their ranks by recruiting more warriors. She'd been out of sorts ever since her association with the Pure Ones' Consul Seth Tremaine ended over a year ago.

Boring was not the right word to describe the situation; it was lonely.

Devlin was lonely.

Taking a determined breath, he refocused on the task at hand.

The Dark Queen's summons earlier had been about recent developments with the fight club networks and the disappearance of many warrior-class Dark Ones and Pure Ones alike.

All linked to a mysterious figure called Medusa, whom Devlin had been hunting for the past fifteen months.

Given their tenuous relationship with humans and fragile truce with the Pure Ones, and given that in many ways, their Kind was an endangered species—only a hundred thousand or so in a world of 7.6 billion people, they kept detailed records of every vampire born and made.

Recently, there had been accountings of far more vampires than records indicated, and many Dark Ones from noble, ancient families had mysteriously fallen off the grid.

If Devlin connected the random series of dots, he'd wager that someone was amassing and *creating* a vampire army.

Ryu Takamura's wife, Ava, was a critical link in the puzzle. Her research in genetic engineering was what had led them to Medusa in the first place.

A year ago they'd disbanded the fight clubs in the epicenter of NYC, but others had sprouted in Tokyo, populous parts of Asia and large Eastern European cities. Not enough to raise much notice from human law enforcement, especially since Ryu had dispatched his network of shadow Ninjas to suppress outbreaks in Tokyo and Seoul, but enough that Devlin detected the pattern from afar.

Their enemies had gotten smarter though, and whenever the Chosen traced a new node of the fight club expansion, it suddenly went underground again. It was like they were chasing ghosts.

Which was also what Devlin had been tracking on the Net. Sometimes it seemed like Medusa and her minions were merely figments of his imagination. Months would go by without any progress or clues. He was a very patient hunter, but even he was starting to seethe with frustration. His prey was getting too far out ahead of him. If he wasn't careful, he could lose the leads entirely.

The only break he had thus far was one Grace Darling.

She was the architect of Medusa's impenetrable cyber fortress. Devlin doubted she knew her part in Medusa's growing global empire of violence, destruction and mass chaos, because their nemesis operated through well-established government agencies and reputable organizations. Tens of thousands of innocent employees were involved, just doing their jobs, unwitting cogs in Medusa's wheel.

At that very thought, a blinking square appeared on the upper right hand corner of Devlin's central monitor.

"I have a question for you," the message appeared out of nowhere.

Devlin quickly checked the encrypted IP address. It was *Mith*, Grace's online handle.

A surprised burst of breath left his chest.

So much for all the security he'd wrapped around the Cove's technology like barbed wire and electric fence heaped with motion lasers and auto-target machine guns.

Grace had apparently infiltrated his secure network like it was child's play. He was both admiring of her skills and chagrinned at his own lack. But now was not the time to dwell on it.

"I'm all ears," he typed back.

"Do you have STDs?"

Devlin blinked. It was rather late for her to be asking the question, but then, he supposed they'd been preoccupied with other things last night. The building could have collapsed around them and he wouldn't have noticed.

Given his pause, she explained, "I always check into these things, but I couldn't find your records."

"No. And I don't have any proof; you'll have to take my word for it," he answered quickly.

This was not something to beat around the bush about. He would have provided medical records, but vampires didn't have any; there wasn't any need. Foreign microorganisms were killed immediately upon entering their bodies. They never fell ill.

The little square blinked for a few seconds, and then, "I don't have any either. STDs, that is. Do you want to see my test results?"

"I believe you."

Christ.

What an awkward post-orgy conversation. Not that any of his online exchanges with Grace had been what one would call smooth or relaxing. It was like a beat-up old car with misfiring spark plugs clunking along inch by inch and stalling every other foot.

At the moment, even though he knew he should be trying to get some answers out of her with respect to her position at Zenn, he didn't know how to start the conversational thread after their... shared experience... the night before.

"You didn't drink my blood last night, why?"

Apparently, she had no such qualms.

Devlin didn't even know how to answer. He'd never hesitated before when Consent was given. It was for survival, after all, and he was due for a good long swill. He'd wanted more than anything to take her blood last night, especially in the throes of sexual ecstasy.

But the truth was, Devlin had never taken a female's blood during intercourse. He'd taken it before and after, and also when sex wasn't involved at all. He liked to keep the two separate, and he'd never had any trouble maintaining the boundary.

Last night, he'd already felt out of control, somewhat terrifyingly at her mercy. He'd wanted desperately to take her blood; it was almost an imperative.

Which was why he resisted to the end.

Somehow he knew that the combination of the two— blood and sex—with Grace Darling was a recipe for an explosive that he couldn't defuse. It was safer for all involved if he never lit the charge.

Flippantly he answered, "Can't reveal all my mysteries in one night. What then would we have to look forward to?"

"Does that mean you're coming tonight?"

Devlin pulled a shaky hand down his face.

What a question. And the unintended double entendre didn't help. He'd crossed the line last night mixing business with pleasure.

As a spy for the British army in his human life, he'd had to play parts to form useful relationships and obtain intel, but he'd been in full control of every situation he entered. He'd charmed women *and* men, pretended to be people he was not, even carried on lengthy flirtations and kissed a number of people he didn't feel any pleasure in kissing.

But sex had been off limits.

Last night with Grace Darling, however, had been limitless. In ways beyond physical. Ways Devlin didn't want to think about right now.

Maybe ever.

"I have questions to ask you," the letters of her typed words trickled onto the screen.

"You can ask them now." Perhaps he could avoid being too close to her again. Or at least stall for some time while he sorted out his jumbled thoughts and emotions.

"Why did you seek me out?"

"We have similar interests and happened to collide on the same topic in the chat—" he typed in response, but she interrupted him.

"No, why are you pretending to be *Azor Ahai* to talk to me and meet with me? I want to know the truth."

Devlin leaned back in his chair.

So much for subterfuge. It might work to his advantage to just be direct with her. She seemed like a direct sort of woman. Perhaps she could even be an ally in his hunt for Medusa.

"I was hoping to borrow your hacking skills," he answered truthfully. "I was hoping you could tell me more about Zenn, the company you work for."

Her conversational square on the screen blinked for a long while.

Just when he thought she wouldn't answer, she typed, "Then come back tonight."

Devlin frowned. Was she suggesting what it sounded like?

He couldn't resist clarifying, "You'll answer my questions and help me... in exchange for favors?"

"Yes, if I can."

Devlin cleared his throat.

"For sex?"

"No," was the immediate response. "I'll give you twelve hours of pleasure in exchange for the use of your body. And I'll answer your questions if you bring dinner."

Well.

Put that way, it sounded downright reasonable as far as trades went. At least that's what Devlin's libido insisted, while more rational parts of him warned that he was playing with fire.

But before he knew what he was doing, his fingers had tapped out the word:

"Deal."

*** *** *** ***

The front door to Dark Dreams jingled a little as Inanna pushed it open.

There was never a sign in the window that indicated whether the shop was open or closed. Probably because it wasn't really a business. It was more like a historic home that was open to visitors whenever its owner felt like entertaining.

It was late afternoon, almost evening, perhaps too late to be having a snack and risk ruining dinner, but Gabriel had called earlier to say that he was running late. Dinner would be closer to eight, and probably wouldn't be fancier than salad and grilled salmon. Even if they didn't stay long at the shop, they could bring home some dessert for later.

The group of four entered the warmly-lit store like Aladdin tiptoeing into a treasure cave. Every time she came here, Inanna was captivated anew by Mama Bear's eclectic collection of trinkets, books and the ever-present scent of spicy tea and freshly-baked pastries.

Inanna didn't announce their presence, as Mama Bear could always hear the bells on her door.

The former-Chosen had always wondered whether it was safe for an elderly lady to open her house at all odd hours for any stranger to come barging in, but it was as if the place was protected by magic. Or perhaps even criminals knew that it was a sacred sanctuary, not to be disturbed, a sweet haven where the weary and the lost could go.

Using her Gift, Inanna could see through the far wall and kitchen shelving on the other side that Mama Bear was busy putting the final touches on a batch of Éclairs. They looked so good, Inanna's mouth started watering.

But first she needed to take care of Papa, who stood unmoving just two feet beyond the threshold while Sophia and Benji roved happily from shelf to shelf, *oohing* and *ahhing* over the intricate wares.

"Floor-to-ceiling shelves line each wall of this square chamber," Inanna described as she took her father's arm.

"It's about five hundred square feet, broken up by antique chests and bureaus. But if you walk straight, the path is four feet wide, unobstructed, and leads you directly to an oval tea table twenty feet ahead, large enough to seat four. Six would be cozy."

He nodded once, and she knew that he could picture clearly what she described.

He never talked of his time as a captive, but she gathered from the Healer that he had been blind for several hundred years at least. At Inanna's urging, Rain had divulged her assessment of how he sustained the injury.

As with every other torture he'd endured, the process of rendering him blind had been vicious, excruciating, calculated. And repeated over and over and over again. Whoever did this made sure that even with his Pure healing abilities at full capacity, he would never see again.

Never use his Gift again.

In time, he'd taught himself to visualize perfectly in his mind's eye the spaces and dimensions around him. His other senses had heightened to compensate.

He moved so easily once he'd familiarized himself with his surroundings that people who didn't know of his disability would never have guessed he was blind. Only the cloudy opacity of his turquoise irises gave him away. That, and the apparent lack of pupils.

As a warrior, he was still one of the best, and getting stronger with each passing day.

But new places were always daunting to him at first, not surprisingly. Inanna suspected that he feared inconveniencing others and shaming himself in the process. He wasn't the type of male who ever asked for help.

Inanna took his hand and put it on the edge of a shelf to his left.

"Many of the wares are fragile, but many are not," meaning, if they were accidentally dropped, they wouldn't break. She wanted to let him know that it was safe to explore the store if he chose.

Besides, if anything did break, her fortune was vast enough to buy small countries, so replacing a trinket in this store shouldn't be a challenge.

Inanna wanted to hover, but she forced herself to let go of her father and move away, giving him space.

He'd let her know during the first few months of his uneasy convalescence without ever raising his voice or uttering a harsh word that he intended to be self-reliant. He would figure it out, whatever challenge came his way in this strange, modern world. Even without the use of his sight.

But oh, how her heart ached for him.

It was a balmy summer day in July. Inanna wore a light, short-sleeved shirt and comfortable slacks. Sophia chose a breezy, colorful sundress, and Benji was in a Batman T-shirt and shorts.

Tal, however, wore a long-sleeved Henley with black jeans. He never wore clothing that revealed more skin than absolutely necessary. The light-weight cotton Henley was the only concession he made to the hot weather, because in cooler times, he always wore a turtleneck.

The better to hide the countless scars he bore all over his body.

Inanna took a shuddering breath. She didn't have enough tears to shed for all the pain he'd endured.

Thankfully, a wondrous exclamation from Benji drew her attention and she went to check on her son.

Alone for the moment, Tal slowly and carefully traced three fingers along the edge of the shelf, level with the middle of his chest.

When nothing wobbled or tipped over, he ventured deeper into the shelf and grazed the top of a small ornate box.

He could feel the jewels embedded in the lid, stones and pearls. Next, he felt something soft and flexible. He took hold of it gently and rubbed his thumb over the outer fabric. A face, two arms, two dangling stuffed legs. A doll of some sort.

His heart clenched involuntarily.

There had been no dolls for his daughter growing up. He'd carved wooden figures for her when he could, but he hadn't known anything about dolls. He hadn't really thought through what little girls played with.

Others in their fort and surrounding villages had been kind, contributing clothes, shoes, feminine accessories. But he couldn't recall that she'd ever had a doll.

Tal replaced the fabric doll on the shelf and moved on.

His fingers grazed the rim of a bowl. The material was thick and sturdy with a smooth glaze to coat. It reminded him of the bowls he used in ancient Akkad for supping. But he guessed that such bowls weren't uncommon even in modern times. Surely he wouldn't find four thousand year old pottery on display in a Brooklyn trinket store.

The aroma of freshly brewed tea and baked goods wafted into his nostrils from the back of the shop.

More than any other modern experience, excepting music, he was always amazed by the different scents in this age from those that had been familiar to him so long ago. Fragrances, perfumes, body odor, foods...some were enticing, some soothing, but others were noxious and unnatural. Like car exhaust, the laying of fresh concrete, the burning of plastic.

This shop had the most wonderful smells. The wares on the shelves reminded him of his ancient homeland, yet the scents from the kitchen gave him the sense of simply being *home*.

Even though he'd never smelled these scents before. Even though he'd never set foot in this shop before.

And then his inquisitive fingers alighted on an object made out of wood, small enough to fit in the palm of his hand. He gingerly took it from the shelf and smoothed his thumb around the shape of it.

An animal. A dog—no, cat, perhaps a large predatory cat—sitting tall on its haunches, its tail curling around one hind paw. From neck to haunches something soft wrapped round and round its body, the material worn thin by time and use.

His breath abruptly froze in his chest. Why did the object feel so familiar? Even the smooth grain of the wood felt like a memory, with warmth of its own that heated even further in his hand.

A sudden, sharp pain splintered through his internal organs, almost taking him to his knees. The wooden sculpture fell with a soft *cluck* to the concrete floor.

"Papa, are you all right?"

Inanna was immediately beside him, taking hold of his arm.

But Tal couldn't hear or feel her. He was engulfed in pain.

Bittersweet memories assailed him. The breaking of his heart devastated him.

There was not a day that went by that he didn't think of *her*. Not a moment without regretting how he'd hurt her, and how he destroyed himself in the process. It took sustained concentration to keep these thoughts at bay, pushed into the back of his mind.

But now they came flooding forth, and he was helpless to stem them.

Where did that wooden carving come from? How did it come to be in this store in this time?

Who—

"Is your friend all right?"

A new voice hovered behind him.

It sounded like an older woman's voice, with a lilting accent, somewhere between Eastern European and American South. It was a voice he'd never heard before, but it raised the fine hairs all over Tal's body.

"Nana, dear," the woman continued to speak in soothing tones, "perhaps we should help him to the tea table to have a seat. A good strong cup of tea and some sugary treats might be just what he needs."

Inanna said something in return that Tal did not catch. All of his attention, all of his senses focused on the source of that voice.

As if time had frozen and everything and everyone around him had disappeared, he slowly turned to face the owner of that voice.

A soft gasp.

So soft, he wouldn't have caught it had he not been ultra attuned to every sound from that direction.

He stared with all his strength in the direction the gasp came from. The figure was short, he knew, so he aimed his gaze lower. It was no use of course. He saw only blackness. Unending blackness.

But a figure took shape in his mind's eye nevertheless. And a face, lovingly rendered by memories and dreams, blossomed in the dark. He reached out a hand toward the haunting vision.

Please. His heart pleaded.

A shuddering draw of breath.

Everything I have endured, every pain and humiliation. It would all be worth it if I could hold you again. Please come back to me.

But no one took hold of his hand. And all he heard was the sound of retreating footsteps, forever leaving him.

Alone in darkness and pain.

Chapter Six

He arrived five minutes after six at her door.

Grace worked through the series of locks and deadbolts to admit him into her studio apartment for their second night. Or at least, she hoped it would be their "second night."

She hoped he understood what his acceptance of her invitation meant, so that she wouldn't have to devote precious time to convincing him to share his body again. Such things had never been in doubt before, but Grace learned quickly never to assume with Devlin Sinclair.

She was starting to glean aspects of his personality and attitude, something she hadn't really bothered to assess in other people she'd encountered in her life. They simply hadn't mattered enough for her to make the attempt.

But Devlin was different somehow. He mattered.

He mattered to Grace.

So she began a mental list of facts and observations about him.

One, he didn't take sex lightly. He needed to feel friendship and affection for his partner.

Note to self, Grace needed to up her friendly game. Whatever that meant. Perhaps she could smile more at him. She'd read the book *How to Win Friends and Influence People* by Dale Carnegie on her Kindle earlier in the day. Smiling seemed to be important for starting friendships.

Two, he was what one might call an old-school gentleman. Open doors. Pull out chairs. Ladies First.

He'd demonstrated impeccable manners all last night, especially the last—in every way—including making sure she preceded him in orgasms every single time.

True, she was at the peak of her hormone surge and it was no difficult task to make her come. And also true, it was all but impossible for men to have multiple orgasms the way women could, so it wasn't like he could ever compete with her on that count, though he'd certainly impressed her with his ability to maintain an erection for hours on end.

Twelve hours. Hard as steel.

Grace's mind hiccupped in remembrance. The logical, curious side of her brain wondered how it was biologically possible for a man to accomplish such a monumental feat, Viagra notwithstanding, while the usually submerged, primitive side of her brain wondered whether he could repeat the minor miracle for a second night in a row and when she could start taking advantage of it.

Devlin cleared his throat.

"I have groceries, where would you like me to put them?"

Grace blinked dazedly at him. How long had he been standing there by the door? He'd greeted her upon entry, hadn't he? But she'd been distracted by her thoughts and hadn't responded.

Right. She needed to pay more attention. The book mentioned that bit.

"Kitchen counter," she finally said. "But you should know that I don't cook."

He moved past her to place two brown paper bags, full of goodies, on the counter.

A corner of his sensuous lips tilted as he said, "Yes, I had a feeling that might be the case. Fortunately, I do cook, and I'm quite proficient at it. But you can judge for yourself."

She sat on one of the barstools and watched him while he unloaded the items, almost getting distracted again by the graceful way he moved, the poetry of his long-fingered hands opening and closing bags, arranging the ingredients he needed in front of him.

"You'll have to show me where everything is," he said. And after she did so, she went back to her stool to watch him work.

"Shrimp and scallops?"

He didn't look up from chopping some vegetables and spices as he said, "Seafood is your favorite, right?"

She tilted her head and considered him.

"I don't recall everything I told you in the chat room, but I do recall that you didn't tell me much about yourself. Only that you like to tinker with programming and that you're an avid gamer in your free time."

He glanced quickly at her through his lashes but continued cutting ingredients.

"What would you like to know?"

What would she like to know about him? It was such a big question. There were endless things she wanted to know, and she surprised herself with the realization.

She started with the basics, because they hadn't really covered that ground yet.

"Do you have family?"

"None that I keep in contact with," he answered readily. "You could say I have some very distant relatives in various parts of the world. But it's just me here in the City."

Though Grace couldn't really empathize, and even if she could, she didn't know how to express it, she did understand what it was like to be mostly alone in the world.

"I don't have anyone either, except my aunt Maria. My parents passed away a long time ago."

He looked at her and she thought that his sapphire eyes shimmered. At the very least they conveyed a warmth that she felt all over her body, as if he'd wrapped his arms around her.

"I'm sorry you lost them so young," he said in that low, husky voice of his. "How did they die?"

"Hurricane. They were driving on a highway that collapsed. I was at home obliviously designing computer games in the basement. It was the next day before I even realized they hadn't come home, I get so wrapped up in my own world. The police came later to tell me what happened."

As she recited the events, Grace's chest started to ache a little, even though she wasn't entirely certain why. Was it possible that she missed her parents? She barely recalled what they looked like.

"Why don't you keep in touch with your family?" she asked him. He seemed like a "normal" guy if extraordinarily beautiful.

Well, and there were the fangs and the bloodsucking. But nobody was perfect.

Didn't normal people want to be close to their families?

"My immediate family members are dead," he answered without inflection, keeping his gaze on his chopping. "But even before that, we weren't exactly a close-knit family."

That sounded...lonely, even to Grace.

"Who are you close to then?"

A brief smile, not particularly happy, just a stretch of his lips, flashed and disappeared.

"I have a few friends. Colleagues from work."

"Do you work for the government?" she immediately asked.

He seemed amused by the question.

"No."

"It took some effort to hack into your network this morning. What is it you do for a living?"

Devlin paused to consider, then resumed his dinner preparations.

"I'm like a bounty hunter you could say. Except I don't hunt for money; I do it because it's necessary, I'm very good at it, and I enjoy it."

He found a brand new baking tray that Grace didn't even realize she had, drizzled some olive oil on the bottom and laid in large, unshelled, deveined tiger shrimp, heaped sauces and Japanese Panko on top and put it in the oven at 400F.

"Why are you an enterprise architect, Grace?" he asked in return. "Why do you work for Zenn?"

"It's necessary, I'm very good at it, and it affords me the lifestyle I want."

He moved on to a large skillet and prepared to sear the jumbo sea scallops on her never-before-used induction range, which was built into the kitchen island so that those seated at the counter could watch the cook in action.

So that Grace could ogle this particular cook.

"Why is it necessary?" he asked.

He was wearing a white collared shirt today with sleeves rolled up to the elbows and the top two buttons undone to reveal the notch between his collarbones and a tantalizing hint of his well-defined pectorals.

That mysterious notch...the suprasternal notch. So mesmerizing in a male—*this* male.

Grace's gaze zeroed in on it and stuck there. She bet if she put the tip of her tongue there, she could feel his heartbeat. And he would feel it quicken his pulse, start a wildfire in his bloodstream, right down to his—

"Grace?"

She struggled to tear her eyes away from that fascinating little crater, but finally met his gaze.

"What did you say?" Her voice had lowered an octave of its own volition. The primitive part of her brain was starting to take over.

He heard the change in her tone and darted a glance at her, immediately picking up the steaming lust that fogged up her eyes.

Grace saw him visibly swallow before turning back to flipping the scallops over in the pan.

"Why is it necessary that you work for Zenn?"

She shifted her gaze from his chest to something safer like the plump, succulent scallops browning on the skillet.

"They keep me out of trouble," she replied. "I don't have a good relationship with the government."

"Because you hacked into their systems at the age of twelve and stole ten million dollars in federal funds?"

She shrugged, not surprised that he knew. He had formidable hacking abilities of his own. Perhaps he knew all about her personal history too. She wondered why he bothered to ask her. But strangely, she was glad to have related it to him.

"They were too slow to release the money to the families that had been devastated by Hurricane Rachel. Thousands were without food, water, never mind shelter. I saw it on the news. I just sped up the process of transferring the funds to the families and the rescue teams on the ground. It seemed like a better use of my time than playing video games in my basement while I waited for things to happen. It's not like I kept any of it."

"Zenn cut a deal with the government to keep you out of prison?"

Grace shrugged again.

"I don't know who did what. I just know that one minute I was locked up in a cell, though I don't think it was in a prison, and the next minute aunt Maria was there to take me away. All I had to do to stay free was to write some programs for this company and get paid well doing it."

She risked looking into the deep pools of his sapphire eyes.

"Why are you so interested in Zenn?"

*** *** *** ***

Devlin bided his time answering by removing the perfectly seared scallops from the skillet to two awaiting plates. He put three on each, drizzled freshly-made lemon butter sauce on top, added some garnish and a few forkfuls of walnut arugula salad. He had about two minutes before the shrimp would be ready.

All the while, he debated internally whether to trust her with the truth. And if so, how much to reveal.

He decided to go with his gut and tell her directly. He didn't think Grace Darling had the capacity for intrigue and subterfuge. Perhaps literally.

"Zenn is connected to a dangerous and powerful network with an entity called Medusa at its helm. I believe she's female, but I have nothing concrete or firsthand to confirm this."

He stared intently into her eyes and said, "I mean to destroy her empire and capture her for questioning. But if all else fails, I'll be satisfied with ending her."

She didn't even blink at the implication of potential murder. As if they were discussing the removal of rotted wood from a termite infestation and then exterminating the critters.

Had to be done. Nothing to it.

"How do you know it's dangerous? What proof do you have?"

He took the shrimp out and used tongs to put four on each of their plates before he answered.

"I can show you my investigation thus far and you can connect your own dots if you don't believe me. But there's no concrete evidence documented anywhere, and it's going to stay that way. We don't want official agencies involved in this."

"Why not?"

He set out their silverware and napkins and sat on a stool across the waterfall quartz counter from her.

"Bon appétit," he said as the oven clock flashed seven o'clock sharp, exactly when Grace always had her dinner.

She looked down at her gorgeously arranged plate, worthy of any five star restaurant, and didn't look particularly impressed. She didn't compliment his effort, didn't voice any thanks.

But when she cut a juicy scallop and put it into her mouth, her eyes closed with near-orgasmic bliss.

Devlin smiled. He'd take that as an indication that his cooking met with her approval.

This was the first time he'd ever made a meal for a woman. If the woman in question weren't Grace, he would have described the ambiance and activity as extremely romantic.

Domestic.

He cringed a bit at the very thought, but another part of him felt a sense of rightness and pure joy, taking care of a female, *feeding* her. It awakened a primitive, animal part of his vampire nature that he'd only ever called upon during the hunt.

It made him want to mark this female, possess her body and soul, bind her to him for eternity.

And that scared the hell out of him.

Besides, this was *Grace Darling*. It would be like binding himself to a glitchy computer. But then, computers didn't betray, so perhaps it wouldn't be so bad.

And they did have incredible, marathon orgies the likes of which Devlin hadn't even dreamed were possible.

They ate in silence for many minutes, lost in mutual enjoyment of the food.

Devlin thought she might have forgotten her question until she suddenly looked up from her plate and repeated, "Why don't you want the police or the FBI to get involved if this Medusa is as dangerous as you say?"

He put down his utensils for a moment to answer her fully.

"First, would you say these government agencies are particularly efficient in your experience?"

"Not particularly."

"Right. Second, do you think they are incorruptible?"

"No. I've seen some of their top secret files. They don't always do the right thing."

Devlin nodded. "I have evidence that Medusa's network is bankrolling some branches of the government, not just here in the U.S., but internationally. Nothing overt enough to call for an investigation, and even if one were to be flagged, Medusa no doubt has ways to suppress it."

Grace focused a couple of minutes to demolishing her meal, and then asked, "There's something else, isn't there? There's another reason."

Devlin inhaled deeply and released a long breath. He might as well go all-in. If his instincts didn't flash giant neon alarm signs when he contemplated eternity with her, he could probably trust her with the full truth, which he'd already begun to reveal last night.

"Yes," he confirmed her suspicion. "There is another reason we can't have official involvement."

He waited until she had finished her food and wiped her mouth, giving him her full attention.

"Medusa isn't human. You might have noticed that neither am I."

She tilted her head to regard him.

"I don't think having fangs and drinking blood makes you inhuman. I looked up some conditions where this happens. It's amazing the types of rare genetic disorders that are out there."

"I don't have a genetic disorder," Devlin said firmly. "This is what I am."

She stacked her hands beneath her chin and set her elbows on the counter, looking intently into his eyes.

"What are you?"

He smiled humorlessly.

"Surely you know of Bram Stoker's *Dracula*? Our kind is often romanticized in books and TV."

She nodded. "Vampires, you mean."

"You seem to take that in stride," he noted, amused.

She shrugged. "There are many things we have no real proof for, that people believe in or swear exist. God. Different kinds of gods. Ghosts. Aliens. Angels. Why not vampires and werewolves and witches too? I'm sure there's a perfectly logical explanation, even if it seems far-fetched. Maybe you're more human than you think. Maybe you just have a genetic mutation. But I get it. Most people might not embrace these anomalies as easily as I do."

"Grace," he couldn't help but admire her, "you are one in a million."

"Actually," she clarified, "one in sixty-eight children are identified with Autism Spectrum Disorder, and of those, one in ten thousand or so have similar symptoms that I exhibit, but not exactly the same. So you might say I am unique."

Oh yes, Devlin would agree emphatically with that.

She got off her barstool and walked around the counter toward him.

Or rather, *stalked* around the counter. Like a feline predator.

"So you're a vampire," she stated solemnly.

"We call ourselves Dark Ones," he informed her, watching her move closer and closer, until she was standing immediately before him.

Without preamble, she touched a fingertip to the notch at the base of his throat.

The sensation was so evocative Devlin almost fell off his stool.

"Do you drink blood to survive or because you enjoy it?"

She used the same fingertip to trace each wing of his collar bones, her eyes following the trail with a mesmerized intensity.

Devlin swallowed. His skin where she touched was breaking out in goosebumps. Fine hairs all over his body raised to attention like reeds in a stiff breeze.

"Definitely the first, and sometimes the latter."

She moved as close to him as his seat on the stool would allow, her hands bracing on each of his spread thighs. He fought to shift restlessly when she flexed her fingers against his denim-clad legs, kneading the tensed muscles beneath like a cat. He thought he even heard her purr.

"I want to know all about your kind," she said softly, almost whispering. "But not right now. Right now I have just one more question."

Devlin's adrenaline revved up as if he were an Olympic triathlete poised at the starting line.

"What's that?"

"What did you bring for dessert?" she inquired in that low, sultry voice of hers, now smoky with lust.

He'd forgotten about dessert. She'd mentioned before in the chat room that she didn't usually like sweets.

"I—"

"How considerate," she interrupted, pressing forward to lick his notch with the flat of her tongue in a long, hot, wet glide.

Fissures of pleasure streaked through Devlin's body like lightning bolts, straight to his cock and hardening it in an instant.

"You brought yourself," she answered for him, and then declared, "I'd like to have my dessert now, Devlin Sinclair. I'd like to have you."

*** *** *** ***

Estelle Martin sat on her bed in the small inner chamber that was little more than a box carved out of the back of the shop, everything built-in, including the bed, closets, shelves, and matching end tables.

No windows to let in any light.

She'd been sitting there for hours now, well into the night. For once, her shop was blanketed in darkness, not a single lamp turned on, not even the twinkle lights she used out front.

She sat there in silence, in her old-woman form, not bothering to change back into her true self, as if being in someone else's body helped to keep her own memories and experiences at bay.

Tal-Telal.

After thousands of years, he was here. In her shop. Not two feet before her.

He'd held out his hand to her.

Her mind skittered away from that image and focused on other aspects of the encounter.

Dark Goddess, but he'd changed!

It was as if her hatred, thirst for vengeance, all her pent up rage and resentment over the millennia toward the world at large and him in particular had manifested in his physical form. She'd only glimpsed him for brief seconds before she all but ran away, but she could recall every single detail of what she saw.

Once, he'd been so golden and bright he rivaled the very sun in the height of summer. And now he was winter incarnate.

His hair had been ruthlessly shaved, and what remained looked tough and brittle whereas she remembered long, silky tresses, thick and soft. It was a dull silver now, streaked with white, instead of the color of finely-spun gold glinting beneath the full blast of sun.

His skin, once a light honeyed tone, was now pale as death and stretched so thin over his flesh and bones she could see clearly every delicate vein beneath it. What she could see of it, at least, given that he'd been mostly covered in black fabric from head to toe.

His face bore lines where it had always been smooth and youthful. There were faint brackets around his mouth, creases between his brows, deep grooves in his cheeks. As if he frowned a lot. Suffered a lot. In contrast, there were no lines at the corners of his eyes. As if he never laughed. Never smiled.

And then there was his most arresting, defining feature: those brilliant turquoise eyes that had shone with an inner light like stars burning within the heart of laser-cut gems.

They no longer shone. They no longer burned.

They were cloudy and opaque like sand kicked up under powerful waves. His eyes seemed turbulent and unfocused now. And whereas once those eyes saw straight into the heart of any matter, any being, now they couldn't see what was immediately in front of him.

He was blind.

A sharp phantom pain exploded in her heart at the realization of how much he must have suffered. How much pain he must have endured. But she ruthlessly shoved the empathetic impulse into the periphery of her consciousness, buried so deep in the dessert wasteland of her heart no one would be able to find it, least of all herself.

There was a time when his pain was hers. When he dictated the rhythm of her heart, the cadence of her breath.

No longer. Never again.

She hadn't painstakingly sawed away her connection to him over hundreds and thousands of years just to be drawn back into his orbit now.

Even so, her hands fisted on her thighs involuntarily, bracing against the maelstrom of emotions that assaulted her.

Anguish. Sorrow. Anger. Regret. Longing. Self-loathing. Confusion. All in their most intense, most concentrated extremes.

But above all, one awareness eclipsed all others and clamored to the fore:

Raw hunger.

She shifted into her natural form as sharp fangs punched through her gums, dripping with saliva. A long, primal hiss emerged from her throat and ended on a growl.

Even now, after millennia apart, after she'd sworn to herself she'd never succumb again to temptation, she wanted him.

Craved him.

His blood in her mouth. His seed in her womb. His body all around and inside of her.

And she would have him, she vowed. She would have him on her own terms this time. She would have her fill until this burning need was exorcised from her body, mind and soul.

Until she fully achieved that ultimate state that was the antithesis of all-consuming, heart-rending love:

Cold indifference.

*** *** *** ***

Twelve miles away in Manhattan, Tal lay awake in bed, staring unseeingly at the ceiling.

Everything over the last few hours were a blur. Somehow, he'd gotten back to the rental apartment Inanna's Mate had prepared. There might have been a cab ride, because he couldn't recall whether his feet or legs were able to function. There had been talk amongst his daughter, Sophia and Benji as they hurried him out of the shop. He'd heard none of it for the roaring blood in his ears.

From the snippets of conversation he'd caught between Inanna and Gabriel when they returned, she seemed to think that his odd behavior was due to stress and exhaustion from being out too long.

She didn't seem to know who the owner of the shop really was.

Tal blinked once. Twice.

It had been centuries since he'd lost the last residuals of sight, but he still kept his eyes open when awake, blinked as if his dead eyeballs still required rest and lubrication, as if he were still a seeing male.

Habits were hard to break.

One habit in particular was etched forever into the very essence of his being.

Arammu, mi shi. My love, breath of my life, my soul.

There was not a day that went by that he didn't think of her. Indeed, it was the image of her in his memory, his dreams, that kept him sane over the years. Although the hope of reuniting with his daughter had given him a goal to strive for, it was the knowledge that *she* was alive somewhere in the world, safe and whole, that kept his heart beating.

He swallowed as tears burned behind his eyes and spread corrosively through his nasal cavity and throat.

She'd seen him.

She'd recognized him.

There was no mistake in her sharp intake of breath when he'd turned to face her.

He should have known better than to reach out to her. It had been an involuntary gesture that he hadn't even realized he was making until he'd absorbed the impact of her rejection as he heard her hastily walk away from him.

Why should it shrivel his heart and shred his soul now, her immediate and unequivocal rejection? After how they'd parted that last time, he should be grateful she hadn't spat at him or cursed him into everlasting hell.

Whether she cursed him or not, he had been to hell and back. Perhaps he was still there.

He almost wished she'd attacked him. He deserved it for hurting her. Betraying her. Breaking the beautiful, loving heart that she'd entrusted into his care. But then she'd have touched him, and he didn't think he could have withstood it.

It didn't matter the whys of what he'd done. It didn't matter the horrors and devastation he'd endured in the millennia that followed. None of it was penance enough for hurting her so irrevocably.

Like shooting down the brightest star in the sky.

The burning pain in his heart spread through his veins and arteries like wildfire, reigniting the countless wounds still unhealed all over his body.

Tal squeezed his eyes shut and clenched his jaw tight against the onslaught. He could not see it, but he felt his old wounds festering within him, roiling under his skin, blooming black and blue and hideous green beneath the paper thin epidermis that stretched tenuously over his decaying flesh and bones.

Rain, the Pure Healer, had warned him of this. The symptoms of his "condition" were similar to the Decline that Pure Ones experienced when they loved the wrong person, someone who could not or would not reciprocate. Except that the Decline lasted thirty days before the Pure One either chose death or became a vampire. Not every Pure One was given the choice, however; the Goddess alone held their Destinies.

Tal's condition had lasted millennia. Somehow, death had not come for him, and though he often battled the desire to take his own life just to stop this breathtaking pain, he stubbornly refused to succumb to a cowardly end.

But now, whatever it was, this gnawing disease within him, had been triggered in full by *her* presence. He could barely draw breath at the mind bending agony that devoured him, as if all the torture he'd endured in captivity were now revisited upon him.

En force. At once.

His blunt nails dug bloody dents into his palms as he fisted his hands at his sides to keep from screaming. Every muscle and sinew tightened to the point of breaking, and his torso arched off the mattress as if stretched raw on a rack.

But even as the unending agony blasted through his body, his blood heated with a different kind of fire, shooting like lightning through his veins, making them stand out like tree roots against his skin. At the same time, his manhood elongated and swelled, becoming so painfully hard that he bucked his hips in helpless need.

The need to feed her. The need to fill her.

The Undeniable. Desperate. Drive.

To Mate.

Chapter Seven

Devlin did not know the exact time he woke up but his body told him it was well into the middle of the day.

Contrary to popularized fiction, vampires did not turn to dust under the sun's rays. At least, not his Kind.

No, they were merely induced to sleep throughout the day. It was a biological imperative so strong, that weaker, newer vampires could pass out stone cold at the slightest exposure. To rest better, safe and undisturbed, vampires of old used sarcophaguses as beds, which led to the modern extrapolation that vampires slept in coffins.

Personally, Devlin preferred the Westin Heavenly bed. He'd had one of gigantic proportions specifically made for his chamber back at the Cove since he was a male who liked to have room to spread out in slumber.

The bed he currently slept on was definitely a Heavenly bed as well, he could tell from the way his body seemed enfolded by clouds, the way his pillow supported his head like soft, comforting arms or a warm, feminine lap.

But the bed was not his own.

He sat up slowly, lethargically, feeling the effects of the sun outside even though no natural light entered Grace's basement apartment, the shutters on the clerestory windows high up in the walls blocking all daylight.

Wow. This was a first.

Devlin had never slept in someone else's home before, much less someone else's bed. He had a fundamental distrust of people, and only through hundreds of years of interaction had he built up enough faith in his Chosen comrades to call them friends.

And look what happened. There had been a traitor amongst them all this time. She was no longer a threat, but it just went to show that deceit was insidious and nothing could be taken for granted.

But here he was, trusting a virtual stranger with his life after just a brief online acquaintance and two nights of no-strings-attached sex.

She could have called some government experimental lab to take him away in a straightjacket in the middle of his dead-to-the-world slumber and he wouldn't have known. She could have put a few bullets into his head and heart (recovery was not impossible, but it sure would have hurt) and he would have been none the wiser.

Thankfully, Grace Darling did none of those things. All of Devlin's limbs were intact. No blood or guts smeared anywhere. No handcuffs or bindings to keep him prisoner.

He looked around the cavernous studio. Where was she anyway?

He got up from the bed and walked around, leisurely taking in the apartment and securing the perimeter. There was nothing out of the ordinary. No hidden cameras, weapons or monsters.

A plate awaited him on the kitchen counter, however. Slices of bananas and two macarons were arranged in the shape of a happy face. A cup of coffee, still hot in its thermos, sat beside it.

A smile involuntarily tilted Devlin's lips at the sight.

She'd made him breakfast.

He couldn't recall the last time anyone had ever made a meal for him, simple though it was. When he'd lived as a human, scores of servants fulfilled his every request. His father the Duke had not been stingy about hiring the best help, the cook included.

But as Devlin dug into the light repast, he couldn't recall a time when his belly had been more satisfied. A feeling of fullness, not just of the stomach, but his very being, enveloped him.

Finishing the last drop of the strong, rich, perfectly brewed coffee, he padded nude into the luxurious bathroom at the back and availed himself to the shower. Afterwards, he wrapped a large towel around his hips and went back into the common area.

Still no Grace.

He wondered briefly whether he should hack into one of the many laptops she had spread out on the large dining table and see if he could find any information on Zenn himself. But not knowing when she'd be back, he didn't want to take the risk.

Besides, she seemed genuinely open to helping him find some answers from her employer. It would certainly save him a lot of trouble, but more importantly, he just couldn't stomach sneaking around behind her back now that they were...

Well, whatever it was they were, he didn't want to betray her trust.

As if his thoughts conjured her, the back door opened behind the kitchen to admit Grace, arms full of something furry along with a bright red notebook.

"It's almost lunch time," she said by way of greeting. "Do you want to go out or eat here?"

Devlin was still half asleep given the fact that A, it was daytime when vampires needed to rest and B, he was yet again exhausted to the roots of his hair from the marathon sex the night before.

Honestly, he didn't know how it was possible the things she got his body to do. It was almost as if she were his Blooded Mate the way his sex obeyed her every command, so hard for so long and used so well he thought the thing might just fall off at the end of it.

So no, he didn't feel up to going out. He wanted to crawl back into bed and sleep for a few uninterrupted days. Maybe weeks.

But he was a bit peckish, despite having just had a snack. His stomach growled in confirmation. His body demanded the replenishment of fuel after all that exertion. A few rare steaks wouldn't go amiss.

"What do you have?" he asked, not particularly hopeful. He'd noticed last night that her fridge was mostly empty.

She put the furry thing—her pet chinchilla—back into its cage, stored the red notebook in a side drawer and walked to the front door.

Instead of opening it, she looked over at the digital clock in the upper oven.

"It's almost noon," she said, as if anticipating an event that was about to happen.

Devlin knew that she always had her lunch promptly at noon, but unless food was about to magically appear, they were going to dine on bread and butter and a few leaves of salad.

Unless...

The buzzer sounded in the front door. And before Devlin could fortify himself (or at least make a mad dash for his pants!) Grace opened the door as her aunt Maria squeezed inside, a loaded bag in each hand.

"Phew!" the elderly woman said as she got across the threshold, "it's hot out there! Just barely July and already ninety-five degrees! Must be that global warming trend everybody's talking about. I just about—"

And that was when she clapped eyes on Devlin, standing in the middle of the room like a twat, buck naked but for a low-slung towel.

"How do you do," Devlin greeted in his most respectful, solemn voice, holding out a hand to shake.

In situations like these, it was better to pretend the Emperor did indeed have new clothes.

The old lady dropped her bags to the floor as her mouth went slack and her eyes rounded into saucers.

"This is my two-week partner, Aunt Maria," Grace said calmly, not at all embarrassed that her only living relative, the mother of her heart, was meeting her gloriously golden lover in the flesh.

Very much in the flesh.

"Devlin," she said, turning to face him, "meet my aunt Maria. She comes over almost every day at lunchtime for a visit before heading off to work at the Little Flower Orphanage in the afternoon."

That's right. Devlin remembered just a tad too late. This was precisely why he didn't sleep in beds that were not his own. He was at the whim of someone else's schedule. An intruder in someone else's home.

Since Aunt Maria didn't take his outstretched hand in hers, Devlin dropped his arm awkwardly and tried to exude a sophisticated confidence despite his state of undress.

"A pleasure to make your acquaintance," he said with a beatific smile, hoping to blind her with its brightness.

A strange gurgle emerged from the woman as she remained rooted to her spot. Only her eyes moved as she slid them to the left to look at her niece.

Not picking up on the vibes of awkwardness and discomfort, Grace stepped forth to retrieve the forgotten bags.

"What did you bring today? We were just deciding whether to stay in or eat out. Now we have our answer. Oh! Tapas from Boqueria. Great choice."

Grace seemed oblivious to her aunt's silence and paralysis as she took the takeout bags to the kitchen counter and began to set out dishware for three.

Devlin scratched the back of his neck with acute embarrassment, but then realized that he was flashing Aunt Maria with his armpit hair as her gaze darted like a nervous rabbit, following his movement.

"Do excuse me," he muttered, dropping the offending arm and attempted to inconspicuously search for his discarded clothes.

The smell of something burning in the kitchen finally got the elderly woman moving.

"Grace! Did you put the aluminum in the microwave again?"

Aunt Maria hurried over to rescue the burnt dish as Grace backed away from the confounding appliance.

"Why do they put food in these trays if we aren't meant to use them?" Grace said curiously, with a touch of exasperation.

"You're supposed to warm them up in the oven," Aunt Maria replied. "They're better that way and it only takes a few minutes."

Grace shrugged. She should have just taken the food out and served them at whatever temperature they happened to be, like she usually did. Strangely, she'd gotten it into her head that lukewarm food was good enough for herself, but not good enough for Devlin. She wanted him to eat well.

She had the most inexplicable desire to take care of him.

Meanwhile, her lover (because somehow calling him sex partner in her head didn't sound quite right) had surreptitiously pulled on his pants and shirt and was edging his way toward the exit.

"Stay," Grace called out before she was even aware she'd opened her mouth. "I want you to stay. Please."

Aunt Maria regarded her with something like a flummoxed expression while Devlin paused in putting on his shoes.

"I don't want to intrude—" he began, but she cut him off.

"Aunt Maria asked me about you yesterday, didn't you, aunt?"

The woman in question grunted a bashful response.

"She can ask you directly now that you're here," Grace continued. "And after lunch, we're going to the Orphanage together to visit the kids. You can come with us if you want."

Despite himself, her grudging invitation spread tingling warmth through Devlin's chest. Strangely, he really wanted to spend more time with her. Get to know her better.

Outside the bedroom.

In his old life, he never would have hesitated to accept such an invitation from a potential collaborator or source of important intelligence. He'd spent months developing this connection with Grace Darling for the explicit purpose of gaining her trust and, through her, find critical leads on Medusa.

Why was he hesitating now?

Because the more time he spent with her, the less Devlin could separate what he did for his mission from the real intimacy that was developing between them. He wasn't sure any more whether he was the Hunter or the man where Grace was concerned.

"Please don't leave on my account," Aunt Maria added her own encouragement. "I so rarely get to meet Grace's... friends." More like never, since Grace had no friends.

Devlin sighed inwardly, resigned to his fate. He curled his lips in an engaging smile and put his shoes back by the door.

"Thank you, I'd be delighted to stay," he said with his best manners. "The food smells fantastic and I'm quite famished."

He joined them at the kitchen counter, taking one of the four available stools, while Aunt Maria prepared their plates.

Conversation was surprisingly easy and thankfully superficial. After her initial shock, Aunt Maria quickly warmed to him as Devlin concentrated on winning over the lady.

He had to concentrate because the noonday sun made him want to hibernate, as if he'd taken a double dose of Temazepam straight through the veins.

It was a monumental effort not to snore off in the middle of dessert. A full belly made him even sleepier. Added to his physical exhaustion, he was surprised he hadn't fallen off his stool and passed out on the kitchen floor by now.

Devlin blinked to refocus his gaze, as his vision grew fuzzy around the edges. But the lowering of his eyelids made them realize that they wanted to stay down. It was like raising a castle drawbridge to peel them apart again.

"Oh, honey," Aunt Maria said, generous with her endearments, "you look beat. Why don't you lie down and take a rest on Grace's bed?"

He meant to argue but his tongue wouldn't cooperate and his mouth didn't want to move.

"Yes, do take a nap," Grace insisted. "You'll want to store up a reserve for tonight."

Aunt Maria gasped and looked away, hiding her rosy cheeks behind a glass of water as she quickly took a few gulps.

Devlin should have been embarrassed but he couldn't muster the energy to care. So what if Grace's only living relative, by all appearances a dear old lady with conservative leanings, knew that he was boning her niece so thoroughly that he was on the verge of losing consciousness from exhaustion? Devlin was afraid he was beyond mortification at this point.

Just as he leaned sideways on his stool, about to topple off, Grace was there beside him, her strong little hands encircling his arm, keeping him steady. She helped him walk the few steps to her bed, guided him under the covers and tucked him in.

Within seconds, Devlin was fast asleep, a smile hovering on his lips as she laid a barely-there kiss on his cheek.

*** *** *** ***

"That is one *fine* man," Aunt Maria said for the umpteenth time as she and Grace rode the Line 4 to Brooklyn.

"He's a keeper, you take my word for it, Grace. I know these things."

Grace couldn't argue with the "fine" part of it, but she didn't know why she'd ever "keep" a man.

Well, okay, Devlin Sinclair was no hardship to have around. He had beautiful manners. He was beautiful to look at. He cooked like a five-star chef. And he certainly served her needs better than anyone in existence, she was absolutely sure, but that didn't mean she'd "keep" him.

How did a woman keep a man anyway?

Marriage could end in divorce. Relationships could be broken. Death could take one or the other or both at any given time—just look at her parents. Nothing was permanent.

"My goodness, that smile of his," Aunt Maria continued, fanning herself with a brochure she picked up at the station, "phew! I don't think my heart's beat that fast since I was decades younger!"

It was true, Grace could attest, Devlin had that effect on her as well. Her pulse raced when he was near. Her heart pounded, her blood roared. She'd wanted nothing better than to go to bed with him instead of coming out to the Orphanage with Aunt Maria, as much as she liked being with the children.

But then he wouldn't have rested at all, given what she had in mind.

"Why haven't you ever married, Aunt Maria?" The question popped into Grace's head all of a sudden and out of her mouth.

Her aunt looked over at her with a tender, reminiscing gaze.

"I was in love once," she confided. "Grew up with him in our neighborhood and went to school with him all the way through high school. Your mother knew him too; he and his brothers were always around."

She sighed and her eyes became unfocused.

"But he was a rebel and my family didn't think his was good enough and I was too young to know whether what I felt for him was merely passion or real love. It felt like real love, but I was only nineteen when I had to decide whether to stay in our small town with him or explore the world on my own and go to college out of state."

She plucked at her skirt and sighed again. "Well, I left. And shortly after that, he left too, never to be seen again."

"That's why you haven't ever married? Because you still love him?" Grace asked, genuinely puzzled. It was a long time ago. Surely her aunt would have gotten over her young obsession by now?

Aunt Maria looked at her and smiled sadly. "I don't know if I still love him, Grace. I don't know if I'd still love him if we grew up together, grew old together. But my heart seems set on him. I don't know how to explain it. Sometimes... sometimes you just *know*."

Grace caught her breath. Her aunt's statement resonated somehow. It struck a chord deep inside of Grace.

"Know what?" she whispered, almost afraid to hear the answer.

"That he's *the one*," Aunt Maria replied. "And no one else would do. For me, no one else ever did."

Damn, Grace thought, as the subway train slowed into their stop. For once, she understood exactly what Aunt Maria meant.

She didn't think any man would ever "do" if he weren't Devlin Sinclair. After two nights of physical passion, Grace had become addicted, obsessed, with the man. She wanted him for longer than two weeks. Even if it took a hundred years, she didn't think she'd ever tire of him or want him less.

She *needed* him. She needed *him*. In a way she'd never wanted or needed anyone before.

Grace was feeling a whole deluge of emotions now. She could even name them—panic, confusion, worry. And most of all:

Fear.

*** *** *** ***

"That's actually a comb, not an eating utensil."

Sophia was so absorbed in her cataloguing that she didn't hear the man enter the small back office in the Persian wing of the MET where she set up her work.

With a start, she looked up abruptly and blinked at the figure half hidden in shadows.

"Excuse me?"

The man shifted slightly so that his face was revealed in the soft light of the lamps.

"This belongs here," he said and reached over Sophia's shoulder to put the forked object in the pile that Sophia was categorizing as feminine toiletries.

"Oh." She looked at the instrument more closely, stroking the four, widely spaced tines. "I guess that makes more sense. But it's so small for a comb, and the handle is so long."

"The handle makes it easier to twist the hair and style it however the woman chooses," the stranger said, "like this."

Before Sophia could object, he took the fork-comb, separated a wavy lock of Sophia's hair with it, wound it around and down, pulled the instrument out at the bottom, leaving a pretty loose spiral knot in its wake.

"Wow," Sophia said, gently patting the spiral of hair on the side of her head, "you're really good with that thing." As if he used the comb daily on women's coiffures.

And then she remembered what she was doing and how ancient the objects in her care were.

"But you shouldn't handle these artifacts so carelessly," she admonished lightly, not wanting to offend but also wanting to do her job properly. "They're really, really old."

The stranger's lips tilted at one corner.

"But they're not fragile for all that," he said. "These are everyday instruments meant to be used. Yet now their fate is to be stored away within display cases, wasting away."

"I wouldn't say that," Sophia retorted. "We'll make sure they're preserved properly."

The stranger tilted his head a bit to regard her.

"If you were the comb, would you rather spend your days sifting through soft, silky hair and helping to make it shine with a glossy sheen, styling it just so to enhance its owner's beauty, or would you rather sit in an airless cage being gawked at by strangers?"

Well, put that way...

Sophia mentally shook her head.

"I'm sorry, I don't believe we've met..."

"You may call me Enlil," the man said. "I am the owner of this exhibit."

Sophia stared at him in confusion. She was relatively certain the Metropolitan Museum of Art owned the exhibit, and that her manager was not named Enlil nor looked like this man before her. She'd made Mr. Richard Sims' acquaintance yesterday when she came by to register and get her intern badge.

"Ah, I don't think—" she began, not certain how she could phrase things to let the deluded man down gently.

"I own the items in the exhibit," Enlil elaborated, "and lent them to the MET for the fall season."

Sophia's eyes goggled. "You *own* the artifacts? But...but they must be priceless!"

That corner of his lips tilted again, hinting at amusement.

"Perhaps to you and the general populace," he granted, "but to me, they are just everyday things that happen to be very, very old."

Sophia looked to the large chest of remaining items to catalogue for the day. There were many more chests stacked on top of each other in the back of the room to continue sifting through.

There engraved on the gold enameled lock were the letters "E. N-A."

"My initials," Enlil supplied, noticing the direction of her gaze.

Sophia felt like she should be standing in the presence of someone of such importance. Either that or someone with an unfathomable fortune. Probably a remote oil-rich country's King or Prince.

She got up from her chair to face him fully.

"Well, I'd just like to say... on behalf of the Museum, we're very grateful for the loan, Mr...?"

"Just Enlil," he insisted softly.

"Mr. Enlil," Sophia amended. "I myself love ancient history and all things Persian. We don't often get these kinds of exhibits in the U.S., though I do recall seeing a small showing once in the Louvre. At least, I haven't seen one of this size with this sort of everyday collection before. It's an honor to be able to help curate the display."

He regarded her closely. She felt almost hypnotized by his stare.

"You are very serious for one so young," he murmured, "almost regal in your bearing."

Sophia huffed a startled laugh. "That's the first time anyone's ever said that about me. I hate to disappoint you, but I'm pretty average and goofy when I'm not surrounded by history."

"Something about these ancient things brings out a different side of you, I suspect," he said easily, looking into her face unblinkingly.

Sophia was beginning to feel just a tad uncomfortable. The man was quite... strange.

His effect on her was eerie. She didn't feel threatened and she didn't sense any evil intent wafting from him, so she knew she was safe. It was her Gift to be able to see into the souls of others.

But she still felt uneasy.

"Um… Mr. Enlil, I should probably get back to work now. It was nice of you to drop by," she said finally with a false bright smile.

His lips quirked again.

"Of course, Sophia St. James," he said, "I'll leave you to it."

And with that, the mysterious man disappeared into the shadows that led down the long dark corridor from the back office.

Literally disappeared.

One moment he was there, and the next Sophia couldn't see any trace of him.

Very weird.

Sophia sat back down and stared at the objects spread out on her back-lit glass table.

Who was that man? Knowing his first name and initials didn't really tell her anything at all about him. But she did discern two things that raised the fine hairs on her arms and neck:

One, he knew her name even though she'd never introduced herself. She'd taken her badge off when she went out for lunch and hadn't yet put it back on, storing it in her purse instead, so he couldn't have read her name tag. Besides, the tag only had her first name on it.

Two, he reminded her of someone she knew. It was not someone she claimed any particular friendship with, though she liked him quite well from their brief interactions, and Enlil looked a lot like him. The large, black, almond shaped, double-lidded eyes. The shape of his mouth and the way he tilted his lips just so.

The man bore an uncanny resemblance to the Dark Assassin Ryu Takamura.

Chapter Eight

Grace sat on the bed beside her still slumbering lover, her eyes taking in every detail, storing each one away covetously.

Lover. Covetous. Words she never thought she would use to describe any aspect of her life. And here she was, coveting her lover.

It was already after ten o'clock at night, after Grace had finished her dinner and fed her creatures. And still, her golden lover slept on, breathing deeply, evenly.

He had worked his way outside of the covers by now and lay diagonally across the king-size bed. His shirt was untucked and rumpled around his body. Most of the buttons had come undone while one bottom corner flapped open to reveal his flat, taut abdomen.

Even relaxed, Grace could see the grooves that delineated his washboard abs. His limbs were thrown every which way, one arm curved at the elbow toward his side, the other arm flung above his head. One leg was extended straight down, while the other was bent at the knee.

He looked like he was sleepwalking a pirouette. Or sleep-lying, rather, since he was horizontally disposed.

She must have really worn him out, Grace thought, and secretly took pride in it. Perhaps she should give him a break tonight. She'd never used a man this thoroughly before.

But on the other hand, as she took in his long, lean, elegantly proportioned frame and exquisitely rendered face, as she inhaled his unique musk and watched, mesmerized, the rise and fall of his magnificent chest... she decided she was too selfish and needy to give him any reprieve.

But she could let him sleep a little bit longer. She could use the time to plot new ways to bring them both pleasure. After all, she'd only found a couple dozen of his body's secrets after two nights. There were so many more just waiting for her to explore and discover.

And she hadn't even kissed him yet.

She didn't really enjoy kissing, to be honest, but sometimes her partners insisted upon it. The mouth had numerous erogenous zones, inside and out, and she already knew that his fangs were two extra ones that no other male of her acquaintance had.

Grace realized with some surprise that she desperately wanted to kiss him.

She leaned over, bracing her weight on her elbows, lying half on her side and half on her stomach, and regarded his generous lips at close proximity.

They opened slightly and his breath quickened. His brow furrowed and his eyelids squeezed tight.

"No..." he murmured, his head jerking in an unconscious motion.

"Devlin," she called gently, "Devlin, are you okay?"

He shook his head to and fro, jerking away from her.

"No...not this...no..."

"Devlin," Grace tried again, cupping her palm against his cheek. "Wake up. You're having a bad dream."

But he didn't, couldn't, hear her, no matter how hard she tried to reach him...

1812. Salamanca, Spain.

"Is there nothing for me?"

The Sergeant Postmaster delivering Wellington's mail shook his head as he distributed the last of the post to awaiting officers.

Devlin escorted the man to his horse and helped him mount, all the while trying to tamp down the coldness of dread.

It had been eight months since he'd received any word from his family or fiancée. At first, when he'd shipped off to the Iberian Peninsula there had been a steady flow of letters.

Short and perfunctory from his brother William. Passionate and gay from Lavinia. Never a word from his father, though Devlin knew better than to expect any. He treasured each and every one of the missives he received.

But then the letters came fewer and farther in between. First William had stopped writing, and then Lavinia too. Her last note had been cold and cryptic. Devlin had memorized every word.

"My dearest Dev,

Just the other day Lady Laura Spencer reunited with her beaux, Major Edward White, second son of the Viscount Berehaven, after he returned from the front and sold his commission.

I can't tell you how often Laura speaks of him while he's been away. One wonders how she's able to enjoy herself at all with the Season in full swing. I certainly grow weary of her endless, depressing talk. But now he's back at last. And I can finally rest my sympathetic ear. Laura wished that you should return soon as well, so that we might both be reunited with our heart's desires.

I must say: I am no longer certain what precisely my heart desires.

Two years is a long time to wait. I barely recall what you look like. What your kisses feel like. It's as if that night at the Summerfield house party never happened. As if we never got engaged. How am I to keep the image of you warm in my heart when the memory of our time together is so distant and elusive?

There is so much to do in London. So many people to see. You might be shocked to know that at the ripe old age of twenty-one, I am still the reigning Queen of Hearts. I have so many invitations that my days and nights are packed to bursting. Every morning, my sitting room is filled with flowers and gifts from admirers.

None to compare with you, my darling, but they are here. You are not.

When will you return to England, Dev? Will you come back? Sometimes I wonder whether it is better if you stayed a distant memory. After all, who can compete with the perfection of my dreams?

—Ever yours, Lavinia"

Well.

Perhaps the letter was not so cryptic after all. She'd all but stated she wished him gone from her life, released from their engagement so that she could fully enjoy other men's attentions. Yet, she didn't explicitly request the break.

Devlin could understand that too. She was engaged to the heir of a Dukedom, after all. It would be foolish to cry off.

He supposed his heart should ache, or at the very least, his pride should be wounded. Didn't he fancy himself in love with her? He'd certainly never been this close with anyone else.

But all he felt was mild disappointment and ready acceptance.

He had hoped that he meant more to her, that she would stay true to him. But he'd always known her voracious appetite for attention, which required time and energy he didn't always possess. And too, if his parents, his own brother, cared so little for him, why should he expect to be worthy of anyone else's admiration and love?

So she couldn't bring herself to jilt him outright. He was man enough to take her rejection for what it was.

And yet...

Something about her letter made the fine hairs on the back of his neck tingle with premonition. Especially when combined with the terse note from his brother a few weeks before:

"Hartington,

I hope you are enjoying your military lark. Everything at home is in good order, you needn't concern yourself. Not that you ever have.

You've never liked being the heir, have you? You were always a studious, awkward chap who preferred mathematical equations to estate management and sport.

And now you've gone off to get yourself killed.

I hear the fighting there is particularly vicious. Everyday there's news in the broadsheets about countless casualties in the war, missing soldiers presumed dead. I can't imagine why you purchased a commission. Wherever did you get the money?

Never mind. It's done. You're out there playing at bravery and I'm here taking care of your concerns. Father has been showing me the ropes, taking me around to his Clubs.

It should have been you, but we're both more comfortable in our current roles, aren't we?

And then there's Lavinia. But don't worry, I'll take care of her too.

—William"

William and Lavinia?

How was his brother planning to take care of his fiancée? Why did Lavinia need William's care?

"Sinclair," Ned Pakenham called out, striding toward Devlin's tent, "a word."

"Sir?" Devlin answered, letting his superior officer and commander of the Third Division precede him into the makeshift chamber.

"We're going to make history tomorrow, my boy," Pakenham said without preamble, "I'm leading the charge on Salamanca after our cavalry clears a path, and you're coming with me."

This was news to Devlin. He was assigned to Wellington's staff as an exploring officer. His job was to gather intel by any means necessary. In a relatively short period of time, he'd built a reputation for himself as reliable, precise, strategic, and daring.

He'd taken quite a few risks already to relay the overall strategy and specific field tactics of Marshal Marmont, commander of the French Army of Portugal.

Because of Devlin's information, they were about to launch a surgical strike against the French through a planned succession of flanking maneuvers in oblique order. It was a huge gamble given they'd be concentrating their forces in one area, but because of Devlin's intel, they had a high probability of success.

As a rule, officers of Devlin's specialization did not participate in field combat. According to Wellington, Devlin in particular was "worth more than an entire brigade."

"What would you have me do?" Devlin asked.

He had the utmost respect for Pakenham. The officer was brave and a solid leader of men. His division always had the highest morale and work ethic. It was no coincidence that he won so many battles.

If Pakenham wanted Devlin to join his ranks for the charge tomorrow, then he wasn't going to question it. He just wanted to do his part. Infantry assaults took a great deal of coordination and team work.

Pakenham gave him a long look, then inhaled deeply and puffed out his chest, taking on an expression of both apology and pride.

"You're going to get yourself captured," he said almost jovially. "We need you behind enemy lines. It's the best way to get more information about Napoleon's next move. We can't let him get too far ahead of us. The plan is to let a small group 'escape' the battle when we round up what's left in the aftermath."

Pakenham paused to see how Devlin was taking this in.

At his nod to continue, Pakenham went on, "You'll wear your officer's uniform. You shouldn't be mistreated—much. Can't guarantee they won't rough you up a bit, but you're a hard-headed chap, you can take a ding or too."

Here, Pakenham raised one eyebrow in question.

Devlin quirked his lips.

"They might use a little force to see if you have anything useful to say about our plans, but I have confidence in your ability to resist sharing."

Pakenham's faith in Devlin was hard won. They didn't get along initially because Ned had little use for non-fighting men in the military.

But over time, and a few "bonding" tussles and boxing matches amongst the men during their idle time, in which Devlin was always a favorite given the ruthless and efficient ways he fought, combined with his insightful intel, Pakenham now held him in high regard.

"There's a collaborator of ours within their ranks. I'll give you all the details. When you've gathered what you need, give him the signal and we'll get you back. You have my word on it."

Devlin nodded. "Wellington knows?"

"Of course," Pakenham answered immediately. "I don't have the brains to come up with this rot. I'm just the messenger. And my infantry is apparently your cover."

With that, he turned to leave, not bothering to wait for Devlin's acceptance of the plan, probably because he knew that Devlin would do whatever it took to help defeat the French.

"You're worth a whole brigade to Old Nosey," Pakenham threw back as he walked away, "don't worry, we won't leave you long with the French. It'll be over before you know it."

Unfortunately, Pakenham's promise didn't come true...

With a sharp intake of breath, Devlin broke away from his nightmare, a reliving of the day before the Battle of Salamanca, before his capture by the French...and the ensuing months of hell.

So close. So close. If he hadn't woken up when he did, it would have been so much worse.

As it was, he was already shaking, his body coated with sweat, his clothes plastered to his skin.

He shot a hand into his hair and clawed it back from his forehead, his fingers digging into his scalp as if physically trying to take a hold of his own head and squeeze the memories out. He focused on calming his breathing and heartbeat, opening his eyes wide and staring ahead.

Grace's apartment. He was in Grace's apartment, not on the fields of battle or in the cold underground prison.

More specifically, he was in Grace's bed. In her—

Arms.

"Are you better now?" she murmured from beside him, one arm bent around his head, as her elbow supported her weight, the other folded on his chest, her hand lightly stroking, patting, the way a mother might comfort a small child who had trouble breathing.

It worked, her touch. His gusty breaths became quieter, easier, his chest felt less constricted.

He looked up into her now familiar face as she leaned over him, eyes filled with something like concern.

It was so hard to read her emotions. Most of the time her eyes were blank, except when they burned with desire. For him.

Her eyebrows still looked like centipedes. Her eyelashes like tarantulas. Her lips still seemed to take up too much of her small, thin face, and her hair looked like it had never met a brush.

And yet.

And yet Devlin found her incredibly...attractive.

Yes, unbearably attractive.

She had this strange ability to bewitch him. He didn't understand it, and he wasn't sure he wanted to. The more he stared, the more he wanted to keep staring. And she gazed just as unblinkingly back at him, her pupils so large her eyes looked entirely black.

He never noticed how clear her eyes were, the sort of translucency only someone with a pure and innocent soul could effect. The eyebrows and lashes served merely as embroidery around those captivating orbs. And her lips...they were pillowy rather than over large and invited one to test their voluptuous softness. Which reminded him—

For all of the dark pleasures they'd given each other, he'd never kissed her. She'd never kissed him. Not mouth to mouth, breath to breath. He wanted desperately to kiss her now.

132

She seemed to be of like mind, for she leaned down more, lowering her face closer to his. But she stopped just shy of meeting his lips, so Devlin raised his head the last inch to claim hers.

She was just as soft and full and ripe as she seemed.

Devlin opened his lips against her closed ones to plump them with his own. Wrapping a hand around the back of her head, he brought her closer still, creating just the right pressure and friction to graduate the kiss from gentle and exploring to carnal and demanding.

He angled his head slightly so that he could more fully devour her, licking along the seam of her closed lips, taking the lower one between his teeth.

"Let me in," he rasped low.

She shivered at the guttural sound and obeyed him, finally parting her moist, swollen lips.

He needed no better welcome, plunging his tongue between them and into her warm, wet core.

Someone groaned long and loud at the first thrust of his tongue. It might have been him, it might have been her. It didn't matter since they were one, connected in a way that transcended the physical.

She slid her tongue against his in an erotic dance, delving into his mouth as he retreated and then inviting him back into hers. They nipped at each other's lips, alternating between playfulness, possessiveness and passionate hunger.

He asked silent questions with his mouth: *Do you want me? Not this shell that I wear, but me, the man inside? Can you care for me, hold me when I'm weak, accept the bestial part of me that wants to mark you, claim you for my own?*

She answered his mouth with equal fervor and made demands in return: *I want you. I want you inside my body, my blood. I want to be inside you too, so deep inside I become a part of you. I want you with a desperation that scares me. So badly I ache when we're not together. So madly my heart splinters to see you in pain.*

They stayed like this, at times exploring leisurely, tenderly, at times turning up the heat to such a feverish pitch, their bodies strained and arched toward each other as they mated with their lips, tongues and teeth.

She didn't touch him and he didn't touch her anywhere else, somehow knowing that they were on the verge of something neither could control, and both feared for the consequences. The erotic dance of their mouths was sexual, sensual, but it was also comforting, caring.

Loving.

Something their bodies, despite all the exertions of the nights before, had never accomplished or attempted to.

But when his fangs descended into his mouth, Devlin reluctantly pulled back and finally answered her, "Better."

He cleared his throat and clarified, "I feel better."

Slowly, as if not wanting this moment in time to end, he opened his eyes and found her staring unblinkingly at him, just as she'd done before he started the kiss.

"Did you keep your eyes open all this while?" he asked, curious and a bit unnerved.

"Yes," she said, still unblinking, "I wanted to see your pleasure. The beauty of it is so mesmerizing I can't look away."

Devlin huffed an abbreviated chuckle and teased to hide his embarrassment, "Kisses are for feeling and tasting, not for seeing. At least, not when you're part of the kiss. Otherwise you'll get cross-eyed."

She finally blinked, slowly and repeatedly, as if attempting to reorient her eyeballs behind their lids.

"You're right, of course. Now that I have the image of you when you kiss stored away, I'll close my eyes next..."

She trailed off, her eyelids drooping, blanketing the brightness within.

Leaving Devlin suddenly cold.

"Good," he said, turning away from her to sit at the edge of the bed.

Inexplicably, he felt deuced awkward, still reeling from the confounding, rather disturbing connection they just shared, and immediately after having his recurring nightmare no less.

He felt raw, laid bare, naked despite being fully clothed.

He needed some space to think, to sort out his emotions. If she touched him now, if she wanted him this night, he didn't think he could keep his body and heart apart.

He wanted to make love with her. To sink his teeth into her throat and gorge himself on her hot, sweet blood. To mark her tender flesh everywhere with love bites. To take a bit of her soul into his.

To bind her to him forever.

And if she used his body merely for pleasure, if that was all she wanted...he thought he might die a little inside.

"I should go," he said, his voice husky with barely restrained emotion.

"Yes, I think you should," she answered so readily he turned to look at her.

She stared at him for long moments without speaking, as if she were in a trance. Or trying to memorize his features.

"I don't think we should see each other again, Devlin Sinclair," she said finally, blinking.

Stunned, Devlin could only look wordlessly back at her.

"I don't like feeling the things I feel when I'm with you," she explained neutrally, "and also when I'm not with you but thinking about you."

What things? He wanted to ask. What feelings?

"I don't want to become attached to you," she continued, her face blank of expression. "I don't like the way you kiss."

She didn't seem to mind while they were in the middle of it, he wanted to retort, but he knew that she was speaking of something deeper.

He was starting to understand her. And he thought she was starting to understand him.

Maybe that was why she no longer wanted him.

Christ.

He shoved his hair back from his forehead and got to his feet. There was a sharp pain burning like acid inside of him, behind his chest bone. He didn't want to examine it too closely.

It was all for the best.

"Very well," he said with remarkable calm, as if being so summarily dismissed by a lover was an everyday occurrence. But he was careful to avoid her eyes.

He had to get out of here. He had to leave *right now*. He wanted to howl and destroy things and lick his wounds in private.

"But before you go, I want to give you something."

What? Another dagger in the gut?

She got up from the bed and went to the gigantic table that held all of her tech equipment and came back with a small glass disc the size of a dime.

"Here, take this," she took his hand, palm up, and placed the disc on it.

"It has all of the data I could download from Zenn's global database and archives. I've removed the encryption for all files. It took me a few hours because I have the so-called 'skeleton key' since I designed most of their IT infrastructure. Otherwise it would have taken weeks, if not months."

Devlin looked at the 5D digital data disc in his palm.

There were only a few like it in the world that could store 360 terabytes of data for some 13.8 billion years. The first one was invented only a year ago. It was not yet mass produced. Somehow, he was not surprised that Grace had one of the prototypes in her possession.

"I don't know what you're looking for, so I made a copy of everything," she continued. "I organized it for easier search in data cubes. And I covered my tracks so that Zenn shouldn't be able to find out."

When she was silent for a long while, Devlin finally looked into her eyes.

She gazed back at him just as she had the first night they'd met: expressionless, emotionless.

"This is as far as I can help you," she told him tonelessly, like a pre-programed smart device, "I hope you have everything you need."

Not by a long shot, Devlin thought.

But what he said was, "Thank you for this. You didn't have to—"

"Yes I did," she interjected, "I did have to. Help you that is. I trust you. What you're looking for must be very important. I trust you to do the right thing."

God. She slayed him.

Why did she say these things? He needed to leave before his compulsion to stay got any stronger.

He gave her a small salute with the disc in hand. And then he left her without another word.

Chapter Nine

"She's in the arts and crafts room," Jaimie Lin, the receptionist, told Grace as she stopped by the front desk of the Little Flower Orphanage.

"You can't miss her. She's the quiet one at the drawing table in the back corner. The one who's always by herself."

Grace had promised Aunt Maria to come by today and try to talk to the new girl who'd been taken in a while back when her parents died in a car accident.

The last couple of times she'd been by, the girl had been in one of her frequent intractable moods, in which she preferred to isolate herself in a small room—a broom closet or pantry—and stay in the dark for hours.

She still hadn't said a word. But they were able to discover that her name was Annie, Annabelle Parker. If Grace was the one to carry a conversation between them, this was going to be a short visit.

As Grace made her way down the hall to the specified room, she tried not to think about one particular topic.

It even had a name, which started with a D and ended with an N.

It had been exactly two weeks since the last time she saw him.

The back of him, rather, as he was leaving her apartment. Two weeks of alternately simmering and broiling in unspent lust, as her hormones remained rampant, but with no focused outlet to diffuse the tension.

She'd coldly and logically thought about replacing him with someone new. It should not have been difficult. And yet, just as logically, she found that she couldn't do it. After all, if one had ridden a champion thoroughbred, would one ever want to go back to a lame donkey?

Grace mentally shook her head, stopping just outside the room in question.

Really, her thoughts were taking flights of fancy. Where did such bewildering analogies come from? She had never ridden a horse in her life. What did she know about thoroughbreds and donkeys?

Enough of this nonsense. She just didn't have the desire to snare someone new. And before she knew it, her sexual crisis had passed.

But her lust for one particular male only increased with each passing day until it reached volcanic proportions. Perhaps she ought to reinvest in some sex toys.

Pushing such depressing thoughts away, she knocked lightly before entering.

There was one caretaker in the room watching over the children. Clara Scott. A quirky, ever-joyful lady who worked part-time here and part-time teaching art classes in her home studio.

Grace practiced diligently to be good at remembering names. It wasn't a skill that came naturally, probably because she had little interest in people in general.

And then there was the fact that she thought mostly in numbers and codes, not letters or sounds. Some names were particularly difficult, especially ones with too many vowels, too many consonants. The ones with silent letters were real beasts. But Grace made every effort to remember names, because Dr. Weisman advised that calling someone by their name was the first step to building rapport.

Grace waved hello to Clara and searched the occupants of the large, well-used playroom for one in particular.

There. Just as Jamie had described. The new girl, Annie, was sitting in the back corner, head down, body hunched in a posture that said "I don't want to be disturbed, don't come near me."

She looked like she was absorbed in a drawing as she painstakingly scribbled on a piece of construction paper with colored crayons.

Grace slowly made her way to the little girl and as inconspicuously as possible pulled up a child-sized wooden chair to her table.

She didn't speak as she sat down and watched the girl draw. Annie didn't speak either, not surprisingly. But she also didn't acknowledge Grace's presence at all, not even to look at who'd sat down at her table.

For a long while, perhaps ten minutes or more, Grace was content just to watch Annie in silence.

It always made Grace wonder why people liked to fill in silences with words. She herself often found silences soothing, calming, enlightening.

For example, the silence let her focus on Annie's features, her curly red hair, lighter brows and lashes and the generous sprinkle of freckles across the bridge of her nose and on both cheeks.

It was a pretty little face, solemn but not sad. Perhaps she'd spent her quota of sadness already. Children had the innate ability not to dwell on painful things. Only as one aged did the ability to let go become more and more difficult to practice, never mind master.

"Is that you in the picture?" Grace couldn't help but ask, pointing to the central figure in the drawing, breaking the quiet finally.

The little girl nodded, though she kept working without interruption. She'd put finishing flourishes on the figure's curly hair, adding a small bow, and was now working on a house and the grass around it.

Quite good with her shapes and lines and color coordination for a four-or-so-year-old, Grace thought. Not that she was an expert on these things.

Still, she'd been helping out at the Orphanage for years now. She'd been acquainted with many children, a few of whom, unfortunately, were still waiting for their family. This little girl was a lot more mature than she looked.

Grace refocused on the drawing as Annie added windows and a door to the house. Within the window frames, she drew two faces looking out at the figure with the bow out in the yard.

"Are those your parents?" Grace asked again.

Another nod. The girl was now coloring in the house, the grass and adding a yellow car to the side.

"I used to live in a house like that with my parents," Grace murmured, more to herself than to her silent companion. "Their names were Judith and Jacob. Isn't that cool? The alliteration of their names?"

Grace peered at the girl, but she gave no indication that she'd heard.

Grace didn't mind.

"They both worked for the same company. I can't recall its name now. I never really paid attention. Their job was in technology though, the same as me now. I still recall the old Nokia phones they carried, their matching Blackberries and their heavy laptop briefs. They went to work early every morning and came home by 6pm sharp so that they could cook dinner together and we would sit down as a family to eat dinner promptly at 7pm."

Grace's eyes unfocused as she tried to remember the details. "I never called them Mom and Dad. I always called them Judith and Jacob for as long as I could recall. All the schools they tried to enroll me in said I was impossible to teach. Said I wouldn't engage on the lessons, I wouldn't listen to instruction. So I stayed home and taught myself from the age of eight."

She looked back at the girl, now adding flowers and trees to the yard in her drawing.

"I was a lot like you are now," Grace continued her one-sided conversation. "I didn't talk a lot. Probably not more than a few words a day. But I listened to everything my parents said when they chatted at dinner. Jacob was like us, you and me, he didn't talk much either. But Judith liked to chatter on. Kind of like the way I'm talking now. For almost the whole thirty minutes it took us to eat our dinner, she chattered on about anything and everything. It was kind of soothing."

"And then one day..." Grace paused, taking a deep breath, unconsciously bracing herself to confront the memory.

"And then one day they were gone."

Grace's voice dropped to a whisper as she stared unblinkingly at nothing in particular.

"That morning they left home early as usual. Jacob had prepared my favorite breakfast, a happy face with sliced bananas and Oreo cookies for eyes. Judith made my favorite morning drink, mildly brewed coffee with a lot of French Vanilla Coffeemate. I stayed all day and most of the night in the basement working on my latest computer game creation. And then... and then they were gone. Died in a bridge collapse during the hurricane."

A small hand touched Grace's arm, snapping her out of her trance, bringing her back to the present.

Annie was gazing at her with wide, intent eyes. She patted her own chest with her other hand and nodded.

"You too?" Grace interpreted. "You lost your parents too."

The girl nodded more vigorously.

"Yes," Grace recalled, "they died in a car accident."

Vehement head shaking. So violent was the motion, the girl's curls went from well-ordered ringlets to a messy cloud of frizz.

Grace put her hands on the girl's shoulders to calm her, still her, before her head spun right off her neck.

"They didn't die in a car accident? The reports are wrong?"

The girl nodded vigorously again. And then she pointed to her drawing.

There, framed in each of the two windows were her parents' faces. Both had mouths rounded in an O. Both had Xs for eyes. What looked like black shadows were colored in around them, extending to the exterior wall of the house in an inky blob.

A blob that ended in the shape of a man beside the yellow car.

*** *** *** ***

"Have a seat, Grace, you're right on time, as always."

Grace sat where Dr. Weisman indicated, in a bone-meltingly comfortable chaise lounge by the floor-to-ceiling window that dominated an entire wall of his spacious uptown office.

It was angled toward his own simple yet ergonomic chair, where he sat down after opening the door and greeting her, elegantly crossing one leg over the other and regarding her with a benign gaze.

Grace was careful not to look at him directly; she had a tendency to stare into people's eyes too long and lost her train of thought when she did.

Instead, she glanced at the tall, well-watered potted plants placed strategically around the room to make it seem less of an office and more of a study. An intellectual sanctuary of sorts. The views of the city from this top-most floor were spectacular, all lush greenery, blue skies and white clouds of summer in New York.

Dr. Weisman's practice obviously did very well, if his luxurious office in the most prime location of real estates was any indication. The strange thing was that Grace never saw a line of patients waiting in the fancy reception area outside. The office always looked empty, except for Dr. Weisman and his assistant. Perhaps he saw all his other appointments elsewhere or on separate days?

"How are your pet fish and chinchilla?" Dr. Weisman broke the prolonged silence to inquire. He always gave her some time to settle in before continuing their on-going conversation.

"They are alive," Grace answered simply. She was actually quite proud of the fact that she'd managed to nurture her creatures this long.

Earlier this morning when she was out with Miu-Miu, the chinchilla had licked her wrist with affection.

Well, Grace assumed it was with affection. For all she knew the animal smelled something sweet on her skin and wanted to have a taste. But Grace did know that she stroked Miu-Miu's baby-soft fur with something like affection. She might have even cooed to the pet.

"That is very good to hear," Dr. Weisman said. "How has your day been going thus far? Did you visit the Orphanage today or take a walk through the Park?"

"Both," Grace answered. She'd cut across Central Park to arrive at the office, though she could have ridden the subway from Brooklyn to a closer stop.

She liked to consolidate the errands and appointments that required her to leave her apartment in one or at most two days a week whenever possible. That way, she got through the perilous human interactions outside of her normal routines all at once, kind of like ripping a Band-Aid off.

Visits with Dr. Weisman were always productive. He was a brilliant and effective psychiatrist.

But he was also extremely disconcerting with his intense, dark stares and portentous silences. Even after seventeen years of twice-a-month visits, he still had the ability to unnerve Grace.

Not because of the way he looked. Though she could imagine his stunning male beauty would make other women squirm or pant or at least pause, he did not attract her. He'd never attracted her. (And strangely, he never seemed to age in all those seventeen years. No wrinkles, not even a few gray hairs.)

Unfortunately for Grace, she suspected she'd only ever been truly attracted to one man, and she'd already severed that acquaintance.

No, Dr. Weisman unnerved her because of the way he looked—at others. As if he could see into their thoughts, emotions and dreams. As if he knew them better than they knew themselves.

He often seemed to know exactly what she was thinking even before she thought it. He sometimes answered unspoken questions before she asked them.

It was downright eerie what this man could discern.

Grace had wondered more than once how a man who looked to be in his late twenties or at most early thirties could reflect lifetimes of knowledge and experience in his bottomless dark eyes.

"Have you been writing in your journal?" he asked after a couple minutes of silence. He seemed to be just as comfortable with silences as Grace was.

In fact, Dr. Weisman's silences sometimes disturbed Grace.

He was not a man who put others at ease. There was something almost predatory about him, though he'd been nothing but kind to her since she first came to him at the age of twelve as part of the deal with the government to excuse her of her computer crimes.

It was Dr. Weisman who helped her get her first tech job, and then recommended her to Zenn.

"Grace?" he prompted when she didn't reply, even after a lengthy pause.

"Yes. Every day," she finally answered.

"Good." He gave a brief nod and smiled at her. His smiles were never real, Grace always thought. They were mere stretches of his lips that didn't reach his eyes.

"And does it get easier each time you write? Have you graduated from nouns and verbs to adjectives and adverbs?"

Grace thought of her recent entries about Devlin Sinclair and the feelings he evoked in her.

"Yes. Lots of adjectives and adverbs."

"Very good," Dr. Weisman murmured approvingly.

Grace looked out the gigantic wall of glass. She would be able to concentrate on the conversation better if she didn't look at her discourse partner.

"Tell me about your dreams lately. Have you had the recurring one again?"

She shook her head. No, she'd been dreaming instead about a particular golden male body wrapped around hers, undulating with hers, thrusting into hers...and she wasn't about to share that with Dr. Weisman.

"But there's something that's disturbing you, I can tell," he said softly, almost hypnotically.

Yes, she was disturbed by the fact that her libido had not calmed down after her hormonal crisis was over.

Every night, she ached for her lover. She felt strangely bereft without him, and she'd never felt this way before. She'd always preferred her own company over that of others, even Aunt Maria.

But now she was restless, and she wanted and wanted and wanted. Endlessly, frustratingly *wanted*.

"What are you thinking right now, Grace?" Dr. Weisman asked.

She continued to stare out the window. "I thought you were omniscient." Or something close to it.

She didn't see his lips quirk at one corner.

"No one is omniscient. I am simply well-trained in discernment. I thought I saw your face darken for a moment, but perhaps that was the shadow from the clouds out—"

"Shadows," Grace suddenly interrupted, turning to face the shrink and looking him straight in the eye.

"There were shadows in my recurring dream. I'd forgotten about them. I saw them again today in a little girl's drawing. The shadows that had moved across the walls in my home when no object had cast them."

She stared unblinkingly into Dr. Weisman's opaque obsidian orbs.

"The day my parents died."

*** *** *** ***

"How was work today?" Inanna asked over a light dinner, as their party of five sat around a glass-top dining table in their rented apartment.

"I made a lot of progress," Sophia said around a forkful of greens, "worked mostly by myself. Only one more chest of artifacts to catalogue. Then I can get started on detailed descriptions for each item."

"Did that man visit you again?" Gabriel asked, "The one called Enlil?"

Gabriel had berated himself for not having been on hand when Sophia received her unexpected visitor.

He'd been her protector that day but wanted to give her some space and was biding the time working on his laptop in the MET's cafeteria. Now that he'd recovered memories of his past life, he was helping the Pure Ones identify possible candidates to recruit into their Dozen; they were still missing one Elite warrior and one Circlet member.

He would have volunteered himself, having been one of the fiercest Pure warriors in ancient times, but he was now a vampire and Inanna's Blooded Mate.

Tal was the next logical choice, but Inanna wouldn't hear of it. Although Tal could still whoop any of the Elite warriors' ass in training, she worried about his blindness and the virulent pain he constantly suffered. One nanosecond lapse in concentration during battle could mean the difference between life and death.

Sophia shook her head. "I haven't seen him again since that one time weeks ago. I asked Mr. Sims, my manager, about him and I asked other employees at the MET, but no one knows a Mr. Enlil. At least not in the flesh."

"Mr. Sims has never been in direct contact with the benefactor of the collection," she recounted. "I pointed out the initials on the chests to him, but he just shrugged, saying they could mean anything, a trademark from where the chests were made, engravings to keep track of cargo on ships...They could have nothing to do with a man's initials."

"Sounds like Mr. Sims either didn't believe your story or didn't believe the man you met is legitimate," Inanna surmised.

"What's le-ji-mit?" Benji chimed in.

"Legitimate. It means real or true," Inanna enunciated precisely and patiently supplied, then spelled out the letters for him.

Benji was expanding his vocabulary at an astounding pace. They enrolled him in a highly-reputed Gifted Center for the majority of the year in Boston, where Inanna, Gabriel and Tal now made their home, in a relatively separate wing of the Pure Ones' Shield.

Still, the six-year-old outpaced quickly everything the school taught him. He was an insatiable sponge for knowledge.

Sophia shrugged. "Maybe I conjured him from my imagination after all. He truly did disappear that day. One moment he was there, and the next he wasn't."

She paused her chewing in memory. "Though I do recall seeing shadows spreading down the corridor from my office, but there was no one there."

Inanna and Gabriel exchanged a brief look, which Sophia did not miss.

"What?" She looked from one to the other. "What did I say?"

"You mentioned that this Enlil looked like Ryu Takamura?" Gabriel inquired.

Sophia gave this some additional thought. "Yes. I mean, I don't know Ryu very well. I've only run into him a couple of times at the Shield when he came to visit with Ava, but yes. Mr. Enlil reminded me of him, close enough in resemblance to be brothers I'd say."

When the two ancient warriors shared another weighty look, Sophia blurted, "What's going on?"

"He is dangerous," Tal spoke for the first time in this discussion. "Stay away from him."

"Papa?" Inanna inquired.

He'd never said a word before now. When they liberated him from his imprisonment, they'd fought against shadow ninjas led by a tall, dark-haired male whom Ryu called the Master.

Inanna suspected that this Enlil and the Master could be one and the same, given Sophia's description of him.

But when they researched the Pure and Dark archives for more information over the last couple of weeks, they came away with nothing. There was no Enlil mentioned anywhere. If he'd been recorded in the Dark Ones' history, then the chapters must have been lost in the War. His only tie that they knew of was to Ryu Takamura.

A tie that Ryu refused to discuss.

As four pair of eyes regarded Inanna's father expectantly, the warrior closed in on himself.

Inanna knew her father well enough to understand that he would reveal no more tonight on this subject.

For reasons she did not comprehend, he was keeping the history of his imprisonment secret. He refused to discuss any aspect of it. What he suffered, who his captor was, why he'd been held prisoner, and now, how he knew this Enlil and what role this man played.

"I am tired," Tal said, getting to his feet, taking his dishes to the kitchen sink without hesitation, having memorized the layout of the apartment to a T.

"I bid you all good night."

After his departure, conversation started up again on lighter topics, engendering much laughter and warmth, as if Tal had physically taken the cold, pain and darkness with him when he left the group.

The only one who was not the slightest disturbed by his reticence was Benji, who requested "Uncle Tal" for story time when his parents tucked him in that night.

Gabriel supposed he should feel slighted since he used to be Benji's bedtime story-teller extraordinaire, but he was just glad that his precocious little boy could bring some light and carefree innocence into the General's spartan existence.

"Tell me about the boy and his pet leopard, Uncle Tal," Benji wheedled, scooting closer to the wall on his full-size bed to make room.

"What's the boy's name, by the way? You never said."

Tal sat down beside him against the upholstered headboard and folded his hands in his lap.

"His name is...Lark," he said, recalling what Inanna called Benji on the rare occasions that he got in trouble—"Benjamin Larkin D'Angelo!" she usually began.

"That's like my name!" Benji noticed happily.

"Indeed. Lark also looked something like you when he was a boy, based on how your mother describes you. Pale blonde and blue-eyed. But without the curls."

Benji shifted excitedly, barely able to keep still.

"When did Lark get his leopard, Uncle Tal? Did he always want to be a warrior?"

Tal answered Benji's second question first.

"Lark never dreamed that he would be a warrior. His father was the village blacksmith, and his mother took care of the home, their small farm, and of course, Lark, until he was old enough to look after himself. Lark loved carving wood, making things, and helping his papa in the forge."

"He wasn't a prince or a demi-god or something?" Benji asked, "I just finished re-reading all of the Greek and Roman mythologies, now starting on the Norse ones. The heroes are always princes or demi-gods, and they have special powers or special friends—like Perseus' flying horse Pegasus."

"Well, I don't know that Lark set out to be a hero, so maybe that's the difference," Tal theorized. "But he does have his magical leopard."

"What's the leopard's name?" Benji asked, always attentive to details.

"Her name is Star," Tal answered. "She's white all over with black spots, a long, thick-furred, curling tail and ears like so that were also thick with fur."

He made two small ears on either side of his head with his index and middle fingers and twitched his nose at Benji, making the boy giggle.

"Star has special powers, doesn't she?"

"Of course," Tal indulged. "She could turn into a little girl, the prettiest girl in all the land."

Tal sensed Benji's deflation rather than saw his look of disappointment. A leopard who turned into a girl was definitely a lot less awesome than a winged horse to a six-year-old boy.

"*And*, she could also turn into a giant leopard with paws bigger than my head, teeth as thick around as your calves, sharper than swords, and whose roar was so mighty it made houses tremble."

Tal roared mightily and held his clawed hands above Benji's head, making the boy shriek with excitement.

"That is *so* cool! Like Power Rangers that morph when they fight the bad guys!"

Tal gave Benji a blank look. He was not anywhere near well versed on modern pop culture, much less the various fascinations of children.

"So the giant leopard fought alongside Lark and protected him?"

Tal nodded. "The leopard saved Lark once from a fate worse than death. She battled a venomous serpent with black eyes, monstrous fangs and spiked tail."

"Ooohh," Benji enthused.

"But we will have to save the battle for another day," Tal said, re-tucking Benji beneath his blankets.

"Tomorrow night?"

"If you wish."

"I love you, Uncle Tal. Good night."

A surge of tenderness nearly overwhelmed Tal as he bent over the boy and kissed his forehead.

This moment. This was his light in the darkness.

Chapter Ten

Fourteen days, five hours and twenty-three minutes.

That was how long, give or take a couple of minutes, it had been since Devlin had been inside Grace Darling's apartment.

He spun a small throwing knife between the fingers of his left hand as he contemplated the giant screens of codes before him. He'd gone through 99.9% of the files Grace had given him with a fine tooth comb over the past two weeks.

Nothing.

There was no incriminating evidence that Zenn was less or more than what it presented itself to be. No cookie crumb trail that led to anything illegal, nefarious or even tangentially suspect. It looked like a perfectly legit, rising star of the tech universe, with sound financial management, operating model and steadily increasing revenues and profits.

Devlin had gone through all of its employee files, suppliers, customers, formal organizations it had any business with...everything checked out. He'd cross-referenced each of the staff members with government databases and found a few marital, misdemeanor, DUI, Internet porn skeletons in the closet but nothing that led him closer to Medusa.

He was at an impasse. Back at square one.

A throaty growl preceded Simca's otherwise silent entry into Devlin's tech center. And where the feline predator went, inevitably, the Chosen's Commander was not far behind.

"Devlin, a word."

Devlin lazily spun his swivel chair around to face the leader of the Chosen, raising one eyebrow slightly to encourage Maximus to continue.

"I depart this night to recruit new warriors into our royal guard," Maximus revealed. "There are a few good candidates, but they are spread across four different continents. Ana has command of the Cove. You are her Second."

"The Queen has issued the order?" Devlin was surprised.

Jade Cicada had been melancholy and self-contained ever since the Pure Ones' Consul, Seth Tremaine, left her side. She'd become even more insular since the departure of Inanna from the Chosen and the betrayal of Simone Lafayette. Now that Ryu had moved out of the Cove with his human wife, the Chosen's number was down to half. The Queen had not seemed eager to fill the vacancies.

In fact, despite the effectiveness of her rule, she didn't seem to relish being Queen, not the way she used to.

"Nay," Maximus shook his head. "I take the initiative unto myself. We cannot keep order with so few. The powerful civilian Hordes have smelled blood in the water and are circling around our Queen like piranhas. I have no doubt they are plotting to depose her and she doesn't seem to care."

"Then why do you care, oh fearless leader?" Devlin quipped casually, though he stiffened with alertness and anger at the threat to his Queen.

Maximus ignored his flippant question, well aware that Devlin was far more loyal and had far deeper attachments than he let on.

He cared just as much as Maximus and Ana did. Devlin was a soldier who recognized a great leader when he met one. Under Jade Cicada's reign, the New England vampires had enjoyed centuries of peace with humans and Pure Ones alike, despite the wars and religious purges that went on in the early years of establishing the Colonies. She hadn't led them astray yet.

"I should be gone no longer than a fortnight," Maximus continued, "Safeguard our Queen well."

Devlin gave a nonchalant wave and turned his chair back around as Maximus and his familiar left without a sound.

Ana was more than capable of protecting the Queen by herself. In fact, Jade Cicada was powerful in her own right, hence her unimpeded rise to the throne. Devlin would do his part to hunt down vampire rogues, of which there had been a lot fewer in the past year since they'd disbanded the fight club network.

But he had bigger fish to fry: finding and bringing down Medusa.

Which reminded him of his impasse, a depressing topic indeed.

So naturally, as he stewed over the lack of results, his mind wandered to more pleasant, more satisfying thoughts, such as a particular computer genius licking her way from his navel to his Adam's apple, or nibbling the tender skin of his inner thighs while pressing her thumb against his perineum just so, or tickling the lobes of his ears and raining kisses along his jaw...

And then Devlin remembered that these were not pleasant thoughts at all. Because he was far from satisfied. He was, at present, and in the foreseeable future if Grace Darling had her way, thoroughly *un*satisfied.

Thoroughly Grace-less.

When the emptiness and loneliness and disappointment had been the sharpest in the first few nights, he'd gone out and flirted with anyone who had a vagina. Got up close and personal with many a beautiful woman in bars and clubs and random public establishments.

Filled himself up with enough blood to last him another month or two, all with his preys' Consent of course, as the Dark Laws dictated. Wouldn't do to break the very rules he enforced as the Hunter of the New England Hive.

But he remained grossly unsatisfied after all the other sort of hunting he'd done, all the blood he'd gorged.

Sexually frustrated. Lonely and angry and confused.

The women were beautiful, but they hadn't been attractive. Not to Devlin, anyway. Grace Darling was attractive, not beautiful. But apparently, at this juncture of Devlin's accumulated experience, Grace was the only female who attracted him. That made her special. Unique.

And it made him resent her just a little. Maybe a lot.

After all, *he* hadn't been the one to seek *her* out for two weeks of orgy. He'd been all about business, trying to make progress on the hunt for Medusa, when she derailed him into having sex with her.

And then she didn't even keep the two week bargain! He'd asked for a little space and she severed the relationship completely! What kind of reaction was that? Blown out of proportion was what it was.

And why was he thinking like a besotted teenager, a pansy-assed, star-struck, hormonal teenager pining for his first crush? With exclamation marks and everything? What's next? Thinking with emojis and hash tags?

Devlin abruptly slammed his head back against the tall headrest of his chair in frustration, but it was deeply unsatisfying as the well-padded cushion bounced his head back with no pain at all.

He needed to feel some pain. Find an outlet for his pent-up emotions. Exorcise this inexplicable obsession with a particularly bushy-browed hacker.

Thus decided, he shot up from his chair, secured the knife back into its hidden pocket and went out in search of satisfaction.

*** *** *** ***

The young man was deep in thought after leaving Estelle Martin's pastry and trinkets shop, Dark Dreams.

The old lady had been out of sorts and distracted.

Usually when he visited, she devoted much time and attention to plying him with treats and freshly-brewed hot beverages. She preferred spicy teas but seemed to know that he liked strong coffee with lots of cream.

She always hung on his every word, though his conversation wasn't the most scintillating. He didn't have many opportunities to converse with others, after all. And when he did engage in dialogue, it was either to play a role or to dissemble. He only ever spoke the truth with Mama Bear.

Tonight she looked every one of her advanced human years. She looked listless and weary, as one who suffered from starvation or thirst would. Yet, she touched none of the cookies and drinks she set before them to share. The cookies had been well-baked, but they tasted bland, as if she'd forgotten to add some important ingredients.

Fancifully, the young man thought she might have forgotten the love.

Having arrived at his residence, he entered through the back door and locked it behind him.

The front of the street where the dance club veritably thumped with loud music and thunderous beats was lit with laser beams in the pitch black night. A long straggling line of humans waited outside the club's doors, all vying for a coveted ticket to enter.

Here in the back, it was eerily quiet. And inside the apartment, the thick sound-proofed walls insulated occupants from all noise. Even the air was still.

Which was why at the slightest breeze, the young man knew he was not alone.

"What brings you here?" he asked into the darkness, no lights to turn on at the flip of a switch. In fact, his chamber could only be illuminated by candles and old-fashioned lamps, as it was not wired for electricity, only sound.

A white-robed figure stepped forth from the shadows. Instead of answering, his visitor made an observation.

"You seem to prefer this form," the female said wonderingly, "You wear it often."

The young man thrust both hands into his hair at the temples and raked his mane back from his face. As he did so, the hair lengthened and waved until it flowed thickly down his back, past his hips. His face also changed until it was impossible to tell the gender. He was simply *the Creature*.

Beautiful. Indefinable. Deadly.

"Better?" the Creature asked in its hauntingly androgynous voice.

The female gave a delicate shrug. "It matters not to me what form you take on. I am merely curious what your real face looks like."

"And why should you be curious?" the Creature hissed, shifting closer to the robed figure.

She seemed undaunted by the threatening vibration within the Creature's casual tone. For all its venom, she'd never seen this particular viper strike. It liked to toy with others, to manipulate and confuse. But it lacked the conviction and ruthlessness of its creator. Like any snake, it had a soft, vulnerable underbelly.

Abruptly, she changed topics, getting to the point of her visit.

"The fight clubs have stalled in Asia, thanks to the Dark Assassin's network of ninjas," she reported.

"Not my problem," the Creature retorted casually.

"You must keep close watch over Enlil Naram-Anu," she urged, "It is an order from *her*."

"What do you expect me to do?" the Creature spread its hands wide in the universal pose of helplessness.

"He's *the* Master shadow ninja. Even the Dark Assassin can't defeat him. He can turn himself into shadows, into the very air and wind, while I can only turn myself into physical, fleshly, blood-and-bone beings. And he kills with his bare hands, while I cringe at the very prospect. How do you expect me to do anything about the great Enlil? And why does he need watching in the first place?"

The female sat upon the only piece of furniture in the cavernous chamber—the Creature's gigantic platform bed.

"He has been acting on his own recently," she revealed. "First, allowing the prisoner to escape—"

"You think that was on purpose?" the Creature was intrigued enough to interject.

"Then, not dealing Ryu Takamura the killing blow."

The Creature merely shrugged.

"And pulling his shadow ninjas out of Asia, giving the Dark Queen opportunity to quell the fight clubs."

"You mean, none of this was on *her* orders?" The Creature was finding each revelation more and more interesting.

"And finally, allowing the human geneticist to use the last of the serum on herself," the female continued as if there were no interruptions, "We have no way of recreating the serum without the prisoner and Ava Monroe's science."

"Fascinating," the Creature said, its tone implying the opposite. It sounded dreadfully bored, which the female knew better than to take at mere face value.

"If Lord Wind is stepping out of place, I'm sure his Mistress will tighten the reins when she sees fit to."

The female eyed the Creature keenly. "Enlil has recently made contact with your precious Sophia."

The absence of a ready quip from the Creature was most telling.

"She wants you to keep an eye on him," the female persisted. "Just report back what you observe. She will deal with him accordingly."

The Creature's continued silence was neither compliance nor rejection, but the female knew that it would do as its liege requested.

"Now come," she said as she beckoned it with her hand. "Take your fill of my blood before yours turn black. I know that regardless of the shape you take, despite that it's all pretense, your favorite form has ever been human."

*** *** *** ***

Devlin sipped his pint of specialty beer from tap in a pub filled with young, good looking people, all of whom had given him the once or twice-over the moment he entered the establishment.

For all the world, he looked like a confident, well-to-do man about town, ready to flirt, handy with compliments, a mysteriously devilish smile teasing the corners of his sculpted lips, just waiting for the right opportunity to spread wide.

This pub would be one of many stops tonight for an experienced Casanova such as he, no doubt. Wherever he went, covetous eyes would follow, hungering to catch a crumb of his careless charm.

But the good looking twenty-somethings was not the reason Devlin had chosen this particular pub. Despite his best intentions, he'd wandered onto this street and into this joint because it sat directly across the road from Grace Darling's apartment.

He sighed into his beer glass, frustrated to no end with himself.

It was bad enough that he pined for her in his thoughts, but now he was stalking her in the flesh. Maybe not stalking per se, but venturing within proximity of her despite her very explicit request to not lay eyes on him again.

Well, if she walked out her front door and looked across the street, she'd see him right away, sitting in front of the window like a besotted, calf-eyed ninnyhammer.

Honestly, two nights of unforgettable, explosive, marathon sex should not make him this…infatuated? Obsessed? Fixated and possessed?

The irony was that it wasn't even the sex that he couldn't let go of—though that was rather memorable, and he feared, unrepeatable with any other female.

It was her insect-like eyebrows and eyelashes, her long, unblinking stares and stuttering conversation. Her deep, clear, innocent eyes. Her pillowy, generous, honeysuckle mouth.

That mouth. That kiss. That mistake of a kiss was what did him in.

Devlin shook himself mentally. He was starting to think with purple prose. What next? Penning desperate, badly conceived love poems and surreptitiously sliding them beneath her front door?

"Mind if I join you?"

A voluptuous brunette sidled up to Devlin's stakeout at the counter that ran along the length of the pub's front window.

He glanced at her briefly, taking in the self-assurance of someone who must be called "gorgeous" and "stunning" several times a day, the come-hither smile on her heart-shaped lips, the blatant sparkle of invitation in her large, arrestingly blue eyes.

She was a bona fide twenty on a scale of ten, and Devlin was not even one iota attracted to her. All she presented was a nuisance.

"Have a seat," he invited nonetheless, the gentleman in him too well-trained to say otherwise.

She slowly maneuvered all her curves into a sitting position on the stool next to his, contorting her long, lithe body this way and that and letting all her bouncy bits jiggle and wiggle just the right amount, as if to say, "look how firm they are, my size-D boobs and peach-like bottom. Test them for springiness and see for yourself. Come on, you know you want to."

Devlin didn't want to. He wanted her company like he wanted a colonoscopy.

But what he said was, "Can I get you a drink?"

She beckoned an envious waitress over and submitted her order. Devlin didn't miss the victorious grin she displayed to the rest of the pub's occupants at large as her proprietary gaze swept across the room, both proclaiming her prize (him) and staking her claim.

Devlin turned to face her while keeping a corner of his eye on the apartment across the street. The woman liked to hear herself talk, apparently, and required very little response from him. He nodded and murmured at the right times and didn't absorb a word she said.

Within himself, he debated whether or not to take her to bed. It went against his usual protocol—he didn't even know her and had no interest in getting to know her. But he needed to purge this strange obsession with Grace Darling.

Maybe it was the novelty of the two-night-stand that threw him off his game. Maybe it was the fact that he'd never slept in a stranger's bed before and he felt too vulnerable and exposed afterwards.

Whatever it was, if he repeated it with someone else, maybe he'd finally get back to his normal self: Devlin Sinclair, the devil-may-care charmer who had no attachments to anyone or anything, and therefore, no chinks in the armor through which he could be hurt.

Never again.

But then a movement across the street took him on a different course.

"This should cover it," he said as he flipped a couple of bills onto the counter, interrupting the brunette mid-sentence, leaving her gaping as he left the pub so fast he nearly knocked down a cadre of four bubbly, eager young things that were just entering through the double doors.

Devlin just hoped he wasn't too late.

*** *** *** ***

It was after ten o'clock at night when Grace's cell phone buzzed with a message.

"Devlin. Door codes. Go to terrace ASAP."

Grace looked at the strange message with knitted brows.

How did he get her number? She supposed he hacked it. And why should she leave her comfortable Westin Heavenly bed to go up to the terrace? It was in the middle of the night and she was only wearing her underwear and an oversized T.

She was snuggled comfortably amongst her blanket and pillows with a pen and her red leather-bound notebook. It was atypical of her to write in her journal at night, but she'd felt inspired to put feelings to paper.

"Grace! Let me in now!"

Was that Devlin's voice just beyond her front door? What was he doing outside her apartment? She'd told him she didn't want to see him again.

Well, that wasn't precisely true. She *wanted* to see him again. She just didn't think it was good for her to do so.

She didn't want to get attached. Pet fish and chinchillas she could handle. One aunt was manageable. But Devlin Sinclair would present a different sort of attachment, one she wasn't confident enough to take on.

In fact, she was just trying to articulate this inner struggle with words. At this rate, she'd have to get a new journal soon. Her thoughts about Devlin Sinclair were quite epic in nature.

Nevertheless. She couldn't leave him locked outside her door in the middle of the night, could she?

"Get out of—*fuck!*"

What was he...

But even as Grace began the thought in her head, a movement caught her eye in the middle of the studio. Something inky slid along the sleek white quartz of her kitchen counter, then oozed down the side facing her.

Grace clutched her notebook tighter and sat up alertly in the bed. Something about that black, oily, yet semi-transparent substance looked eerily familiar. It spread like spilled water, or more accurately, spilled liquid glue, viscous and thick yet diffused and stretched like...

Shadows.

As if a gun went off in her head, Grace leapt off the bed and scrambled for the back door to the terrace. The shadow seemed to sense the frenzied attempt at escape and immediately shot forward in pursuit.

But Grace was faster, closer to her destination, and reached the door sooner, wrenching it open and dashing out, not bothering to close it behind her. If her pursuer was truly as amorphous as shadows, a solid obstruction wouldn't deter it anyway.

She ran barefoot up the back stairs all the way to the roof of the building until she burst through the terrace door and into the balmy, summer night. The sky was covered in layers of thick, ominous clouds, preventing a wan moon from shedding any light on the concrete rooftop.

Darkness was everywhere. Somehow, the light from the streetlamps and still-open bars and restaurants below failed to reach up this high. Grace wondered whether the unsuspecting pedestrians and party-goers would be able to hear her scream from this far away.

The shadow poured through the terrace door opening and slowed in its approach, as if knowing that she had nowhere else to go. Gradually, it heaped upon itself and lengthened into the shape of a man.

Grace hoped she'd be able to scream. She didn't recall having done so before.

For all she knew, she was one of those people who, when frightened or confronted with a nasty shock, went dumb and mute instead of using the full force of her lungs to draw attention. The most noise she'd ever made when facing something unpleasant, like a giant cockroach crawling into her shower, was squeak with dismay.

She drew breath to shout now, for whatever good it did her. She wouldn't go down without a fight.

But before she had to exercise her vocal cords, something large and cat-like vaulted onto the rooftop and charged at the shadowy figure, slicing right through it with glinting, silver slashes.

Grace heard a rough grunt as the shadow separated into three equal parts, each elongating into a black-robed man.

In their midst, almost entirely blocked by their darkness, was Devlin Sinclair, a lethal looking curved knife in one hand, a long stiletto in the other.

Before her very eyes, the shadow men closed in on Devlin, their forms dissipating like smoke in the wind. But Grace saw the dark swirls swarming around Devlin's person as he slashed and stabbed at them with deadly precision and speed.

There was no other noise or movement, save the strange, mortal dance that was taking place right in front of her on her rooftop terrace.

Devlin used his left arm mainly for defense and his right for attack. When he hit something solid, she could hear a gasp or expulsion of breath, but no other sounds emerged.

Once in a while, a spurt of blood or some other fluid would projectile out from their relatively contained death match to splatter onto the leaves of the potted plants or stain the gray concrete with dark red.

And of course, Devlin received his fair share of counterattacks in turn. Even under the pale, scattered moonlight, Grace could see his black shirt rip in places, his pants tear in one thigh and at the back of the knees. She could see that his arms where they were bare were coated with blood. Whether his or his enemies, she could not guess.

And then he stopped her heart by going down to one knee, his left arm falling limp by his side.

Before she knew what she was doing, Grace launched into action, using strength she didn't know she possessed to pick up a nearby potted Fiddle Leaf Fig by its stalk and swinging the heavy steel planter with enough centrifugal force at the shadows that surrounded Devlin that they dispersed with an audible *whoosh*.

Clutching the potted plant firmly in both hands, Grace stood over Devlin's crouched form like a she-lion defending her cub. She didn't know how she was going to fend off shadowy assassins, but she was going to die trying.

Thankfully, she didn't have to put her shot of wild courage to the test, for the momentary distraction she provided gave Devlin enough time to get back to his feet and pick off the shadows one by one, moving with a lethal efficiency that Grace found oddly mesmerizing.

Soon, each shadow collapsed into the form of a man, and each man briefly held his shape before suddenly disintegrating into specks of black debris, like ashes from a violently smothered conflagration. Until there was nothing left but dust.

And a heaving, bleeding, mess of a man.

Grace let go of the potted fig and reached for Devlin just as he collapsed heavily against her shoulder, almost knocking her to the ground.

"Can you make it back downstairs?" she asked, though she didn't really expect an answer given his condition.

His head fell forward, and she took that as a nod.

Gingerly, supporting much of his weight on her shoulders, with one of his long arms wrapped around her, she half carried, half dragged her severely wounded rescuer back to her basement apartment.

But when she finally got him to her back door and tried to haul him inside, he shook his head and rasped, "Not safe here. Must go."

"But where?" she asked.

She wasn't sure if she could help him move another inch to save her life. She'd already performed a superhuman feat having dragged him this far.

"The Cove," he breathed, his voice reduced to a croak.

With a squeak of dismay, Grace lost her footing as Devlin toppled on top of her, squashing her under his full weight.

"Ana..." he seemed to say, "...come...wait..."

And then he lost all consciousness. At which point Grace discovered that she could in fact scream.

Chapter Eleven

"You're very strong for a woman," Grace couldn't help but comment as she stared openly and unblinkingly at the statuesque warrior-princess-like female who carried Devlin's prone body in her arms like a babe.

The female spared Grace an arrogant look and spread her lips in the simile of a smile to show off a top row of bright white teeth bracketed by two gleaming, sharp fangs.

Grace swallowed but didn't withdraw her stare. She was too fascinated to look away.

"I guess vampires are extra strong, huh?" she asked no one in particular.

She certainly didn't expect the Amazon to reply, as the woman hadn't said a word throughout her miraculously timed arrival to Grace's apartment (Grace didn't have to scream for very long, and cut the sound at one pointed look from this awe-inspiring female), and her taking charge of the situation with Devlin and transporting them to the "Cove" in her black SUV.

Grace guessed that this would be where Devlin intended for them to go, though she would have told the taxi driver, had they taken a cab, to go to the Chrysler Building instead. Because that was apparently where the Cove was based.

Once at the tower, they went below ground into a tunnel Grace didn't know existed and then into a shiny elevator with no buttons or panels, illuminated by three overhead halogen lights.

Good thing she didn't suffer from claustrophobia.

She assumed they were going up, though the ride was so smooth and soundless, she couldn't really feel the movement. The slight pressure in her stomach told her they were indeed rising, and rapidly.

Finally, after an interminable period of time, during which she barely breathed, because she was that in awe of the female carrying Devlin and because the situation seemed to require the solemnity, the double doors of the elevator opened, revealing their destination.

And what a destination it was.

The female warrior exited the elevator with Devlin in long, confident strides, but Grace shuffled her feet slowly behind, slightly overwhelmed by everything she was taking in.

They were apparently in the Chrysler Crown, which Grace thought had long ago been closed to visitors. But someone had invested a great deal of money to build a veritable palace within the Crown that took up three floors in height and square footage.

A magnificently opulent, gigantic Great Hall rose thirty feet from the floor to meet at the intricately decorated point of a vaulted dome, surrounded on all sides by floor to ceiling triangular windows, alternating with ribbed and riveted stainless-steel cladding, radiating outwards in the world-famous sunburst pattern.

Toward the far end of what could only be called a throne room, sat an enormous Chinese styled...well...throne. The palatial chamber also contained a variety of seating arrangements, thick, plush rugs and jeweled ornaments. Ornate, but not ostentatious. Lavish, yet tasteful.

And upon the luxurious throne sat the most beautiful woman Grace had ever seen. No one else was present.

Aesthetically speaking, the alchemy of her features did not produce perfection, but rather a mesmerizing collection of imperfections that gave her beauty a fragility that haunted, enchanted—seduced.

The female warrior who still carried Devlin in her arms said something Grace couldn't hear to the woman on the throne.

"Take him to the healing chamber and set up the transfusion. I shall be along shortly to see to him myself."

Grace was able to hear the Great Beauty's words now that she was close enough.

"I need to go with him," she spoke up, before the Amazon could take off with Devlin, and realized belatedly upon receiving a gimlet glare from the Great Beauty that perhaps she'd spoken out of turn.

"And who might you be, human?" GB (as Grace shortened Great Beauty in her head) asked softly. Strange, that softness could menace.

"My name is Grace Darling," Grace answered at face value. "Devlin and I are...friends."

"Are you indeed," GB said this more like a statement, less like a question.

Grace nodded. "He got injured while defending me from some sort of shadowy assassins. If he needs blood to recover, he can take mine."

"How generous of you to offer," GB demurred, then added, "But in his current state, I'm afraid he would drain you dry—as in dead—if he were to take you up on it."

"Oh." Grace felt oddly disappointed that Devlin wouldn't be taking her blood, and alarmingly, she wasn't so worried by the "drain you dead" part.

But apparently, GB had come to a conclusion in those couple minutes of conversing with Grace. She whispered some more instructions to the Amazon carrying Devlin, who promptly began marching out the throne room.

As she did so, she jerked her head toward Grace, indicating that Grace was to follow. And Grace hurriedly did so, not looking back at GB.

Belatedly, she wondered whether she should have curtsied or bowed or something before departing the Great Beauty's presence.

In silence, they exited the Crown, going down a curved corridor and a set of spiral stairs, reaching a nexus of hallways that contained many doors. The female warrior walked purposefully down one hallway and entered one unmarked door that looked like all the rest.

They arrived at some sort of clinic, the "healing chamber" GB had mentioned. It was a lot more luxurious than the grandest of hospital suites. Everything was pristine white, Grace could tell, even with the lights dimmed to a low setting. There were windows carved into the walls, but nothing to look out at. Grace supposed they were more for looking in, like observation windows.

With soundless efficiency, the Amazon got Devlin hooked up to some monitors and bags of blood on a mechanical bed that looked too comfortable for its purpose, like one of those deluxe adjustable Sleep Number beds.

If ever Grace was this incapacitated, she'd like to book a room in this "healing chamber" please.

"He should be awake within twenty-four hours," the Amazon finally deigned to speak to Grace. "His deep sleep now is his body's way of conserving energy to mend itself. He's sustained heavy injuries."

"But none are fatal?" Grace wanted to make sure.

How did the Amazon even know the extent of injuries Devlin suffered? It wasn't as if she or anyone else had done a thorough examination. She hadn't even taken his vitals or felt around his wounds.

The female quirked her lips. "If any were mortal, he'd be a pile of dust by now. But since he is still in his physical form and his body is intact, he will make a full recovery."

"Oh." Grace was saying that one paltry word a lot. It was a sound she uttered when she wanted to indicate that she'd heard what was said but that she didn't really understand the meaning of words.

"So you're Grace Darling," the Amazon said, as if embarking on a casual conversation.

"And you are?" Grace asked, slightly annoyed.

If *she* had the manners to remind others to provide their names, it just went to show how little manners the others had.

"Anastasia Zima, at your service," she answered with a slight inclination of her head. "I am one of Devlin's comrade in arms."

That sounded quite... soldiery, Grace thought. No wonder she conjured up the image of an Amazon warrior.

"And you're a vampire too, I guess?" Grace ventured, taking a seat in a cushy armchair beside Devlin's bed.

She was suddenly beyond exhausted. The adrenaline rush that had sustained her thus far ebbed to nothingness and she felt weighed down by worry, fear and uncertainty.

"What gave me away?" Anastasia quipped, baring the tips of her fangs again.

Grace nodded, not because she fully grasped the situation but because the motion of nodding made her feel as if she had more control than she did. Sort of like the advice of smiling to feel happy when you're sad.

"Tell me exactly, in detail, what happened back there." Now that the friendly preliminaries were out of the way, Anastasia was all business.

Grace efficiently explained the events as she recalled them. She didn't know why Devlin happened to be outside her apartment at just the right time; she was just grateful he had been.

"What did they want with you, these shadow assassins?"

"I don't know," Grace answered, "I didn't wait around to ask."

She gazed unblinkingly at the even rise and fall of Devlin's chest.

He was still in his tattered clothes, still smeared with blood, but he seemed so calm and contented lying there.

A contrast of black clothes, red blood, golden skin and hair amidst all the sterile white of the bed sheets, pillows and surrounding ivory furniture and décor. He looked like he was submerged in a deep, dreamless slumber.

And as Grace's eyes fixed on a particularly nasty gash on his forearm, she thought she could see the skin knitting together as if his tissues had taken on a life of their own.

Anastasia regarded her in silence for a long, long time.

Grace distantly wondered what the female was hoping to see in her. Something special to explain why Devlin sought her out?

It certainly wouldn't be found in her looks, Grace thought. She'd seen two women tonight who surpassed the beauty of all the supermodels and movie stars that had ever graced the giant billboards of Times Square. If this was the type of women Devlin surrounded himself with on a regular basis, he definitely didn't seek Grace's company for the visual feast.

"I'm a tech genius," Grace blurted out, to save the other woman from having to puzzle it out all by herself. "I can design, build and hack into anything digital."

"Ah." This seemed to satisfy Anastasia's curiosity. "Devlin has been trying to find a way into Zenn's secure files for the past few months."

Grace nodded. "He has all of them now."

Anastasia arched one elegant eyebrow slightly as if to say, "not bad."

"So you're an... aide of sorts to Devlin?" the female warrior ventured, still trying to figure out the exact nature of their relationship.

"We're lovers."

There.

Grace hurled that out there like throwing down a gauntlet. She raised her eyes from Devlin to stare directly into the other woman's gaze, locking eyeball to eyeball.

Mine. Grace wanted to say, though the mad desire to lay claim on a man she'd told both to him and herself that she didn't want to get attached, was a blatant and alarming contradiction.

The other elegant eyebrow lifted too, until both wing-like sable beauties were raised aloft to give the female warrior an expression of both surprise and surrender, as if she heard Grace's claim on her comrade and forfeited the right to challenge her.

"You must be very proud," Anastasia said quietly.

For a second Grace thought she was making fun—that someone as ordinary as herself could claim to be lovers with someone as extraordinary as Devlin Sinclair.

But then the warrior added, "Be good to him, Grace Darling. He is well worth keeping."

Anastasia drew closer to Devlin's bed side and brusquely checked the monitors and changed out his bags of blood for the transfusion.

Goodness, Grace thought, he'd already used up a half dozen bags! The Great Beauty wasn't kidding when she said Grace would be drained dead if he took her blood instead.

"This should be enough until he wakes up," Anastasia said, getting ready to depart the chamber.

"You may stay here if you like," she told Grace. "There is more than one bed to sleep on. Toilet and shower just in there. I'll have food and water brought to you shortly. If you need anything else, just say it. The walls are wired for sound. We will hear you no matter where we are."

How efficient and...creepy.

Grace didn't ask who "we" referred to. She'd only just met two women in this giant palace.

"Actually, I would like something," Grace ventured, just as Anastasia was about to step outside the chamber door.

"Could someone bring some clothes, my phone, any one of the laptops on my dining table, and a red notebook from my apartment? It should still be on my bed."

Anastasia inclined her head.

"And—"

One eyebrow arched again, this time with subtle impatience.

But Grace was not intimidated. She didn't know how long she would be here and she had her needs.

"Could they also bring my two goldfish and my chinchilla? They're on a strict feeding schedule."

Anastasia's expression did not change, but Grace could almost hear the "are you kidding me" in her thoughts.

Nevertheless, the warrior inclined her head in acquiescence and departed.

Satisfied, Grace turned back to Devlin, her gaze fixing on the gash on his forearm, as if the healing of that wound marked how he was getting along in general.

Remarkable.

The previously puckered flesh around the gash was now smooth and seamlessly pulled together. Only a thin pink line indicated where some sharp object had sliced through his skin and muscle before. The rest of him must be healing quickly too.

Vampires were such fascinating creatures, Grace thought in a scientific vein.

She would ask him many questions when he woke up, but for now, she was bone-weary.

She took hold of the large, long-fingered, gloriously masculine hand attached to that healing forearm in her own much smaller hand and pulled it to rest underneath her cheek as she laid her head on the armrest of her chair and curled into the fetal position to sleep.

*** *** *** ***

Enlil Naram-Anu blended into the shadows of the night and watched as two of Jade Cicada's well-trained vampire guards gathered some of Grace Darling's belongings and exited her apartment as if they were never there.

He then became one with the wind and floated in a swirl of black up upon the rooftop terrace. Gathering into solid form again, he surveyed the area for signs of the struggle that took place here only an hour or so before. There was some blood splatter and three black stains upon the concrete ground, as if someone had held three bonfires there.

That was all. None of the dead vampires' dust remained.

Enlil wasn't well pleased.

Very few beings had the ability to become shadows. This ability was rare in all the races that he knew. And even when their bodies contained this special gift of *qi* or energy, it took decades, sometimes centuries, of brutal, relentless training to harness it properly, to manipulate their own bodies and the surrounding air to become so fluid and amorphous, they become one.

Only Enlil himself had ever achieved the ultimate formless state; all others trained in the same arts were at most shadows.

Enlil's shadow warriors, or shadow ninjas, as they were more often called in the East, ranked among the deadliest and fiercest fighters ever created. Once upon a time, they held the elite privilege of being the Dark Queen's personal guards. They were also the special forces she sent out to battle when the strike was surgical and required speed and efficiency.

The majority of his army perished during the Great War eons ago. He'd tried to recoup some of the numbers during his time in Asia, for he discovered that a disproportionate amount of that special gift could be found in both vampires and humans from that part of the world.

But after hundreds of years, he'd only managed to successfully train a few dozen shadow warriors, including his half-human son.

Then, one of his earlier human disciples, a truly gifted Master of *qi*, had set up his own *Gakko kage yushi* (school of shadow warriors) to counteract the forces that Enlil was building for Medusa. He passed down his arts from generation to generation, forming a secret warrior society that could be called upon to combat chaos and evil.

Enlil's own son had joined his ranks, even taking on the human Master's name.

Ryu Takamura was only able to quell the wildfire of fight clubs spreading throughout Asia a year ago through his network of shadow *shinobi*.

Approximately a dozen of Enlil's shadow assassins remained today. And he just lost another three.

No, he was not well pleased.

The Mistress commanded all, including him and his warriors, but she had never dispatched his soldiers without involving him. Perhaps in this instance, she knew that he would not have agreed to send them on this task, though he was not certain whether she had intended to capture or kill Grace Darling.

Well. It seemed they were both acting without consulting the other. Enlil knew that she was having him watched. If he were her, he would do the same.

For, after thousands of years of dutiful, unquestioning service, Enlil had started veering from his well-trodden path.

His life, his very blood and body, had ever been inextricably entwined with hers. He'd always thought that they shared one soul, one heart, like the gnarled and twisting giant cherry tree that guarded the gates of his Shinto shrine back in Japan.

But ever so slowly, infinitesimally, since the discovery that he had a son perhaps, if he were to pin point the exact moment of the change, a hair-line fracture had formed and spread at the root of their figurative tree.

He could feel himself desiring, for the first time since he'd devoted himself to her as a young and untried True Blood, to be his own person, with his own mind and purpose, to pull away from the darkness.

She no longer trusted him, it seemed. For good reason. For he *had* allowed the prisoner to escape. One might argue, if presented all the evidence, that he had even facilitated the prisoner's escape.

He had also allowed Ryu Takamura and Ava Monroe to live, taking with them the one-in-a-billion, never-again-replicable sequences now embedded in her not-quite-human DNA.

Enlil gave one last regretful look at the black burn marks on the concrete where his soldiers had perished. Such waste.

Even now, he would not voluntarily go against the Mistress. He would not stand in the way of her plans.

But he would be party to them no longer.

From his back holster, he unsheathed a long, thin blade, flashing silver in the night. Holding both hands around the hilt, the tip pointing down, he bowed his head over his clasped hands and murmured sacred words in an ancient language. The edge of the dagger glinted a pale blue, as if heated by an internal flame.

With one smooth motion, he plunged the dagger into his heart, deeply inside until it reached its ultimate destination, the notch that bound the Mistress and him together.

The white hot blade filled his heart with fire and pain; he could hear the sizzle as it cauterized the wound his devotion to the Mistress had created. And just as swiftly, he pulled it back out of his body, falling weakly to his knees, the wound in his chest gaping and dripping dark blood onto the concrete ground.

It was done, he thought as he fell forward onto his face, his limbs spread limply upon the cold, hard ground, his eyes open but unseeing.

He could feel his body trying to unravel.

Only time would tell if he would retain his physical form and live or if he'd just committed suicide. The severing of a Blooded Bond could go one way or the other, depending on the Bond in question.

Whatever the outcome, he'd made his choice. And now he would live—or die with it.

*** *** *** ***

Devlin awoke sometime during the next night, having slept almost an entire day.

Though he'd been submerged in a deep, healing slumber, he could recall faintly glimpses of what occurred while he'd been mostly unconscious.

He recalled the humiliation of Anastasia carrying him to and fro, something she'd probably tease him mercilessly about for years.

He remembered the Queen entering the chamber and putting soft, warm, healing hands on his shoulders, chest and legs. Jade Cicada had once been a healer, like the Pure One, Rain Ambrosius. Devlin didn't know why she'd quit the arts, but he was grateful for her soothing touch.

Mostly, he recalled a small hand grasping his (it was hard to forget when his hand sometimes lost feeling from being used as a pillow), the even breaths that accompanied his own, the soft sighs in that sultry voice he knew so well by now.

When he tentatively peeled his eyes open, Grace Darling was standing over his bed, staring unblinking down at him. Something he was becoming accustomed to seeing her do.

"You're awake."

Simply, tonelessly said. No leaps of jubilation or dances of rapture at his remaining among the living. But strangely, Devlin heard the affection and concern in those sparsely uttered words nonetheless.

"How do you feel?" she asked matter-of-factly.

"Better," he replied.

"Are you still in pain?"

"It's manageable."

They stared at each other for long moments, and then:

"Thank you for saving me."

They'd said it at the same time, to each other. Then, simultaneously, as if each were a mirror of the other, they smiled.

"I didn't really save you," she said, somewhat shyly.

"You were very brave," he declared firmly, in a tone that brooked no argument.

"You were magnificent," she blurted out, something fierce brightening her eyes, a mix of bloodthirstiness and pride.

He shook his head.

"I got lucky. And I had a little help." He squeezed her hand in his to emphasize the point.

He'd never forget the way she charged in with the potted plant, wielding that thing clumsily but effectively. He'd never been on the receiving end of such fierce protectiveness and bravery before. Particularly from someone so much smaller and weaker than himself.

"If my closest comrade didn't happen to be a shadow ninja himself and showed me some tricks in the decades that we've trained and fought together, I wouldn't have lasted two blows with those assassins. I'll have to confer with Ryu when he's back in the City."

He pulled her closer so that she sat down beside him on the bed.

"What did they want with you, Grace?"

"I don't know," she said, almost apologetically, frustrated.

Then she blinked in memory. "It's not the first time that I saw them," she said slowly.

"Just this morning I saw them in a little girl's drawing, and when I went to my bi-monthly session with my psychiatrist, I remembered a little more."

Her eyes unfocused on a distant white blob of furniture as she lost herself in thought.

"I have these recurring dreams, so vivid and real when I'm having them that I wake up in a cold sweat, often at the foot of my bed, having fallen off in the process, heart pounding and pulse racing. But I can never remember what the dream was about. My psychiatrist encourages me to write down everything I feel and anything I can recall after each episode, but aside from what I just told you, I never have much more to write about."

She looked back at Devlin and remembered the way he fought the shadows so fearlessly, with lethal grace and efficiency. The shadows had enveloped him like fog, dissipated like smoke when he tried to pin them down.

"I recall some of the dream now," she said softly, as if afraid that she'd lose hold of the fragments and images in her mind if she voiced them too loudly.

"But it's less of a dream and more of a memory. When I was twelve, on the day that my parents left for work, I went upstairs in the morning to have my favorite breakfast that they left me. Then I spent the whole day until late at night in the basement working on my programs."

"They always call for me to come up to dinner when they get home from work because I lose track of time. But no one called me to dinner that day. I fell asleep on my computer keyboard, and by the time I went up, it was well into the night, maybe even early hours of the morning."

She looked down at their clasped hands as if focusing on their bond would give her courage to recall the rest.

"The kitchen looked exactly as I left it in the morning. There was no dinner on the table or even stored away in the fridge, as sometimes they did when they didn't want to disturb me. I made myself a sandwich and ate it at the kitchen counter. I was still groggy from sleep and didn't think much."

"Then I saw a large black shadow sliding down the stairs that led to our bedrooms, even though there was no object to cast it. As I stared at it, the shadow stopped moving. And then, it simply pooled onto the floor of the kitchen and flowed like spilled water out onto the patio until it disappeared into the night."

She was breathing in quick little bursts now, and didn't notice that Devlin was gently rubbing her back with his free hand to soothe her rising anxiety.

"It was so bizarre I thought I'd imagined it. After I finished my food, I went back to the basement to finish my coding. I didn't hear any of the heavy gales and rain outside that had apparently hit my neighborhood and several others around it. It wasn't until the next day that the police came to tell me my parents had d-died in the hurricane because of a collapsed bridge."

At this, her voice dropped to a raspy whisper.

"I never even saw their bodies. The police just presented me with what remained of their things. A couple of beat-up Blackberries and work badges. They said my parents were crushed beyond recognition. But somewhere, deep down, I think I always knew that they had died the night before. Perhaps in our own home..."

She raised her eyes and looked directly into Devlin's bright blue orbs.

"And that the shadow I saw had something to do with it."

Chapter Twelve

"We'll figure this out together," Devlin made the promise to Grace.

She might not know it, but he'd make it his personal mission to keep her safe, to hunt down those responsible for her parents' death as well as the attack on her, and ruthlessly end them.

He wouldn't rest until he did.

He let go of her hand to use both of his to push himself to a sitting position. Pulling out the IVs for his blood transfusion, he swung his legs to the side of the bed and attempted to stand. He would have fallen on his ass had Grace not rushed around to provide support, looping one of his arms around her shoulders.

"Are you sure you're well enough to move about?" she asked.

She didn't sound worried as much as simply making a logical inquiry given the extent of injuries he received just twenty-four hours ago, but a little furrow appeared between her striking brows.

Devlin was starting to appreciate those fulsome brows.

"Well enough to leave this chamber—with your help," he replied with reluctant qualification. "The tech center adjoins my personal quarters. All of Zenn's files are there. Maybe you can work your magic and find something useful that I missed over the last two weeks."

"Later," she said firmly. "First, we should get you washed up and changed into clean clothes. I can't even tell how your injuries are healing for all the blood and stains."

"Are you planning to give me a sponge bath, my faithful little nurse?" the teasing quip was out of his mouth before Devlin could stop it. He didn't mean to flirt with her, given how she felt about their...non-relationship.

Grace stopped in their slow hobble down the corridor from the healing chamber and looked intensely into Devlin's eyes.

"Grace, I didn't mean—"

"I was thinking I would help wash you in the shower instead," she said succinctly, her dark, clear eyes almost hypnotic as they regarded him unblinkingly.

"I think…" Her brows scrunched slightly as she concentrated on finding the right words. "I think I've missed you, Devlin Sinclair."

"Have you?" He meant to say it with smooth nonchalance in his usual devil-may-care tone, but it came out instead like a breathless, needy query filled with uncertainty.

She didn't answer, simply providing the crutch he needed to move down the corridor again.

When they reached his quarters, he opened an unmarked door just like that of the healing chamber, and they hobbled inside together.

Grace paused just beyond the threshold for a few moments taking in his spacious apartment.

The place was as large, if not larger, than her own basement studio. Also open floor plan and with clearly delineated areas for different purposes. No windows. Lots of books.

Instead of a kitchen and dining area, there was an entire alcove lined with shelves full of books, with a laddered loft that provided the perfect place to relax and read. The bathroom was separated from the living space by an intricate ceramic and metal screen. A gigantic platform bed dominated almost an entire wall on the other side.

"Very elegant and masculine," Grace commented matter-of-factly.

"Like you."

Devlin rubbed the back of his neck with an alarming degree of shyness.

He'd never brought anyone inside his private quarters before, not even the other Chosen. He had always been extremely reserved in the sharing of personal details, perhaps because he didn't fully trust anyone.

He'd always been the friendly yet unknowable member of the Dark Queen's guard. Ryu was his closest friend, and not even he knew Devlin's story.

"Make yourself comfortable," he murmured, feeling decidedly uncomfortable, "I'll go wash up."

"Let me help you," she said, and took hold of the bottom of his shirt to pull over his head, not waiting for permission.

"I can do this," he insisted, staying her hands in his.

She looked up at him questioningly. "I thought you wanted me to be your faithful nurse."

He tried to smile with cavalier flair, but it came out more like a wince. "I'm not sure your touching... more than my hands... is such a good idea."

"But I want to touch you," she said firmly. "I've been thinking about it. A lot."

"Touching me," he echoed weakly.

She nodded. "And kissing you."

"Huh."

"All over."

All Devlin could do was inhale and exhale deeply. This was all music to his ears, but he had to get something straight first.

"I thought you didn't want to become attached," he reminded her cautiously, as if he didn't really want to remind her of any such thing.

She frowned a little and he worried.

"I don't like attachments, this is true."

A gust of breath left his body at her words, as if his chest suddenly deflated.

"I don't know if I'll become attached," she continued, still trying to puzzle it out. "But I think I'm already obsessed."

"Obsessed," he repeated inanely.

She held his gaze directly and declared, "I want you, Devlin. I just want… *you*."

At this her eyes widened, and he watched it happen right in front of him—the dilation of her large black pupils, the brilliant light that entered her clear brown irises, as if something sparked within her, a realization perhaps of a profound truth.

She didn't elaborate on whatever insight that had dawned upon her, however.

What she said was, "Can we get you washed up so I can check your wounds, maybe give each other a few orgasms—if you're up to it—and talk about this afterwards?"

Devlin made a sound in the back of his throat that was somewhat strangled, as if he didn't know whether to laugh or cry.

This time, when she tried to lift his shirt, he didn't stop her. He stood mutely while she undressed him, focusing on staying on his feet. When she undressed herself just as efficiently, he wobbled and swayed a bit, struck hard by how much he wanted her.

Needed her.

Wordlessly, she led him to his luxurious rain forest shower tucked in the back of the suite. She turned the water to the right temperature and looked around for something to scrub his body with.

"I just use soap," Devlin explained, "Habit from my human life."

Grace found the large, man-sized bar of soap in a corner cutout within the shower wall and built up a lather in her hands. The fresh, clean scent infused through the heated fog the hot water created.

It was a simple fragrance, one that wouldn't cover up the original scent of a person's skin, but rather enhance it, embrace it.

Grace realized that this was the unique combination she'd inhaled from Devlin's skin, but only when she was close enough to pick it up. He wore no other colognes or even strong deodorants.

You wouldn't pick up any smells on him in passing, only when he let you come close. And then... you'd never want to leave the orbit of his body again.

At least this was Grace's particular dilemma. She was helplessly addicted to everything Devlin.

It wouldn't do to melt into a puddle of lusty urges now, she thought. She had work to do. All business-like, she began running her frothy hands all over his body, beginning with his arms.

"So you weren't always a vampire?" she asked, finally getting to appease some of her curiosity.

Devlin tried to be as no-nonsense about this naked-shower-touchy-feely stuff as Grace was apparently being, but it was an extremely difficult act to pull off. Even if he could keep his expressions and voice neutral, there was one part of his body that flatly refused to remain dispassionate.

"I was born human and turned into a vampire," he managed to reply.

"When were you born?"

Her meticulous little hands were traveling up his shoulders and neck now, as far as she could reach on tiptoe, then down his collar bone and pectorals, her thumbs rubbing across his nipples.

Devlin was struggling mightily to concentrate on the conversation.

"Ah… seventeen…seventeen ninety, that's the year I was born," he finally got out. "July eighteenth."

She paused in her soaping for a moment to gape at him. "You're *two-hundred thirty years old*?"

"If you round a little, yes," he said, then added, "I'm practically an infant in vampire terms." Lest she thought him too old.

Grace's right hand pressed over something puckered near his shoulder high up on his chest. Curious, she stepped closer to take a better look. The wound appeared to be old and scarred over, unlike the faint lines and discolorations left by his recent injuries.

"How did you get this?" she asked, a bit mesmerized.

It looked like it must have hurt terribly. A bayonet wound? A bullet wound? She hadn't seen enough severe injuries first hand to know.

"It's not important," he answered gruffly.

Immediately, she noticed a drop in temperature despite the hot shower blasting overhead. Despite its age, the wound still seemed fresh in Devlin's psyche.

She didn't press for more information. Instead, she rubbed the soap bar vigorously between her hands again to build up more bubbles.

"A two hundred and thirty year-old vampire. Fascinating," was all she said as she went back to his body, moving her hands down his ribs.

As she pushed against a particularly sensitive area where a few broken ribs had yet to heal completely, he angled away a little.

"Sorry," she murmured, gentling her touch. "There are no more open wounds, it seems, but I guess not everything has healed on the inside?"

He merely shook his head, as if to say it was nothing to be concerned about.

As her hands became less purposeful in terms of cleaning and more sympathetic to his wounds, her touch became caresses.

Caresses that stoked a different kind of pain within him. A pain that was somehow pleasurable. A pleasure so acute it resembled pain.

"How did you become a vampire, then?" she continued to ask, seemingly unaffected by his naked, aroused body beneath her roaming hands.

They moved around his narrow waist and then slowly from his obliques up the symmetrical sides of the upside-down trapezoid that defined his broad back. Her fingers and thumbs rubbed gently in a circular motion to clear his skin of grime.

"It's a long story," he bit out, barely managing to prevent a hiss of pleasure as her hands massaged their way down the deep groove of his spine.

"I'd like to hear it someday," she said leisurely, in no hurry to interrogate him further this night.

And maybe he'd tell her, Devlin thought. She would be the only person apart from himself who knew his story. It might even be a relief to share with her. He'd been so alone and isolated for so long.

They were alike in that way.

"Where else do you hurt?" she asked briskly, coming back to his injuries, "How do you know if there is internal bleeding?"

"My body will sort itself out," he answered, "there's no need to worry. It just takes time."

She looked up at him. "Is there anything to speed up the healing process? Have you received enough blood?"

Devlin swallowed, his eyes involuntarily straying to her throat, elongated and exposed as she craned her head up to look into his face.

"Fresh blood... taken from the source..." he swallowed again and unconsciously wet his suddenly parched lips, "...accelerates the process."

"Would you like to drink from me?"

Oh *God*, the things she said.

Devlin didn't trust himself to speak. He wanted to sink his fangs into her throat more than anything right now, apart from perhaps sinking something else of his into a different part of her body. And he knew he was well enough to have the self-control to stop before he took too much. But somehow he felt that tasting her sweet nectar would take too much out of *him*.

"You may take my blood, Devlin," Grace invited, oblivious to his inner battle. "I want to make you better."

"Grace..." Her name hissed out through his teeth like a prayer. His fangs had already descended in his mouth, pulling his lips slightly apart.

"Does it hurt?" she asked, curious and unafraid.

"Not... not between you and me. Not given the way we feel."

Her adorable bushy brows furrowed a bit. "What do you mean? Isn't it like two little stabs? Your teeth are bigger than needles, smaller than knives, so the pain is somewhere in between the kind caused by one or the other?"

He closed the couple of inches of distance between their bodies and surrounded her with his much larger frame.

"Let me show you," he whispered and bent his head down to brush his lips against the tender skin of her neck.

But instead of striking, he simply nuzzled her as he enfolded her in his arms loosely, almost protectively, bringing her stomach flush against his hard, pulsing sex.

"Show me," she couldn't help but to urge when he still didn't bite her. Instead of lacing her with fear or doubt, the anticipation was making her unbearably aroused.

"I want to feed you."

Where were these words coming from, Grace was distantly amazed at herself.

She *wanted* to be someone's *food*?

She wanted it so badly, in fact, she was ready to slice open a vein herself and make him take it! It was a biological imperative to give him her blood, her body, her—*everything*.

It didn't make any sense, but Grace couldn't fight it. Not with cold logic, not with all the reason in her formidable, computer-like brain. For once, some other part of her was calling the shots. It wasn't her libido either, though she was hyper sexed up; it was something primitive and unconscious, involuntary and undeniable.

Just when she thought she'd self-combust with this white hot need to *be his*, she felt the slow burning sting of his penetration.

*** *** *** ***

The long, loud, vibrating moan Grace uttered as Devlin sank his fangs into her throat spiked his bloodlust even further.

Lust for blood. Lust for sex. Lust for *her*.

He'd tasted her sweetness before, when she'd purposely pricked her finger against his fangs the first night of their acquaintance. He knew that her blood had the power to enslave him, make him weak even as it filled him with vigor. It was unlike any other he'd tasted over the two centuries he'd been a Dark One.

Tangy like raspberries. Thick and sweet like honey. Salty like caramel. So indescribably potent. Addictive.

As her blood blossomed on his tongue, bursting with the unique flavors and essence of Grace, Devlin knew he was changed forever.

No other's blood would satisfy him now. Perhaps his basic needs for survival, but not the needs of his heart, body, mind and soul. Her blood changed him, as surely as if her red blood cells carrying the unique coding of her DNA had infused and combined and metamorphosed with his, awakening a part of him that had always lain dormant, a part that clamored to claim her as: *Mine.*

He crushed her into his body more forcefully as he fed, no longer gentle, or in the least gentlemanly. The engorged head of his sex prodded demandingly at her belly, frustrated to be trapped between their bodies rather than squeezed within her hot, wet cunny, weeping with its own ravenous hunger, straining for release.

He backed her into the wall of the shower and lifted her. When she obligingly wrapped her arms tightly around his neck, he grasped her hips and brought them flush against his groin, his long, thick, pulsing penis sliding slowly through her swollen nether lips from tip to base.

"Please," she urged in her low, sultry voice, her fingernails digging into the muscles of his upper back, breaking the skin with her ferocity.

"Now, Devlin. *Please.*"

He hesitated only for a split second, pausing on the edge of a precipice, knowing that in choosing to fall into the unknown abyss he'd be taking a leap of faith. He'd be giving a part of himself up. To her.

To Grace.

Slowly, painstakingly, he pulled her hips back and positioned himself at her entrance. His draws on her vein slowed as well, but deepened at the same time.

And then he began to push into her, inch by voluptuous inch, making her feel every magnified sensation of his hot, satiny cock grinding through her tight, throbbing tunnel, the drag of their most sensitive flesh against one another igniting incendiary sparks of pleasure that harkened explosive fireworks to come.

"*Oh my God,*" she groaned helplessly as he was finally, *finally*, seated within her to the hilt, the head of his penis rubbing fully against the hard ball of her pleasure deep inside. The exquisite, perfect pressure he created within her set off the first of her orgasms, like the split of lightning before a long roll of thunder.

Steadily, slowly, he continued to draw at her vein, in the same unhurried, frustrating and devastating manner in which he pulled a few inches out of her and pushed deliberately back in. Deeper and deeper with every stroke, grinding unerringly against the hard knot of her pleasure.

One roll of thunder led to another, punctuating the endless chain of orgasms he set off within her. Her voracious core pulled and squeezed at his sex, demanding more, demanding all of him. She wrapped her legs tightly around his hips, used them as leverage to move in counterpoint to his slow, measured thrusts, amplifying and multiplying the pressure and pleasure of his claiming of her and her possession of him.

"Devlin," she sighed, nearly overwhelmed by the incredible bliss of feeling him move so deeply and powerfully within her.

"Come with me," she urged, needing desperately to feel the flood of his seed against her womb.

He was working her with a single-minded determination to maximize her pleasure and minimize his own. The achingly slow, shallow thrusts against her G-spot deep inside were driving her mad with ecstasy, so intense and so continuous she could barely breathe. But she wanted him to feel the same helpless surrender. She wanted him to release all of himself into her. Again and again and again.

Pinned like a butterfly to the shower wall, she didn't have much mobility. But fortunately, she knew a few secrets of his body to unleash the wildness within him.

She took her hands from behind his neck to squeeze between their bodies and drag down his muscled chest. She pressed her thumbs against his hardened nipples and felt his breath hitch.

Flattening her palms against his pectorals, she raked her fingernails gently and repeatedly across his areolas and their tight little buds, and used the leverage she gained with her hands to push herself farther away from his body, sliding him out almost to the tip. Then she gyrated her hips with a surge of power and forcefully impaled herself onto his staff again.

Faster and faster her lower body pushed and pulled against him, creating a friction so raw, so blazing it bordered on pain. But her vagina was slick with juices from her countless orgasms and melted the pain into blinding, building pleasure.

And as she reached the zenith and arched her back until it cracked, bending to ecstasy's will, he too lost control and pulled away from her throat with a muted roar.

Hot gushes of his semen flooded her core like tidal waves breaking against the cliff of her desire. Endlessly, he released into her, his painfully hard erection jerking and pulsing within the tight clasp of her sex, the strength of her blood exploding within him.

In this moment, infinite and timeless, their bodies were one, their blood united. He experienced her climax as his own; she lived his release through her blood inside of him.

When the gusts of his breathing subsided to a gentler breeze, Devlin licked the puncture wounds in Grace's neck closed and lingered there to nuzzle.

And partly to hide his face from her.

He was afraid he might have tears in his eyes if she looked at him just now. Tears that wouldn't be camouflaged completely by the ongoing shower.

She wasn't to know it, but everything had changed. At least for him. There was no turning back now.

He loved her.

This strange, awkward, brilliant, mysterious conundrum of a female. A woman who might not be able to return his feelings, perhaps inherently incapable of it. A human who would grow old with time while his youth was evergreen and eternal. Even if she were willing to be Turned, Devlin, as a vampire made himself could not do the turning.

Their bond seemed doomed before it truly began. How would he ever survive the loss of her?

Still, there was no turning back. And even were it possible, he would choose no other but Grace.

As if she somehow sensed his need for her, not just body, blood and sex, but something deeper, raw and undefinable, her hands cupped the sides of his face and brought his mouth to hers.

Her eyes were indeed closed this time, Devlin saw as his own remained open. At first she simply rubbed her lips along his, plumping them, teasing them. And then she began to suck at his upper and lower lips separately, treating each one to the same amount of attention and ardor.

Tasting his breath, lapping the water from the shower that mingled with his unique flavor. Minty and fresh. Spicy and bold.

When her tongue plunged between his swollen lips and into his mouth, Devlin's eyes involuntarily slid shut, as if the sensations of her possession were too much to bear.

It was she who laid claim to him this time, as poignantly as his still throbbing, aching, swollen cock buried deep inside her core.

She thrust her tongue languorously, voluptuously into his mouth, at times demanding, at times teasing. She held his face immobile as she plundered, as she feasted upon him like a starving woman at an all-you-can-eat buffet.

"You taste so good," she groaned into his mouth. "I can't get enough..."

More, her lips demanded as they abraded his. More, her teeth commanded, biting into his full lower lip and drawing blood. More, her tongue insisted, as it swept across the sensitive inner flesh of his mouth from roof to sides to tangle with his.

More, her body urged, as her hips gyrated against him, screwing his erection tighter and tighter within her, as if to lock him there forever.

More, an unnamed part of her clamored, blowing past her fear at the overwhelming feelings he evoked within her, past all logic, sense and sanity.

It was no longer pleasure she was after. Unlike any sexual congress she'd ever engaged in, there was no distance between her mind, her body and her unconscious desires with Devlin. They were all melded into one hot mess.

All she wanted was to devour him, brand him, *own* him.

There was no more finesse in the way she kissed, clanging her teeth against his, biting, sucking with her mouth, scratching, clawing with her hands, losing all rhythm and control below. Simply driving herself into him, onto him, all around him.

With a gasp, he staggered, then braced both arms against the wall beside her shoulders to steady them both.

She was the one in control now, or out of control, depending how one looked at it, using the strength of her limbs and back muscles to pump powerfully against him, at the same time as she consumed his mouth.

Her orgasm was raw and explosive, her strong inner muscles milking his sex in a velvet vice, savagely pulling the answering climax out of him.

He moaned helplessly into her mouth, their lips still sealed together, their tongues still dueling. She took it all inside of her—his sigh of surrender, the harsh, battering beat of his heart, the jerking and shuddering of his tortured sex, the hot, thick flood of his seed. If only she had fangs of her own. She'd take his blood too.

She'd take all of him.

As their breathing slowed and their pulses calmed, he stepped further into her, pinning her with the full weight and heat of his body against the wall.

She reluctantly released his mouth, but couldn't resist peppering butterfly kisses against his lips, at the corners where his dimples rested in slight grooves, along his chiseled jawline and over his perfect cheekbones.

Her gentleness now was almost an apology for the ferocity with which she'd ridden him and taken him just moments before.

Not that he seemed to mind.

"I thought you don't like kissing me," he rasped when he recovered enough breath to speak.

"I never said that," she argued, ever a stickler to details. "I said 'I don't like the way you kiss.' Because you made me... feel things I wasn't ready to feel."

"And now you're ready?" he whispered, gazing into her eyes, searching.

She shook her head, staring back at him solemnly.

"They overwhelm me, the feelings. But I don't think I care anymore."

A huff of breath left his chest like an abbreviated laugh or a release of tension. He reached beside her to turn off the shower and dropped his forehead to hers, closing his eyes.

"Grace."

It was all he said, just her name. It sounded like an endearment, a vow, a fervent prayer.

So she returned the sentiment with equal gravity.

"Devlin."

It wasn't a declaration of love, he knew, but it was close enough to soothe his vulnerable, aching heart.

Chapter Thirteen

He's disappeared.

The Creature communicated telepathically with its Mistress through their special connection.

It didn't know whether this connection also existed between her and others she commanded, and once upon a time it might have cared, enough to be jealous even, of her bond with the rest of her minions. But now it felt weary and numb.

Prolonged pain and violence could do that to a soul, especially when it dragged on for years.

Millennia.

She offered no response through the link between their minds. It supposed that she already knew, then, that Enlil Naram-Anu could not be found.

Was he dead? The Creature wondered. Perhaps the Mistress knew the answer already. It wouldn't ask her, however, it didn't want to show any curiosity.

Curiosity implied that it cared about the answer. It really didn't.

Care, that was. About anything.

What do you want to do about Grace Darling? Now that she seems to recall parts of her past?

A long silence on the brainwaves. The Creature thought she just wasn't in a conversing mood today.

And then she gave it the message, *Keep watching her. Tell me what she's doing and where she's going.*

She's under the protection of Jade Cicada now, the creature noted, strongly implying that it would be very tricky to know her actions. The Cove was a fortress they had yet to find a way to break through, even when they had a traitor planted on the inside.

She will come out of hiding soon enough, the Mistress shot back. *She will come looking for answers. She will want to know what exactly happened to her parents the day they died. And we will be ready for her when she comes.*

And the prisoner? the Creature reminded her.

Well, it supposed the correct term would be "ex-prisoner" since Tal-Telal was no longer in the Mistress's possession.

A dark portentous silence bloomed between them like the mushroom cloud of an atomic bomb. In retrospect, the Creature realized it probably shouldn't have brought up the Akkadian General. The Mistress's moods were extremely volatile when she thought of him.

He will return to me in the end, she finally hissed across the unknown distance between them. *Else he stands to lose everything he holds dear. He knows that I always keep my promises.*

The creature quickly switched topics, not wanting to linger on her venom for the General.

This tentative truce between the Pure Ones and the New England Dark Queen is erecting obstacles in the way of our progress, it communicated. *The Asian fight clubs have all but fizzled out and the expansion in Eastern Europe and Latin America has been slow at best.*

You trouble me with trifles, the Mistress deplored. *Have you not the most cunning of minds? Wield it accordingly. Drive a wedge into the alliance. Jade Cicada is not without weakness.*

Indeed she was not, the Creature knew. The traitor had shared quite a few juicy details with it before she met her mortal reward.

It knew just what to do.

*** *** *** ***

As Devlin slept deeply in his bed, a white cotton sheet twisted haphazardly around his hips, Grace climbed the ladder to his library alcove with Miu-Miu and her red notebook tucked in one arm, which had been delivered along with all the other items she'd requested through a built-in lift beside the bedroom door.

Her pets had already been fed, it seemed, and Antony and Cleopatra were now swimming contentedly in their borrowed new bowl. It even had a little castle and some pretty seashells on the bottom for decor.

Whoever her host was, Grace thought, the Great Beauty was most considerate of details.

She didn't know what time it was, and for the first time since her parents died, she didn't particularly care.

Maybe if she didn't measure it, her time with Devlin could stretch forever.

She let Miu-Miu snuffle around the cozy enclosure, surrounded on three sides with shelves of books, the fourth side open to the room below with a glass railing that was so clear and fine it was all but invisible.

There was a half-moon arrangement of cushions and pillows at one end and a low round table sandwiched between two large, plush bean-bag chairs on the other. All on top of a weave of thick, fluffy sheepskin rugs that covered the entire floor of the alcove.

Grace slowly wandered from one corner of the built-in library to the other, perusing Devlin's private collection. The shelves of books stretched from floor to ceiling, but downstairs the volumes were all related to IT, programming, gaming, mathematics, statistics and even business accounting. She'd glimpsed a couple of thick tomes on the random walk of stock markets and financial derivatives.

Up here, the collection was much more personal. On one side, there were history books for every ancient civilization. On the other side were legacies by famous British novelists and poets, including the complete works of Shakespeare. Grace even recognized some of the others they were so renowned: Wordsworth, Dickens, Austen, Bronte, Byron, Milton, Keats, Blake, to name a few.

But by far, the works of Shakespeare dominated the library. One book in particular protruded slightly outwards from the shelf, as if it were often read or extending an invitation to be read.

Grace gently pulled it out, and it opened directly to a ribbon-marked page.

> *Sonnet 147:*
> *My love is as a fever longing still,*
> *For that which longer nurseth the disease;*
> *Feeding on that which doth preserve the ill,*
> *The uncertain sickly appetite to please.*
> *My reason, the physician to my love,*
> *Angry that his prescriptions are not kept,*
> *Hath left me, and I desperate now approve*
> *Desire is death, which physic did except.*
> *Past cure I am, now Reason is past care,*
> *And frantic-mad with evermore unrest;*
> *My thoughts and my discourse as madmen's are,*
> *At random from the truth vainly expressed;*
> *For I have sworn thee fair, and thought thee bright,*
> *Who art as black as hell, as dark as night.*

Huh.

Grace didn't understand the exact meaning, but it seemed to her that the gist of the writing was to point out that to love was to embrace insanity. Not terribly complimentary of love, this sonnet.

She flipped over to another well-marked page and read:

Sonnet 116:
Let me not to the marriage of true minds
Admit impediments. Love is not love
Which alters when it alteration finds,
Or bends with the remover to remove:
O, no! it is an ever-fixed mark,
That looks on tempests and is never shaken;
It is the star to every wandering bark,
Whose worth's unknown, although his height be taken.
Love's not Time's fool, though rosy lips and cheeks
Within his bending sickle's compass come;
Love alters not with his brief hours and weeks,
But bears it out even to the edge of doom.
If this be error and upon me proved,
I never writ, nor no man ever loved.

Hmm. Grace was somewhat more familiar with the lines of this sonnet. It was probably very famous. It still didn't make a lot of logical sense to her. How could love be immutable?

Everything changed. The world changed. Nothing remained the same. This was why love was a figment of human beings' imagination.

"Ever-fixed mark" indeed.

Grace felt like everything she had in common with Devlin was downstairs. But up here, in his inner sanctuary, she felt like an intruder. Stuck out like a sore thumb.

Nevertheless, the thick, luxurious sheepskin rugs called to her. Even though she didn't belong, she felt safe and content here. As if Devlin's very arms were wrapped closely and warmly about her. She couldn't resist any longer and hunkered down into the soft fleece.

Heaven, Grace sighed, making herself comfortable in the cushions and pillows. The only thing that would complete her bliss was Devlin's body inside her. Or better yet, Devlin orgasming endlessly inside her.

But the male needed his much deserved rest. He wasn't quite ready for twelve-hour orgies in his current state, though his unwavering erection would have protested this assessment. She'd tucked him in bed anyway and reluctantly disengaged from his embrace to take temptation away.

Temptation to her own self-control that was, for she couldn't have resisted taking him again and again had she stayed in bed with him.

Her blood did seem to help, for he no longer seemed as tender in the torso as he was before, and the pink lines on his skin from puncture wounds and slashes had faded almost to invisibility.

A swelling of pride and bone-deep satisfaction filled her to the brim as she realized that *she* did that for him. Made him strong again. Fed his needs.

Could one make a career out of being a vampire's food?

But it was more than a job. It was a duty. Heck, it was her very own *calling*.

But only Devlin. Everything she had to give, it was only for him.

What did it all *mean*?

Grace didn't know the answers, so she tried instead to write down everything she thought of, starting with the recovered memories of the day her parents died.

It was hours before she came down from the loft with her notebook and Miu-Miu in tow.

She put the chinchilla back in her cage and spread some old newspapers she found beneath it. Devlin had stacks and stacks of them in a corner of the loft, neatly tucked away in a large woven basket. They were mostly sports and financial pages. And he seemed particularly fond of the *Economist*. Some of the newspapers were decades old.

On second thought, perhaps she shouldn't have used them to catch chinchilla droppings.

Grace darted a glance in Miu-Miu's direction. Too late. Her pet was very regular with her bowel movements. There was nothing she could do about it now.

Grace checked her cell and answered her aunt's worried texts, having not heard from her in a couple of days. She even let Maria know that she was with "her man," to which she received a series of emojis and exclamation marks in reply, a level of expressiveness uncharacteristic of the older woman.

Grace smiled and turned off her phone.

She then seated herself at the built-in ledge that served as a work station along one wall and began tapping away on her laptop.

Soon, she was in the Cove's secure network and searching through Devlin's files, the ones on Zenn that she copied for him.

He'd already flagged bundles of data that might require further digging. There weren't many of them. A quick scan told Grace that everything was as it should be, nothing noteworthy or suspicious in any of Zenn's archives all the way back to the company's inception. Because she was intimately familiar with its architecture and file logic, having built the structure and security around it, Grace's scrub of the information took much less time than Devlin had taken.

As she came back for a second pass, she agreed with Devlin's assessment that there were only two source files worth digging into. Grace wondered why he hadn't already done it himself. But she quickly realized that an extra layer of encryption was wrapped around the files like electric barbed wire, a firewall unfamiliar to her own algorithms.

She leaned back in her swivel chair and laced her hands together, stretching her arms taut and cracking her knuckles. She'd never met a puzzle yet that she couldn't crack.

As Grace concentrated on hacking the firewall, Devlin twitched and murmured in his sleep. The nightmare he'd been able to evade for weeks had finally caught him in its jaws again…

1812. Somewhere in Spain.

He'd been starved, beaten and left to rot in a dark, square cell in the bloody middle of nowhere Spain for weeks.

Devlin resisted scratching the open, festering wounds in the middle of his back from the countless lashes he'd received while tied to a couple of stakes in the ground. The wounds were burning and itchy at the same time, no doubt oozing pus as well. At this rate, he just might die of infection. He was already feeling feverish.

It was the only time he'd been dragged outside, to receive the most recent bout of punishment (or rather, "inducement," as his captors would say) and even then it was the middle of the night. He'd lost track of the last time he'd seen and felt sunlight on his skin. All of the other tortures were efficiently conducted in a large, windowless chamber next to his underground cell.

Officers were supposed to be treated with some semblance of respect and dignity when captured by enemy ranks, but they'd stripped him of his clothes the moment he and two of Ned Pakenham's infantry soldiers had been taken. Devlin had tried to negotiate their release, given that those men knew nothing and were useless as prisoners when the battle had already been won.

But all words and persuasion had fallen on deaf ears. Before his very eyes, one of the soldiers was shot dead on the spot. Just to make the point that there would be no concessions. After that, it became abundantly clear that Pakenham and Wellington's plan for Devlin's mission had gone horribly awry.

It took a day and a half of being dragged walking or running, or just face down in the dirt clawing, behind the horses upon which their captors rode to reach their destination—an isolated fortress far away from any sign of civilization. There, Devlin was brought before the leader of this little band of what appeared to be hired mercenaries instead of regular, law-abiding soldiers.

The leader was neither Spanish, Portuguese nor French. He was most definitely not English, though he spoke the language quite fluently. Devlin had come to think of him as "the Greek," given his accent and his looks.

As an avid student of ancient history, one of the many scholarly pursuits his family deplored in him, Devlin called the term kaloskagathos *to mind when looking upon the Greek. It meant "gorgeous to look at, blessed by the gods, and therefore in possession of a beautiful mind."*

The Greek's mind was many things, but beautiful was not one of them. Devlin would have used adjectives like twisted, depraved and sadistic.

He was always smiling, the Greek.

Smiling while his men rained agony upon the captives. Smiling when he interrogated Devlin the way he might enjoy a scintillating conversation. Smiling every time he came to visit Devlin in his cell, as if he were genuinely happy to find him there, rotting in his own filth and countless unhealed wounds.

As if his thoughts conjured the male in question, the Greek appeared just beyond the iron gate of his cell.

"How are you feeling today, Devlin?" The Greek always greeted him by his Christian name, insinuating a closeness that didn't exist.

Devlin distantly wondered how he even knew his name, given that Devlin had certainly never revealed it. He'd only given his title and rank when captured.

"I could use some good French wine, a beefsteak and some salve for my back," Devlin replied cheerfully. He liked to think it needled the Greek, his gracious acceptance of his current lot.

His captor's smile grew wider, almost but not quite revealing his teeth.

"You'll have your reward after you tell me about the English commander's plans," the Greek doled out his oft repeated line.

Devlin was beginning to wonder whether the Greek really cared to know Wellington's strategies. At times the interrogation seemed a mere excuse to torture Devlin and the other soldier.

"Not today," he answered. "My memory doesn't work well when I'm feeling peckish."

The Greek shook his head almost admiringly. "I'm sorry to hear that," he said, his tone all sympathy and concern.

Abruptly, he smiled again. "I'll have to see what I can do to jog your memory, then."

Bring it on, Devlin thought.

Enough with the pointless banter. He didn't know what else the Greek had up his sleeve by way of torture, but he wouldn't crack. He was made of sterner stuff.

"I thought I'd change things up a bit today and tell you a little story you might be interested to hear," the Greek declared, a glint of excitement entering his eyes.

Or perhaps it was madness. Devlin couldn't really tell the difference where the Greek was concerned.

His captor made himself comfortable by sitting down on the dirt ground and stretching out his legs while leaning his back against the deep frame of Devlin's cell door. Looking for all the world as if he was settling in for the duration.

Devlin could care less. If the Greek wanted to be chatty today, it was no skin off Devlin's back. Let's hope literally.

"Once upon a time there was a beautiful Marquess," the Greek began, "let's call him the Marquess of Hart."

A shiver of awareness goosed down Devlin's spine.

"He was the eldest son of the Duke of... Devon."

Devlin deepened his breathing in an effort to calm his quickening pulse. How did the Greek know?

"He was born into the wrong family, sadly," the Greek continued, seemingly immersed in his story-telling. "Like a cuckoo in a nest of eagles. Or rather, an eagle in a nest of cuckoos."

Helplessly, Devlin raised his eyes to the Greek, staring intently at his face as he spoke.

"He took after his mother, this beautiful boy, all golden and bright—fair skin, rosy cheeks and stunning sapphire blue eyes."

At this, the Greek's gaze unfocused, as if he were as much describing the boy in his story as someone else from his memory.

"He had none of his father's dark looks. You couldn't find any trace of the Duke in him, in fact, which was probably why he was widely regarded as the usurper in this noble, ancient lineage."

The Greek turned slightly so that he could see Devlin's face out of the corner of his eye as he spoke.

"The poor, beautiful child was hated by his mother, because for her at least, if not for anyone else, he was a product of his beast of a father, the result of countless copulations forced upon her in the early years of their marriage. For, after all, she was exquisitely beautiful, he was randy and robust, and she was his property, his wife. Her duty was to beget an heir for the Dukedom. There was not one single night during that terrible first year that he didn't visit her bed."

Devlin swallowed, memories of his childhood flooding his mind as the Greek continued to weave his gruesome spell.

"She told him often, her first-born son, how much she hated him. How much she despised his sire. How she wished he were never born. The only advantage of his birth was that her husband began to visit her less often and turned a blind eye to her affairs."

The Greek regarded Devlin fully for a moment, smiling beatifically. "How do you like my story so far, Devlin Sinclair?"

Devlin barely managed to shrug, but his ashen face betrayed the pain he carried inside.

"Not interesting enough?" the Greek inquired solicitously. "Let's see if I can make the story more exciting."

He settled back against the door frame and looked away again.

"Before the boy turned one, the Duchess was with child again. It was her duty too, after all, to beget a spare. Within the year, she gave birth to another boy, an ordinary, dark-haired, wrinkly thing who nevertheless became the apple of the old Duke's eye."

Devlin flinched despite his efforts to keep still.

"This boy didn't take after his mother at all. And while one couldn't be entirely sure if he inherited the Duke's austere dark good-looks, for the boy grew up to be exceedingly average in every physical way, he seemed to take on his father's mannerisms, interests and personality."

"They were two happy peas in a pod, those two. And the Duchess was pleased, for now she could be free to do anything she wanted, take as many lovers as she liked, freed from her husband's slavering and incompetent nightly visits. She removed herself from the lives of these three males and promptly died with one of her numerous paramours a year thereafter."

Devlin wanted to shut his ears, but he knew that the Greek would find a way to make him listen. If this was his torture of the day, the Greek had certainly found Devlin's soft, vulnerable underbelly.

"Only the heir seemed saddened by her passing. I can't begin to comprehend why, since the Duchess had never shown him even an ounce of affection. The Duke was relieved in a way, given that he thought of her as a burden, but his hatred toward her, all the years she spurned him, all the vitriol she threw at him, remained after her death."

"After all, she had the audacity to get herself killed in the most embarrassing way, entwined with her lover to the very end, making the Duke a laughingstock. She made him a cuckold and it was widespread public knowledge among the ton."

"Is there a point to this rambling?" Devlin couldn't resist interrupting.

He was shaking now, and he couldn't control it. It was as if his captor had taken a dagger and was using it to slowly carve out Devlin's heart.

"Oh I'm just getting to the good part, don't be impatient," the Greek said. "We haven't even reached the climax of the story yet."

Devlin ground his teeth and kept silent. He could hear the glee in the Greek's voice when he'd uttered his objection. It was a sign of weakness. He wouldn't show it again.

"So the Duke refocused the full force of his hatred and venom on his elder son, the one who looked so much like his late wife, the one everyone whispered behind his back that the poor child wasn't really a product of the Duke's loins after all."

"And the little Marquess of Hart didn't do himself any favors. He was a quiet child, studious and careful. Unlike his younger brother who voiced his opinions and demands often and loudly. His reservedness reminded the Duke of his mother's frigidity, so the Duke turned all of his attentions and any affection and regard he had in his beastly heart toward the younger son."

"Naturally, there formed a rift of insurmountable proportions between the two brothers, one who was secure in his father's regard but wouldn't inherit his title and one who loved but never received in turn."

The Greek looked at Devlin again, who kept his gaze on the floor in front of him.

"And now we get to the good part. I know you've been waiting with anticipation."

With relish, he turned to face fully Devlin's cell, staring unblinkingly at Devlin's face as he continued his uncanny story, sitting with his long legs drawn up and enfolded loosely by his arms, like an eager fortune teller at a campfire.

"The boys grew up, as boys are wont to do. The older brother dedicated himself to scholarly pursuits, but the heart of a warrior burned within. The younger brother reveled in being a rogue, a sportsman, a dandy about town, but deep inside, a cold ball of resentment and jealousy grew. For though he had his father's approval, an exclusive pack of chums, money and privilege, he did not have that coveted title; he was merely a second-born son."

Devlin's cheek twitched. It was the only outward sign of distress he showed. But the Greek caught it, and it seemed to fuel his sadistic joy.

"And then it came to pass that our little Hart fell under the spell of a beautiful woman at last. She was vivacious and bold, smart and passionate, a true belle of the ball. And she had set her sights on Hart."

"He was not easy to win, but she was persistent and cunning. So he decided to let her have him, accepting his duty to marry and carry on the line, though he never could tell if she wanted the man or the title. After all, no one in his life had ever given him the impression that he was worth having as simply himself."

Devlin stared unblinkingly at the ground, oblivious to all else save the sound of the Greek's dark, hypnotic voice.

"Sensing that something was not quite sturdy in their little love boat, Hart went off to serve his country, putting some time and distance between them, putting to patriotic use the special skills he'd secretly developed under the guise of scholarly pursuits."

"He'd learned how to fight, how to shoot the heart out of any target, how to unravel the most complicated puzzles. How to kill. He learned how to flirt too, because charm and friendliness opened doors and made connections better than introversion and bookishness. And he learned that being a charmer, a devil-may-care rake, was a fantastic disguise that sheltered the real man inside."

Devlin refused to look at the Greek. He could feel the male staring avidly at him with those wild, haunted eyes.

"And that brings us to his fool-hardy mission to purposely get himself captured by enemy troops so that he could discover Napoleon's next moves."

The Greek paused for effect, gaging Devlin's mood. Devlin refused to twitch even a hair.

"Our heroic little Hart endured beating after beating, under the misguided notion that his countrymen were looking for him, that they would eventually find and liberate him. Wisely, he did not attempt escape, because the probability of success was quite abysmal. But what he didn't realize was that no one was searching for him. They'd given up a long time ago."

Devlin's eyelid flickered.

The Greek opened the prison cell and prowled inside. Devlin noticed that he'd left the gate wide open, and there seemed to be none of the other mercenaries around.

There were no sounds at all, in fact.

Devlin was not chained or bound. He could easily make a run for it. But the Greek seemed confident he wouldn't make it very far, or perhaps he wanted him to make the attempt just to have the pleasure of hunting him down.

The Greek crouched on his haunches in front of Devlin, close enough to strike if Devlin timed it just right. Perhaps a jab to the eyes and throat or a kick to the groin.

"Do you know why no one is searching for you, Devlin Sinclair?" the Greek asked softly. "Because your brother William has already declared you dead."

Devlin raised his eyes to the Greek, burning with rage. What nonsense was he spouting now?

"It's true, I'm afraid," the Greek continued apologetically. "You see, it was his idea to have you sent out on this foolhardy mission. He planted confidantes within the General's camp, convinced Wellington of the beauty of such a plot and arranged to have you dispatched. Dispatched and dispatched with, so to speak."

The Greek chuckled low at his little pun. "We were supposed to... take care of you immediately once we confirmed your identity, but..."

The Greek cocked his head at Devlin, raking him with a slow, unfathomable gaze from the top of his dirt-streaked hair to his blackened, blistered toes.

He smiled a snake-like smile.

"Well. I thought I'd play with you for a bit first. 'Twould be such a waste to end something so bright and beautiful too quickly."

Devlin held his unholy stare for a long time.

Finally, he said, "Interesting story you tell; you missed your calling as a raconteur."

The Greek's smile spread into a grin, revealing two extra sharp canines.

"It's more interesting because it's your story, Devlin Sinclair. I know you do not believe me. I can see in your eyes that you're telling yourself lies. I do have proof, you know, insurance against the eventuality that my men are not paid in a timely manner."

The Greek reached into his coat jacket and retrieved two letters. He gently laid them on the ground in front of Devlin's feet.

"Surely you'd recognize your brother's handwriting. The first letter is addressed to me, detailing every part of our arrangement. The second letter is from your fiancée to your brother, or shall I say, from the new Marchioness?"

Devlin flinched.

"Miss Lavinia Highwood and the Marquess of Hartington, the new one that is, since you were pronounced dead, married two weeks after your demise was deemed official."

The Greek pulled out a carefully folded newssheet from his inner pocket and laid that on the ground too.

"It was a quiet affair, apparently, since the wedding was hastily planned. The bride was rumored to be gaining some girth about her middle, which was why she urged her lover to take action against his inconvenient older brother."

"You lie," Devlin seethed, unable to control his pain and rage any longer.

For a moment, the Greek's ever-present smile slipped. For a mere split second, he looked truly sympathetic to Devlin's heartbreak, saddened on his behalf.

"Alas, I do not," he said softly. "You can read the letters for yourself. And in case you hold out some remote hope that your troops are still looking for you, they stopped long ago when they discovered the burnt, disfigured body a few miles south of here in your officer's uniform."

Devlin thought of the other soldier who'd been brought alive to the fortress with him. He'd not heard or seen the other man for days.

"Yes, you guess rightly," the Greek said, seeming to read his thoughts. "That soldier died in your stead, I'm afraid. I had to provide evidence of your demise, after all, to collect my payment."

"Then why am I still here?" Devlin demanded, furious that someone totally unrelated and innocent had lost his life for him.

"Why keep me alive?"

The Greek remained silent for so long, Devlin thought he wouldn't answer.

But then he said in his dark, haunting voice, "You remind me of a boy I used to know. The most beautiful, golden boy you've ever seen. His name was Xanthos and I loved him very, very much. He was studious and serious, like you, but full of passion with an unerring sense of righteousness. In the end, he loved justice and truth more than me, and I had the unfortunate task of... killing him."

His dark, red-centered eyes bore into Devlin, so commanding Devlin couldn't look away, not even to blink.

"In doing so, I killed myself," the Greek said softly. "Xanthos had been the best part of me."

He let out a long, shuddering breath, and before Devlin's eyes, the Greek seemed to deflate and age. The ever-present careless smile was gone. A cold bleakness settled into his demeanor, and for once, he was entirely solemn.

"I am tired of this endless existence and despicable human treachery. You will be my resting place, Devlin Sinclair."

Devlin could not begin to understand what he meant. So he said, "If you plan to end your life, by all means be my guest."

A low, humorless chuckle rattled through the Greek's chest and out between his lips. "I must give you my gift first, beautiful boy, the gift I should have given him."

"What—"

But the Greek was suddenly upon him, cutting Devlin's words right out of his throat.

Twin daggers struck the side of Devlin's neck while the heavy weight of his captor trapped him against the wall. The Greek's hands held Devlin's arms immobile at his sides, as strong as iron manacles. He knelt directly on top of Devlin's legs, keeping him pinned helplessly to the ground.

Devlin's eyes bulged, his nostrils flaring. He couldn't move even one muscle of his body, but he could hear the grotesque sounds of the Greek sucking at his throat and swallowing thirstily.

He was drinking Devlin's blood! He'd bitten Devlin in the neck with his teeth! It was too mind boggling to take in.

Soon, the blood loss caught up with Devlin, sawing away at his tenuous grasp on consciousness. When his eyelids slid shut, he heard the Greek's voice in his head:

I will inject the last of my soul into your body when you are in the in-between, the ephemeral yet infinite gateway between life and death. When you awake, you will see the world with different eyes. You may even have some version of my Gift, the ability to see into others' memories. And you will be very, very thirsty. My men are passed out outside in a drunken stupor. They will be easy prey for a newly made vampire.

Why? Devlin pushed the question out in his rapidly fogging mind.

You look exactly like him, my Xanthos, the Greek answered in his head. You have his courage and his strength as well. And I am tired of living this pointless life without him. You, Devlin Sinclair, have much more living to do. Xanthos would have approved.

And then, just before Devlin breathed his last as a human, he heard a long sigh and a crumbling rustle. The weight was lifted off of him, as if it had simply disintegrated into the air.

Chapter Fourteen

Devlin woke up gasping, his heart pounding, his vision blurred.

Grace was beside him immediately, helping him to a sitting position, rubbing her hand in soothing circles up and down his back.

"Devlin, what is it? Did you have that dream again?"

He shook his head. He couldn't speak yet. Every time he had the nightmare, he relived the process of dying and coming back to life. Becoming a vampire.

But it wasn't the Change or the physical torture during the weeks he'd been imprisoned that made him dread this particular dream. It was the story his captor told.

And when he'd drank his fill of the band of drunken mercenaries' blood, when his vampire senses had sharpened to a razor point, he'd gone back to his cell and read the two letters the Greek had left behind. The marriage announcement in the papers as well.

Next to them had littered a pile of unassuming black ashes, so contradictory to the larger-than-life presence of the *kaloskagathos* Greek.

There had been no escape from the truth of it: the murderous designs on his life by the two people he cared for the most in the world.

"Devlin, are you all right? Would it help if you talked to me? Dr. Weisman says talking helps to 'unburden and demystify.'"

He still couldn't speak, simply doing all he could to breathe in and out.

"Would you rather write it down? I know I don't respond the right way in these situations."

"Grace," he rasped, putting a hand on her arm, stilling her.

She didn't show it in her tone, which was without inflection as usual. But a little furrow appeared between her bushy brows and her eyes were dark and intent.

Devlin recognized this as her way of worrying. She was distressed for him, perhaps even frightened.

The need to comfort her outweighed the pain of his own memories for the moment. He pulled her into his embrace and laid them both back on the bed, her much smaller body curled into his side, her head nestled on his chest, tucked beneath his chin.

"Who is this Dr. Weisman you keep talking about?" he asked irrelevantly to distract them both. "Is it a man or a woman?"

"A man," she answered dutifully, going with the flow of his conversation.

She would probably never be one of those women who spoke with an agenda. Only if she fixated on something would she pursue a topic like a homing beacon, without artifice or dissemblance. For the most part, she was easily distracted and because of that, unthreatening to talk to. There was never any judgment or presumption in the way she viewed the world.

"Good looking?"

"Very."

Devlin gave a short huff of laughter. "That was an instant and adamant assertion," he noted. "Should I be worried?"

"About what?"

He looked down at the crown of her head as she snuggled warmly against him.

"A male often has cause to worry when his female is regularly in the company of a 'very good looking' man who is not himself," he explained, because her question was genuine, not an attempt at coyness.

She gave a small shrug. "Why should you worry? I'm not attracted to him. I'm only attracted to you."

Ah, music to his ears. Devlin was feeling better already.

Emboldened, he decided to needle her further, "What about all of your previous... partners? I have a feeling I wasn't the first you recruited for that..." he flipped his hand idly in the air, looking for the least offensive phrase—offensive to his own ears that was, "...two week engagement."

"Oh, I wasn't attracted to any of them," she quickly replied. "They were bodies that fulfilled a purpose for me."

Devlin's breath stalled.

Her words hurt more than he could have imagined. Even though she was speaking of other men, he'd been "recruited" for her purpose in much the same way. Was he deluding himself that he meant more to her? And if so, that the attachment would last?

Perhaps he was a masochist, perhaps he was still too vulnerable from the dream and had forgotten to guard his raw, stumbling heart, but he couldn't help whispering the question:

"What about me? What am I to you?"

Grace took his question very seriously. She propped herself up on her arms to look down into his face, holding his gaze.

For the longest time she stared at him, in the same intense, unblinking way she did from time to time over the duration of their acquaintance. He wasn't sure what he saw, or what she was searching for in his eyes. It was as if she'd locked herself in a trance while probing into him with her clear, dark gaze.

Finally, she said, low and wondering, "I don't know what you are to me. You make me feel things I've never felt before. Feelings I can't describe. Sometimes I'm afraid of them. Sometimes they make me full to bursting. I think..."

She cupped his face with one palm and rubbed her thumb across his mouth. Back and forth she caressed him, as if mesmerized by the feel of his lips and the perfect fullness of their shape.

He waited with baited breath, not wanting to rush her, hanging on her every word. Hoping she'd finish her thought and dreading the rest of her sentence at the same time.

"I think you're my drug, Devlin Sinclair," she murmured reflectively, as if talking more to herself than to him. "You're my obsession and addiction. A habit I don't want to form but one I can't seem to break."

Well.

He wasn't thrilled with the "don't want" part of it, but for now he'd settle for the rest of her confession.

"I want to make love with you, Grace," he said solemnly, his words carefully chosen.

She'd never referred to the joining of their bodies as anything remotely resembling love, but for him, it could never be anything else. He wanted her to know what this meant to him, what *she* meant to him.

He was putting a stake in the ground.

A line of concentration appeared between her brows, as if she were trying to puzzle out what he meant.

"How do we make love?" she asked, "love is a concept, not a product. How do you make it when it's not real?"

"We'll find a way together," he whispered, drawing her down to him, taking her lips in a slow, soft kiss.

"I've never made love before you," he breathed into her mouth, "Never truly loved before you."

She draped herself, still dressed in one of his long-sleeved shirts, over his naked body, and angled her head to deepen their kiss.

She was wet from wanting him already and wanted to race toward the climax, but when she tried to push his passion higher, he deftly retreated and came back at her with a simmering warmth, playful and teasing.

She tried to take control by holding his head in her hands, thrusting her fingers into his thick, wavy hair, thrusting her tongue deeply into his mouth, making him groan with the carnality of it. But even as he let her take the lead, his hands smoothed up and down her sides in a calming motion, gentling her urgency.

She wanted him now, she wanted him hard and fast. So she tried to capture his erection between her thighs and take it into her naked core.

At this, he flipped them smoothly so that she was trapped beneath his much heavier frame. He captured her wrists and held them beside her head, leaving her mouth to trail kisses down her throat, her chest, plumping her small breasts wetly through the fabric of the shirt with gentle sucks.

Frustrated noises gurgled from Grace's throat. She didn't like not being in control. She wanted to be the one to play his body like a harp, to find all his secrets and take him to the edge, hold him prisoner there. She'd never had the same done to herself, because that meant relinquishing command, submitting herself to another's will.

"Let me," he entreated huskily, nuzzling his face against her belly, moving steadily lower to her bare hips, upper thighs and the nest of curls between them.

Grace writhed helplessly against him, but he held her firm, holding her hands at her sides now, his muscular torso between her spread legs.

She dug her heels into the mattress trying to gain purchase, trying to take back control of this runaway train, but he was already upon her, his mouth hot and heavenly against her sex, his tongue sweeping along her labia, then paying exquisite homage to her clitoris, swirling and teasing, lapping and gliding.

"Devlin..." she groaned, frustrated and unbearably aroused. "I want you now, inside..."

But he ignored her, taking his time with his sweet torture of her, and some distant part of her recognized what he was doing and the difference between what she'd done to him the first night they'd been together.

He wasn't analytically and detachedly trying to draw out calculated reactions from her body. His every touch, every kiss, every breath was instinctual, as if his body was an extension of hers and he made it come alive in ways she'd never thought possible.

She felt her orgasm build relentlessly, but whereas she would have rode it consciously and eagerly started another right on its heels, giving her body the release it craved, she purposely held back this time. She wanted to wait for him to join her. Because, somehow, it mattered.

Whatever they had, it was more than physical pleasure.

"Devlin," she moaned softly, "come inside of me. I want to see your eyes when you come apart."

He heeded her this time, levering himself up on his elbows, releasing her wrists. She opened her thighs and wrapped her legs around his hips, bringing his pulsing erection to her weeping core.

Eyes locked with his, she stared into those amazing sapphire orbs as he slowly entered her, thick and long and hard and satiny. He pushed deeply to the hilt and held there as she quivered with sparks of incandescent pleasure around him, comprehending with crystal clarity that no one could ever make her feel this way.

Only him. Only Devlin.

"I love you, Grace," he said in that low, smoky baritone, husky with emotion, staring deeply into her eyes.

She gasped, caught unawares as her body came apart at the seams, as her heart pounded its way out of her chest, and her spirit soared to dizzying heights.

And only then did he begin to move, stroking her higher, deeper, harder. Keeping her suspended at that glorious peak, crashing wave after wave of ecstasy upon her.

"Devlin," she breathed, holding his face in her hands, lost in the glistening pools of his eyes. "Come with me."

His body obeyed, and she saw with vivid fascination the crimson flush of his pleasure that traveled up his chest, his throat, his cheeks, the beauty of his crisis blooming on his face, contorting his features in something like anguish, a breathtaking pain, as if he were dying, as if she had slain him.

She felt the hot gush of his seed wash over her womb, the shaking of his body as he lost himself to passion, the voracious pulls of her sex for more of him.

All of him.

She pulled him down to her finally and sealed his mouth with hers, breaking their gaze.

But it was too late.

She would never forget the way he looked as he released his seed, along with his heart and soul, into her.

The devastating way he loved her.

*** *** *** ***

The Creature had a simple plan to drive a veritable chasm between the New England Dark Queen and her Pure allies.

But it was in no hurry to execute the scheme. Preparation and planning were key. It enjoyed games that required cunning and strategy. And it absolutely delighted in building the anticipation for a glorious climax.

No, the Dark Queen could wait while it set wheels in motion.

Meanwhile, it had a few tricks up its sleeve to accelerate the expansion of the fight clubs.

Recreating the Genesis serum, on the other hand, presented a larger challenge. Fortunately, it was one that its Mistress seemed less concerned about. Perhaps she had some tricks of her own that she didn't share.

Shrugging the responsibility of engendering mass chaos, violence and destruction aside for a moment, the Creature decided to take a stroll down its favorite street in Brooklyn, to visit its favorite shop.

As it passed by the gleaming, newly washed window of a flower shop, it looked to make sure it was in the right skin, like an insecure teenager checking her makeup.

Just to be sure. It wouldn't do to reveal its real face to the lovely old Mama Bear, Estelle Martin. She'd never call it Binu again.

The sun had just set as it arrived at Dark Dreams. It loved the sound of the little wreath of bells jingling as it opened the door.

Estelle was facing it as it entered, sitting at her oval tea table.

She was not alone.

"Welcome, Binu," she smiled, though her smile seemed dimmed at half its usual wattage. "Come join us for some biscuits and tea. It will only take me a few minutes to prepare your favorite coffee."

She hustled away without waiting for its reply, leaving it to awkwardly face two individuals it had never met and one who made its stomach tie itself in knots.

"Hello," Sophia said warmly, smiling shyly in greeting. "There's plenty of space for one more. Come sit by me."

She pulled over a nearby chair and patted its cushion as if to advertise its comforts.

"Is that your name—Binu?" the blonde woman it had never met in person, but knew about from reports, asked curiously. "What a coincidence. The word has a special meaning where I come from."

She smiled and stood up, gesturing for it to take the seat that Sophia offered. "Please do join us. We don't bite. My name is Nana Chastain and this is my son Benjamin."

Its eyes finally riveted on the little boy with golden curls, who at first sight appeared to be a miniature version of his mother, but when it looked closely, the shape of the boy's face, its angles and planes, curves and valleys looked nothing like his mother's.

"Hi," Benjamin chirped happily, unaware that a real life monster was not two feet in front of him.

The boy's face was so familiar it couldn't look away, even as it was aware that it had been staring for an uncomfortable length of time.

What was it about the boy? Where had it seen that nose before? That chin and those cheeks?

"Are you all right?" it heard Sophia's voice like a distant echo through a fog. She had stood up too and was coming closer to it.

"Have we met before?" she asked, almost close enough to touch. "There's something familiar about you."

"Here we are," Estelle called out as she reemerged from the kitchen. "Black and smooth with a dollop of cream. Just the way you like it, Binu."

It didn't realize it was backing away until its back met the front door. The three women and child stared after it with similarly puzzled and worried expressions.

"I—" it couldn't finish the thought as it turned and all but fled the shop.

Its long strides ate up the sidewalk as it headed away from Dark Dreams, heedless of the direction and distance.

The only image in its mind was the little boy's face, *Olivia's* face.

Olivia, the human woman who had been obsessed with it, whom it had toyed with and destroyed.

The woman who'd claimed it had a son.

*** *** *** ***

"We have to go to London."

Devlin finished buttoning his shirt and watched Grace gather her belongings by the door of his chamber, now texting someone on her phone.

"Why London?" he asked casually, down-playing the bomb she'd just set off at his feet.

He hadn't been back on English soil since his ill-fated confrontation with Lavinia after he'd returned from the Peninsula. If he never set foot on Britain again it would be too soon.

"Zenn's HQ is there. And so is its mainframe. I can't break the encryption of the two files you flagged from afar, but if I hardwire directly into the mainframe, I can get through."

She looked up at him. "Can someone transport my things back to my apartment? Aunt Maria has agreed to come by daily to take care of Miu-Miu, Antony and Cleopatra. I want to take them with me on the trip, but I don't think it would be practical."

A corner of Devlin's lips quirked.

No, hefting a fish bowl and a chinchilla cage around while they broke into Zenn's fortified HQ in the middle of London's financial district right across the street from St. Paul's Cathedral would definitely not be practical.

"I'll have their safe transport arranged," he assured her. "But do you think it absolutely necessary to go to London?"

She came to stand before him, trapping him with her intense, dark eyes.

"Don't you want to solve the puzzle?" she asked, her voice filled with a strange sort of urgency, one he'd never heard in her tone before.

"Don't you want to find what you're looking for?" she continued relentlessly. "You sought me out to help you crack Zenn. Cracking Zenn would lead you closer to your target. Isn't that right? So let's do this together. I want to know why they encrypted my parents' files."

"Did you know that they worked for Zenn's parent company before Zenn was spun off and rebuilt as a start-up? I need to unlock those files, Devlin. I need your help. I've never traveled so far by myself. I've only ever been in two cities my whole life."

She was growing agitated, and her nervousness made Devlin forget his own troubles for the time being. He smoothed his hands comfortingly up and down her arms, then kissed her quickly on the forehead.

"Of course we'll go together. We can leave within the hour." He flashed one of his signature disarming grins. "How does First Class on Virgin Atlantic Airways sound, darling?"

She frowned at him. "I wouldn't know."

And then her brow cleared and she even smiled tentatively back at him.

"But I like the way you call me 'darling.'"

His eyes crinkled at the corners as his grin grew wider.

"Are you better now?" she asked, solemn again. "Have you healed completely?"

Devlin puffed up his chest and put her hands on his abdomen, putting pressure on his ribs. "Doesn't hurt at all. Good as new."

"Devlin," she said, looking at her hands on his fine white shirt, covering those chiseled abs and steely ribs, "how big is the plane?"

"Airbus 350. It can hold over four hundred passengers, why?"

"Maybe we should sit at opposite ends of the plane," she said seriously. "I don't think I can keep my hands off you otherwise."

She said the damnedest things, Devlin mused, a bubble of happiness floating through his heart. Perhaps London wouldn't be so bad after all if Grace was by his side.

*** *** *** ***

"It was very strange," Inanna murmured while snuggled into her Mate's side after a slow, wondrous session of love-making.

She was flushed with the strength of his blood and seed within her, radiant with the sometimes unbelievable happiness she felt since they'd reunited after millennia of being lost to one another. But this evening's encounter inserted a shadow of apprehension into her resplendent bliss.

"I feel like I know him somehow, the young man who came to Mama Bear's shop, even though I've never met him before. And he must have felt something too, because he ran right back out as if demons were on his heels. Sophia said the same thing when he was gone. It's as if she knew him too but couldn't place him. Just a feeling, an awareness."

"I wish I'd been with you," Gabriel said, tightening his arms around her, willing his body heat to soothe her.

"My body would hurt a lot less if I could have skipped training with Tal." He deliberately put a teasing note in his voice to help ease her tension.

"How is Papa?" Inanna asked, her worry shifting focus instead of lessening. "He hasn't been the same since..."

She turned her face toward Gabriel as she realized something important.

"He hasn't been the same since we visited Dark Dreams together," she finished her thought. "A lot seems to coincide with that shop, I wonder why."

Gabriel knew it was better to help her sort her thoughts out rather than try to distract her. This topic was important for reasons they didn't yet know.

"What do you know about the shop and its owner? How long has it been there?"

Inanna thought back briefly to the first time she'd noticed the place, the first time she'd met Mama Bear.

"It must have been a couple of years ago," she mused. "I used to walk often down those streets at night because there are many Lost Souls to be found in the area."

Inanna was once the Angle of Death among her Kind. Her role had been to release Lost Souls back into the Universal Balance so that they could be reborn with hopefully a better life.

Now that she'd found her one true Mate and no longer needed to feed off the blood and souls of others, sustained completely by Gabriel's body, she'd tentatively taken on the new moniker of Light-Bringer, as the fabled, destined hero from the Zodiac Prophesies.

Though she hadn't the first idea what it was she was supposed to do to save the races from imminent destruction. Right now, she just focused on living and enjoying life to the fullest with her small family nucleus of Gabriel, Benji and Tal.

As well as finding her mother. Inanna believed in her heart of hearts that her mother was still alive.

"One night I passed by this shop, brand new and sparkling like the gingerbread house from the fairytales Benji likes to read, and something about it just beckoned to me. I had to go inside. And that was when I met Mama Bear."

Inanna smiled fondly in memory. "If I were to envision the most wonderful mother, kind and sassy, full of wisdom but knowing when to let me make my own decisions and mistakes, I couldn't have picked a more perfect person to fill the role than Mama Bear."

She gazed into her Mate's eyes and nuzzled his nose briefly with hers. "She helped me to fight for you, you know. She never gave me any direct advice, and I never asked for it, but she helped me understand my own heart better. She helped to embolden me to go after what I want. You."

She kissed him slowly and lingeringly. "My love. My Mate. My everything."

With one smooth motion, Gabriel rolled her on top of his body and entered her hot, slick passage, joining them intimately, knowing that she needed the connection.

They took not a moment of their time together for granted, having been separated for so long. She still feared losing him like she did once before. He did everything he could to reassure her, but he knew that only time would lessen her doubt.

In moments like these, he just needed to remind her that he was here. They were one. He simply held there, buried to the hilt, the full head of his sex exerting the perfect pressure on her G spot deep inside.

"Does Mama Bear have a name?" he asked, helping her continue her train of thought as she sighed with pleasure and wrapped herself more tightly around him, holding him as close as she could.

"Estelle Martin, I believe," Inanna said, her eyes drifting closed as a warm, tingling orgasm began to build within her.

Just having him inside of her did that. Made her senses come alive, her spirit soar.

"What do you know about her?"

Inanna took some time to reflect.

Finally, she said, "Not much, really. I've never asked about her past or even her present, and she's never volunteered. I know that she bakes mostly to supply the orphanage a few blocks down with treats for the children. She doesn't sell anything in her shop, but I've seen her give items away to strangers. It seems to make her happy to do so. And sad at the same time too, as if she were letting go of something precious to her, some part of herself."

"She seems like a kind lady," Gabriel recalled.

He'd met Mama Bear a couple of times now, but Inanna was right. Although they would spend an hour or two partaking of tea and baked delights at the shop, usually chatting much of the time with its owner, he didn't know anything pertinent about her. Where she was from, why she was here, whether she had any family or a significant other.

It was only a feeling they had of her, that she was a sweet, generous lady, for the most part joyful and ready to smile.

But there was also a darker side, Gabriel could tell. A pervasive sadness and...anger...that sometimes rose to the surface.

"Perhaps it's just a coincidence," Inanna said, not knowing what to make of what happened and her own feelings about it.

"Perhaps it was nothing. The young man might have remembered an appointment he was late for. And Papa...maybe something in the shop triggered a hurtful memory. He'd been through so much. Rain won't tell me the details of her medical assessment, but she revealed enough. He is in constant, unending pain."

Tears welled in her eyes as she held Gabriel's gaze.

"I've barely just gotten him back and I already feel like I'm losing him again."

Gabriel enfolded her snugly in his embrace and kissed her tears away, whispering words of comfort and reassurance in the old language.

She deepened their kiss and infused it with a desperate passion and carnality, devouring his mouth and tongue, nipping at his lips.

She needed him to come for her again, deep inside where she held him tightly, wash away her fears and doubts. And so he would.

Always.

Chapter Fifteen

London had certainly changed in the last two hundred and thirty years, Devlin reflected as he and Grace rode in one of the famous black hackneys from Heathrow to their temporary residence.

He'd watched many other cities transform with time, as if they had lives of their own, growing and sprawling and expanding in ways he could never have imagined as a human in the early nineteenth century.

But he'd always managed to avoid any news about England, or Britain in general. It took a lot of diligence to close his eyes and ears to current events given how important England was as a global economic and political powerhouse, but he'd been creative and for the most part successful in his efforts.

And now he was finally here. The place he'd been born. The place where he'd died, if not physically, then emotionally and psychologically.

He never should have confronted Lavinia. Sometimes truth shed no light. It only brought darkness.

"Devlin, are you okay?"

If Grace noticed his silence and reticence enough to ask the question, the situation must be dire indeed.

He took her hand in his and squeezed.

"Perfectly fine," he lied.

"Where are we going?"

Devlin wished they were headed to the Ritz Carlton on St. Jame's, or any other hotel or B&B for that matter, but while he'd been able to procure two last-minute First Class direct flights from New York to London, he wasn't able to get a hotel room.

It was Wimbledon season and there was also some sort of international diplomatic gathering being held in the city. Everything was booked solid. No amount of charm and negotiation, and even bribery, worked.

"We're going to Devonshire House," Devlin said tightly, unsuccessfully trying to sound off-handed.

"Do you not want to go there, Devlin?" Grace asked, a familiar furrow appearing between her brows.

"Why not? It's only the house in which I grew up," he answered, "And only during the Season."

"You don't have good memories there," she stated rather than asked.

He swallowed and gave her hand another squeeze, as if to brace himself.

"No. I do not."

"We can stay at a YMCA if you'd rather not go," Grace said, "I'm sure one will have a bed or some place on the floor available."

He loved her, he really did. And in moments like these, Devlin knew precisely why.

"It's fine," he said again, as if repeating the words would make it so. "I have you. You'll come to my rescue if I'm besieged by bad dreams or unhappy thoughts."

"I will try," she stated solemnly.

He gave her a small smile, which he almost felt, and brought her hand to his lips for a kiss.

"We're here," he said as the cab slowed to a stop in front of an enormous gated mansion at Hyde Park Corner on Piccadilly.

Grace got out without waiting for Devlin to come around and open her door, as she was mostly a New Yorker and never expected others to open her doors, and craned her neck way back to look up at the gigantic edifice which could easily be called a palace.

"This is a 'house'?" she breathed, awe-struck, "You lived here?"

Devlin paid the cab driver and unlocked the gate, ushering Grace inside the expansive courtyard.

"I resided here when I was human for a number of months each year when Parliament was in session, from October to June. The rest of the time I stayed at my family's country estate."

"Estate," Grace echoed. "Was your family an important one?"

"You could say that," he answered, "if you consider members of the English nobility important."

They entered through the stately front door. The building must have been hundreds of years old, older perhaps, than Devlin, but it was outfitted with modern security safeguards, and as Grace took in the interior, modern conveniences and décor as well.

"We're going to stay here, just the two of us?"

"Yes."

His reply was clipped, and she could already notice the brooding tension within him, as if the house itself threatened him.

"We're not intruding?" she wanted to make sure, because it felt like they were in a museum and everything was priceless, despite the renovation updates she could see.

"I own it," Devlin said. "It's used as a heritage museum, open to visitors most weeks of the year, but I called my estate manager before we got on the flight to close it to the public for the time being so that we'd have a place to stay."

He didn't pause to look around, instead leading her directly up a flight of very long, very grand curving stairs.

"It probably worked out for the best actually. We have a lot more privacy to conduct our mission from here."

There were paintings everywhere, some landscapes but mostly portraits.

"Are these paintings of your family?" Grace asked, slowing her gait to look at some more closely.

There were several paintings, larger-than-life-sized, of a beautiful, blonde woman whose eyes seemed to follow Grace as she moved along.

"Yes." His tone was curt.

"Where are the paintings of you?" Grace was eager to see what Devlin looked like in his human life. Perhaps there were a few of him as a boy. She'd passed by a couple already that depicted a dark-haired boy and young man who looked nothing like Devlin.

"There are none."

"Are they kept at the country estate or...I suppose you have more than one estate?"

"There are no paintings of me anywhere," he said flatly. "My parents never commissioned any. Perhaps even they knew that I would never inherit."

"But..." Grace didn't understand.

Even if Devlin's human life was cut short, he must have been the age he looked now when he was turned. So somewhere in his twenties. His parents would have had plenty of opportunities to commission any number of paintings of him growing up.

And he must have been a gorgeous little boy, a breathtakingly handsome young man, she thought. What parents wouldn't want to capture his beauty and charm for posterity?

He didn't explain more, guiding her into a room at the very back of the house on the uppermost level. It was like an attic, but it was renovated into a studio office with a large, modern platform bed, and she could see the bathroom through a slightly opened door in the corner. There was also a small kitchenette with a portable stove and refrigerator-freezer.

"Who stays here usually?" she asked, looking around.

"My estate manager," he answered. "He comes to London, from Bristol where he lives, to oversee things personally during the busiest tourist season in the summer. I had this outfitted for his convenience. He's delaying his trip here by a week or so while we're in town. That should be enough time for us to get what we need from Zenn."

"The fridge is fully stocked," Grace noted as she opened the door to check, impressed.

"I only hire the best."

She closed the fridge and turned to face him fully.

"There's so much I don't know about you," she murmured, more to herself than to him. "You're obviously very rich. You were born into English nobility. You had a family. And you hate being in this house."

"All true," he confirmed, but didn't elaborate. He wondered whether she'd ask the questions that were on the tip of her tongue, whether she'd scratch the itch of her curiosity.

She regarded him unblinkingly for a long time, as if she were trying to puzzle him out just by looking at him. But then he saw the tiniest shrug, just a nudge of one shoulder really, to indicate that she wasn't going to pursue his past.

At least not today.

"Shower first or set up our tech?" she asked, refocusing their attention on the mission.

"I'll set up. You go freshen up," he decided, relieved more than he could say to have something other than his disaster of a history to concentrate on.

Two hours later, they agreed on the plan of attack.

Tomorrow, they would visit Zenn's HQ for reconnaissance to take note of the security protocols and assess the number and quality of guards. Grace had already retrieved the building blueprints from secured archives, though not secure enough to prevent her infiltration.

"I feel like I'm in a movie, not real life," Grace confessed when they finally called it a day and settled in bed after a light repast. "Mission Impossible or Jason Bourne or James Bond. Ones of those action thrillers. In times like these I'm glad I'm not quite normal. A normal person might have a heart attack."

Devlin was amused for the first time since they'd arrived in London.

"I'm glad you're not normal," he said, pulling her closer. "You're my kind of unique."

She propped her head up on her hand and looked down into his face.

"I want to find out the truth about my parents, but what are you planning to find about...what was that entity's name again?"

"Medusa," he supplied darkly. "Anu Medusa. Although she's only referred to as A. Medusa in almost all of the documentation that connects her. She, or a conglomerate she controls, owns Zenn, one of many such companies in her portfolio. She also has majority stake in several biotech and genetic engineering research facilities."

"Everything we've been dealing with as a race, we Dark Ones and our allies, points back to her. She's at the nexus of much chaos and destruction, most of which humans aren't yet aware. But I don't think her intention is to stay in the shadows for long. We need to stop her before she launches full-scale open war."

"Why is she doing this?" It seemed a logical question to ask.

Devlin shook his head. "I've researched my race's histories meticulously. The last time there loomed such a threat was the Great War between my Kind and the Pure Ones, a race similar to mine but also different in many ways. There are many of the same patterns today as there was millennia ago. But whereas the Great War started because the Pure Ones rose up to fight for their freedom from Dark Ones' rule, what Medusa is stirring is sinister. Evil."

Devlin took a deep breath and let it out slowly.

"I've seen it first hand, this evil. The world has known quite a few dictators in the last few centuries. It's a voracious, unqualified greed for power. It's about domination and fear. We have to stop her."

Grace briefly reflected with awe on the strange, surreal universe she'd landed herself in by associating with Devlin. Even if they parted ways in the future, she'd never look at the world the same way again.

Mythical monsters, legendary heroes, vampires and shadow demons apparently did exist. It was a lot to take in for a human woman who liked to manage her life just so.

"I knew I had to help you," she said simply. "I could tell you're one of the good guys."

He quirked his lips. "Depends on whose perspective you take."

"From any perspective," she emphasized firmly.

He looked into her eyes with a small smile. "I don't think the humans whose blood and souls we sometimes take as fuel for our bodies would agree with that assessment."

"But you've taken my blood," she argued. "I don't feel any ill effects."

"Because I stopped when I needed to. Not all vampires would."

"That's why you're good, Devlin," she reasoned. "Whether you are a human or a vampire, or whatever else you might become in the future, you're always one of the good guys. Because you're you."

But was being good the same as being lovable? Devlin wondered. Where his family and his fiancée had been concerned, it hadn't paid to be good.

Or perhaps something was simply wrong with him, and that was why he was surrounded with, and attracted to, people who didn't—couldn't—love him.

"What are you thinking about?" She stared deeply into his eyes and seemed troubled by what she saw.

"It doesn't matter," he murmured, pulling her down to him for a heady kiss, trying to take his mind off of hurtful thoughts.

She responded readily, her body immediately aflame for him.

Ravenously, they made love. Then again slowly, losing themselves in a simmering pleasure that warmed them from the inside out.

At last they slept, limbs entwined, bodies joined. There were no hauntings from the past for Devlin this time. Only dreams of Grace.

But Grace...

Through her blood still unfurling inside his body, communicating with the blood inside her own, she saw everything.

All of his memories, pain and self-doubt. Including his ill-fated visit to the new Duchess of Devonshire in this very house.

June 1814. Devonshire House, London, England.

Devlin waited until her latest lover unhurriedly left, after performing his services in the Duchess's bed. Her chair, the Aubusson carpet, and back again in the bed.

This one was different from the one a few days ago. There had been four different men in the two weeks that Devlin had staked out the house, watching, assessing, deciding.

But William never visited the Duchess's chambers.

It had been a month since his return from the Continent, since the end of the Peninsula War. He'd continued to collect intelligence for the English after his...rebirth, never revealing his identity. His efforts had helped the Allied forces rout Napoleon in a decisive victory at the battle of Toulouse and the capture of Paris.

He'd discovered new powers as a vampire in the process, including an eidetic memory, only more precise.

He'd always had a good memory and was able to store an inordinate amount of knowledge in his insatiable mind. But now he recalled with perfect detail everything he saw—faces, words, pictures, places. Even symbols and languages he didn't understand.

He supposed this was what the Greek had meant when he said that Devlin would take on some version of his Gift.

He'd debated coming back to England. There was nothing for him here. The old Duke, his father, had died in a hunting accident a year after his own "death." William was now the Duke, Lavinia his Duchess. Devlin wanted nothing to do with either of them. Not revenge, not justice. Nothing.

And yet here he was, lurking behind Lavinia's sitting room door, with an unobstructed view to her bedroom and everything—everyone—in it.

She was now sitting at her vanity, brushing out the tangles in her long, golden curls. Her lady's maid always made herself scarce when she knew her mistress was entertaining, so Lavinia tended to her own toilette this night.

She was more beautiful than ever. Even after giving birth, not once but twice.

An heir and a spare were already ensconced in the nursery, keeping the nurse and housemaids busy.

Ironically, the heir looked nothing like his father, instead taking solely after his mother, all golden curls and big green eyes. The spare didn't look like William either, though if one didn't look too closely and the boy was camouflaged by shadows, one could perhaps make a tenuous connection. In full sunlight, the boy's brown hair had fiery undertones and his fine, delicate features had no trace of William in them.

He looked rather a lot like lover number three.

William didn't seem to care. He and Lavinia treated each other with cool regard. They kept up all the social graces and dined together always for breakfast. During which half hour words were seldom exchanged.

William then went off to his Clubs and Parliament, the races and his mistress's apartment not three blocks from the house, and Lavinia went off to shopping, paying social calls, rides with ardent beaus in the latest chariots. The most recent trend tended toward cabriolets, a special import from France, now that the war was over.

In the evenings, they might attend some of the same amusements, but usually arrived separately and hardly even greeted one another at the same party. For the most part, they lived entirely separate lives and seemed content to keep it that way.

At least, there seemed to be no seething resentment or overt disdain. They each seemed satisfied with their part of the partnership.

They each got what they wanted: William, the title, all its wealth and privileges, and the most beautiful and coveted woman in England as his wife; Lavinia, the title, wealth and privileges, an undemanding husband and continuing reign as Queen of the Season and Belle of the Ball.

Her parties at Devonshire House were famous for their elaborateness and flair, not only in England but on the Continent as well.

Without fully realizing what he did, Devlin quietly approached Lavinia, edging across the darkened room where the candlelight from her vanity and bedside table did not touch.

He was not three feet behind her to the right, his dark clothes blending in with the dark colors of the velvet draperies half drawn over the beveled glass French doors of her balcony.

"Lavinia."

Her name was but a whisper, but she stopped her brushing and lowered her hand. Her eyes slid to a corner of her vanity mirror and unerringly met his gaze in the near darkness of her chamber.

"Are you a ghost attempting to haunt me?"

Her voice was calm and low. She did not seem surprised to see a man in her bedroom who was supposed to be dead.

Whom she'd urged others to murder.

"I have no interest in haunting you," Devlin answered, taking one step closer to the flickering candlelight, revealing more of himself to her unblinking perusal.

"Since I am no ghost."

She took him in leisurely from top to bottom, an appreciative glint entering her eyes as she did so.

"No, I can see that you're not," she murmured silkily. "What is it you want then, pray tell?"

"Why did you do it?" Devlin got straight to the heart of his misery. "Why did you and William do it?"

With a flick of his hand he threw the two incriminating letters on the carpet at her feet.

Slowly, she reached for them, and just as leisurely, she took them to the low-burning fire in the grate opposite her bed and tossed them inside, without reading the contents. The letters quickly disappeared in the flames as if they'd never existed.

"You made me wait," she answered finally, turning to face him. "I am not a patient woman. It took me the better part of a year to land you and then you went off to that stupid war and made me waste the best time of my youth waiting for a soldier who might never return."

Her volume increased as she spoke, the frisson of anger in her tone building quickly into rage.

"Do you know how many proposals I turned down while I waited that first year? And all anyone wanted to talk about was my heroic, dashing soldier of a fiancé. Who risked all to fight for his country, his love.*" Her emphasis on the last word could only be termed as derisive.*

"You were the heir to a Dukedom! You were supposed to behave like one! But no, I understood from your letters all your misguided notions of saving your country and duty and blah blah blah."

She turned away, and her voice quieted again.

"And I realized that I'd made a terrible mistake. You were as strange and awkward as people said you were. You didn't behave as a normal man should. But I was taken in by your beauty, so perfect and bright. I wanted it."

She could have been speaking of the latest Parisian fashions, Devlin realized, her tone was just as covetous and detached, as if she were talking of possessing a thing instead of a flesh-and-blood man.

"But I could have never controlled you," she continued, still facing away from him. "You had all these righteous ideals. You probably expected faithfulness in marriage when it's simply an alliance, a business arrangement. You were already doubting me, I could tell. Doubting what we had together. You would have found a way to cry off our engagement when you came back from the front. If you came back."

She turned so suddenly and fired without warning that even Devlin's honed reflexes couldn't avoid the bullet that embedded itself in the muscle and sinew of his upper chest, near his left shoulder.

The impact and shock of being shot made him stagger a step backwards, but he remained standing, otherwise unmoved.

He didn't even flinch at the searing pain.

Lavinia lowered her smoking pistol and regarded her handy work. She'd always been a crack shot. It was one of her less feminine pursuits that made her all the rage with the young bucks.

"Hmm," she mused, unperturbed by the sight of blood welling from his wound through his clothes, seeping down his arm, and dripping into the expensive carpet.

"I missed. A couple of inches lower and it would have gone straight into your heart. I guess you really aren't a ghost. What are you?"

Devlin didn't answer. Words deserted him.

This was the woman he'd thought he loved? This was the woman he'd made love to for the first time?

Heartless. Capricious. Deceitful. Egotistical and selfish. Cold-blooded. Ruthless.

Yet loved by half of the men in England. The fame of her beauty, wit and passion even made it across the Channel.

Devlin was numb with grief. For the lonely, pitiable, stupid boy he used to be. How could he have been so blind?

"Are you planning to bleed to death—again—on my bedroom floor?" she asked emotionlessly. "What do you want, Dev? It's too late to retake the Dukedom. You have no power here."

Footsteps could be heard rushing up the grand staircase. Heavy and many.

"It's probably the footmen," she said nonchalantly, "alerted by the shot. So what do you intend to do? You can't win, Devlin. I will never give up what is mine."

"Then enjoy it, Lavinia," he rasped, taking a step back toward the French doors. "You and William deserve each other."

When the footmen could be heard outside her bedroom door and Lavinia rushed over to open it, Devlin deftly slipped out onto the balcony, leapt off it to the manicured grounds two stories below and disappeared into the darkness.

He never saw Lavinia and his brother again. He left England that very night, on a ship bound for the Colonies.

When he finally holed himself up in one of the tight quarters below deck, he dug out the bullet from his flesh with a knife. But before the ruptured skin could start knitting together again, he rubbed sea salt into the wound, clenching his jaw at the blazing agony. The skin puckered angrily as the salt rendered the damaged tissues extremely hypertonic, curling the edges instead of mending across the gap.

But his body did eventually heal, leaving behind an ugly scar that he would carry with him for the rest of his existence as a reminder of his folly: he trusted too easily, loved too readily. Even a family that had always spurned him.

He would never make the same mistake again.

Chapter Sixteen

Grace woke up in the middle of the afternoon with dried tears on her cheeks, caking her eyelashes.

She remembered every bit of the dream she had—no, Devlin's *memories* that she saw, as if she'd lived through them herself in his place.

All of it.

How did he bear it? So much betrayal and hurt. How could he still be so good? So noble? Grace didn't think she could survive as he had. He even had the strength to open his heart again.

He'd told her he loved her.

Grace didn't know what love was, but she was certain about one thing: she wasn't worthy of this beautiful, gentle, courageous male. After everything he'd been through, he deserved a woman who could love him back wholeheartedly and faithfully.

Eternally.

Grace could manage faithful—what woman in their right mind would stray when she had Devlin in her bed? But wholeheartedly and eternally Grace had no way of promising.

She was human. She had at most seventy or so years left of her life, maybe forty or fifty of them physically productive if her health held up.

She had a computer processor for a brain and a blood-pumping muscle for a heart. Sentiment was something she found extremely elusive, bothersome and confounding.

How could she possibly give him what he deserved?

She knew her limitations well. She could barely recall loving her own parents, though she knew she had good memories. But for the most part they were blurry and fragmented, as if her feelings for them were encased in ice.

It didn't logically compute, Devlin being with her. If she ran the algorithm in her head a billion times, a billion to the exponential of ten, there was no logical scenario that would ever match someone like her with someone like him.

Devlin slept soundly, breathed deeply, his body wrapped around hers, his half-hard erection still thickly filling the covetous notch inside of her.

She noticed this about him during the day. He slept like the dead, oblivious to sounds and motion. She gently disengaged from him and went to the bathroom to wash her face. She stared at her reflection in the mirror over the sink, water dripping down her chin.

You don't deserve him, her reflection told her. *He needs much more than you could ever give.*

But I don't want to let him go, she told her reflection. *I want him more than anything in the world. And I don't recall ever wanting anything before.*

Her reflection glared disapprovingly back at her, silently condemning.

Grace sighed heavily and went back into the common area, got out her journal from her small carryon duffle and began to write.

*** *** *** ***

It took Grace and Devlin three hours to scope out the crystal-like tower that encapsulated Zenn's headquarters, sprouting like an alien obelisk in the middle of London's booming financial district.

While he'd slept, she prepared their digital employee badges and inserted them surreptitiously into Zenn's security system. Ever resourceful, truly Bond-like, Devlin then procured real badges for them to wear when they visited the building just after sunset.

The identities she created for them were those of IT security workers with the highest-level clearance, the sort who resolved difficult hardware and server issues, who had the access codes to all of Zenn's mainframes.

Still, they realized when they reached the central enclave at the top of the fifty-story skyscraper, the level where all the mainframes were stored, that they needed more than their badges and codes to access the tubular vault.

There were only two guards stationed with un-holstered semi-automatic rifles by the air-tight, steel-reinforced, bomb and fire-proof concrete doors.

They didn't blink an eye as Grace and Devlin appeared from the fiberglass capsule lift that opened to the vault entrance. Didn't so much as twitch as they made some half-baked excuses on why they were there and clumsily snooped around.

But Devlin had a feeling they'd react with instant, deadly force if he tried to break into the chamber.

They weren't human, that much he could tell. But he didn't know whether they were Pure or Dark. Their eyes were blank, and they never blinked, as if whatever consciousness that inhabited their bodies was remotely controlled.

It only took a few moments, but he saw immediately that the vault security clearance required retinal scans, five-fingered palm prints, as well as an access code that reset every five seconds.

He and Grace had a lot more homework to do before coming back here again.

The good news was, they had help. Jade Cicada would never send them off on such a critical mission (though they hadn't asked for her permission) without reinforcements.

Maximus was waiting for them in the formal sitting room of Devonshire House with Simca crouched comfortably at his feet, her long, whip-like tail swinging to and fro, when Devlin and Grace returned to their temporary base of operations.

"I hope this didn't take you out of your way?" Devlin said as he clasped forearms with the Chosen's Commander.

Maximus gave one brief shake of his head. "I was already in the vicinity, trying to track down a potential recruit."

"How do you manage to tote her around wherever you go?" Devlin inquired as he nodded a greeting to Maximus' feline companion, who merely eyed him with a bored look and a toothsome yawn.

"I have ways," was all the Commander said.

Devlin briskly introduced Grace, then wrapped an arm about her waist and pulled her tightly into his side, as if to declare: *mine*.

Maximus' mouth quirked in a rare half-smile of amusement.

"So this is the female who depleted your strength and made you boneless," he murmured and watched in fascination as Devlin's fair-skinned face and neck immediately went up in flames.

Grace, however, felt no embarrassment whatsoever.

"Oh, did Devlin tell you about the night we met? He performed exceptionally well. Would have kept going but I needed my rest," she said in his defense, lest his comrade was impugning her lover's virility.

As Devlin turned a brilliant, yet-undocumented shade of crimson, a low rumble of laughter rolled forth from Maximus' deep, broad chest.

"An honor to meet you, Grace Darling," the Commander said meaningfully.

Grace solemnly pumped the hand he extended.

"Did you manage to make contact with the recruit?" Devlin abruptly and desperately changed the focus of the conversation back to business.

"I did," Maximus replied, as they all headed up to the estate manager's quarters.

"He goes by the name Alend Ramses these days. Extremely ancient, older than me."

"That *is* ancient," Devlin quipped, "positively decrepit."

"Yet very much alive," Maximus noted. "The ancient power all but radiates from him. He is one of the few remaining True Bloods in existence."

"What are True Bloods?" Grace chimed in.

"Dark Ones born," Devlin answered. "Not made."

"Fascinating."

"And his answer?" Devlin asked of Maximus.

"He did not give one," the leader of the Chosen replied, thoughtful. "He merely thanked me for the invitation. I don't blame him if he refuses. He has been ruler of his own domain for thousands of years—literally. Why subjugate himself now to a vampire Queen who isn't even a True Blood? On a different continent?"

"I hope that wasn't your recruitment speech," Devlin winced.

"I gave him the gist of what we're fighting against," Maximus said. "He did not seem eager to participate in yet another war of the races, having gone through countless wars in his lifetime."

"Next time, let me do the recruiting," Devlin muttered. "Your charm needs polishing, Max."

Maximus slid the Hunter a look of pure annoyance. He hated being called Max and Devlin was the only member of the Chosen who had the gall to do it.

"Well, it's good timing that you're here," Devlin continued, unperturbed. "I've been going through the scenarios in my head on how best to break into Zenn's vault, and the most expedient, if most risky, one I can come up with is to just blow the doors clean off."

"We don't have weeks to waste on getting all the security protocols in place. And by then, A, Medusa might be alerted to our presence, or B, we might have to blow the doors off anyway as a contingency plan. Might as well cut to the chase."

"I can round up the ammunition," Maximus agreed. He was the Yoda of explosives.

"I was hoping you'd say that." Devlin gestured for the Commander to sit before a laptop displaying the 3D blueprints of Zenn's secure vault where the mainframes were kept.

For the next couple of hours while the two males plotted, Grace slept fitfully in the back of the room.

Fitfully, because she was afraid of having to live through Devlin's memories again, and because she was haunted by her own misgivings about their future together.

It was all happening so fast. By this time tomorrow night, she might learn the truth about her parents' deaths, and Devlin would hopefully obtain critical information to help win the war against Medusa.

And then?

Logically, Grace knew that the best way to break an addiction was to remove oneself from temptation.

The pain of quitting cold turkey might be brutal, but it was healthier in the long run.

*** *** *** ***

Back in New York City, Sophia had an unexpected visitor in her little nook at the MET.

Not the mysterious Mr. Enlil, but someone she knew and was quite thrilled to see again.

"Ere," she breathed as she stood from her desk and rushed to him, stopping just shy of wrapping him in a bear hug.

No matter how happy she was to see him, they did not have that kind of a relationship.

Or any relationship at all, for that matter, except perhaps in some of her girlish fantasies when she was too frustrated with Dalair.

For the most part, she considered him a close acquaintance, perhaps a friend. And though she'd grown accustomed to his striking beauty and poise, she was still just a little in awe of him.

"I was in town for a couple of days and looked up my old friend Mr. Sims," Ere said as he smiled down at Sophia from his superior height, a simmering warmth in his eyes.

"He mentioned that he's taken on a sort of an apprentice to help put the Persian exhibition together."

Ere swept Sophia from head to toe admiringly. "And here you are, Sophia Victoria St. James. As lovely as ever."

Sophia practically glowed at her ex-teaching assistant's compliment. But she was two years older and wiser now, and did not become nonplussed at his easy flirtation.

"You look as hot as ever yourself," she shot back, not trying to be coy but simply stating the truth. "What have you been up to?"

"Oh, this and that," he replied, which wasn't really much by way of an answer, but it was his usual style. Not revealing much about himself, even though he'd invited her into his home and entertained her there for hours when she'd helped him with his research.

"Mostly up to no good," he said this with a disarming grin, flashing brilliant white teeth bracketed by deep dimples on each side of his generous lips.

"I doubt that," Sophia said, shaking her head. "You might pretend to be a baddie, Ere, but I can tell you're really one of the good guys."

Abruptly, his smile collapsed and his eyes darkened. It was only a moment, but Sophia saw the bleak, almost frightening expression on his face, and something cold and sinister in his black, black eyes.

But just as quickly, he smiled again, this time more reservedly, as if the smile was a fragile thing that his lips had trouble propping up.

"How can you tell, little Sophia?" he murmured, and Sophia had the bizarre impression that Red Riding Hood might have heard the same silky voice when confronted with the Big Bad Wolf.

"Can you see into the hearts of monsters?"

Perplexed by his question, Sophia just answered the first thing that came to mind, "I don't see monsters, Ere. Just...souls."

She shrugged at the nonsense she was spouting, for nonsense it must be for a "normal" person like Ere.

But then again, she'd always sensed that there was something different about Ere.

"Some are pure, some are troubled. Some are lost, some are confused. Some are whole and deeply fulfilled. Those are the most beautiful souls—the ones who found their place in life and the partners to share it with."

She huffed a small laugh. "You must think I'm the strangest girl you've ever met," she admitted.

He regarded her intensely for one long moment, and then the easy-going demeanor was back.

Like a mask he conveniently slipped in place.

"I think you're charming, lovely Sophia," he murmured.

"But I must be going." He took a breath and briskly surveyed her work room. "I just came by to say hello. It's been ages since we've seen each other, has it not?"

She nodded. "We never did get to have that dance."

The last time they were supposed to meet up had been over a year ago at an exclusive night club Ere had recommended.

It was also one of the rare occasions she'd seen Dalair.

"Perhaps next time we can visit a dessert shop instead," he proposed. "I know a particular place in Brooklyn that's quite the treasure trove for all kinds of treats."

"You aren't talking of Dark Dreams, by any chance?" she inquired, amazed at the coincidence.

"That's the one," he concurred.

He hesitated briefly, but then said, "Perhaps we can bring that little man sitting in the alcove just outside, the blonde one with the curly hair that I passed. He looks like he favors desserts and treasure hunts."

As an afterthought, Ere added, "He says he's protecting you. Probably from the likes of me. What a fierce warrior heart he has."

Did Ere like children? It seemed rather sudden to invite a boy he didn't know on an outing with her, Sophia thought. But then, maybe he was trying to downplay the outing so she wouldn't confuse it with a date.

He always flirted with her, and there was a time in the beginning that he could make her blush with just a look, but he also seemed quite diligent in the avoidance of any real attachment.

"You mean Benji?"

Inanna was on Sophia's guard duty today and brought Benjamin with her to the MET to pass the time. The boy could spend days in a museum this size without getting bored. He was fascinated by all things of antiquity.

"I'll have to check with his parents, but sure, I think he'd like that," Sophia replied. "He loves history, by the way, so I'm sure he'll love you. How many PhDs do you have on ancient civilizations again?"

But Ere seemed to have frozen at something she'd said. There was that darkness and bleakness in his eyes again.

"More than I need," he managed to rasp in response.

At the sound of approaching footsteps, most likely Inanna's, Ere turned abruptly and walked away.

"I'll contact you," he called out over his shoulder before disappearing down the dimly lit corridor.

Sophia didn't even have the chance to say goodbye.

Shortly, Inanna appeared at the door to Sophia's makeshift office, Benji at her side.

"Did you have a visitor?" the ex-Chosen inquired. "I did not want to intrude, but I wasn't sure whether you were safe."

Inanna and Gabriel had never guarded a human before. And not just that, but the human incarnation of the long-awaited Pure Queen. They weren't yet familiar with how to best balance between being protector and friend. And as Sophia had no powers beyond recognizing Pure souls and minimal fighting skills, it was always a gamble to give her too much privacy.

Sophia shook her head. "He's an acquaintance of mine, I'd like to think a friend as well. He was the teaching assistant for one of my classes my Freshman year."

And then she added irrelevantly: "Dalair doesn't like him."

"But you do?"

Sophia looked down the corridor where Ere had gone.

"Yes," she admitted. "I do like him. I wish we were truly friends."

Perhaps then, she could help dispel the darkness she sensed within him, eating away at the edges, sometimes even engulfing the incandescent orange flames of his soul.

*** *** *** ***

It was midnight when Maximus and Simca, Devlin and Grace entered Zenn's headquarters through a service tunnel a couple of levels beneath the tower.

On their seventy-five second ride to the top floor in the small, fiberglass capsule lift that shot through the center of the building, the two vampire warriors readied their weapons while Simca poised in a powerful crouch, her long rope of a tail lying still and tensed behind her, like a sword drawn.

Grace knew her role and position well within this deadly quartet: always stay in the middle so that she was well protected and concentrate only on cracking the security firewalls once they had access to the mainframes. She was to ignore everything she heard and anything she caught out of the corner of her eyes while she worked.

After all, Maximus had reasoned earlier, seeing and hearing her party get cut down or killed wouldn't affect her own situation in any way. If they died, she wouldn't be able to outrun her foes. If they lived, then everything was going to work out just fine. Distracting her attention away from breaking the codes would only slow them down.

It was all quite logical, Grace would be the first to admit. But Maximus could really work on his pep talks.

By the time she took a few deep breaths, they had arrived.

But when the clear glass door of the lift slid open, an empty corridor greeted them.

Maximus slid Devlin a meaningful look, one that said, "I don't like this."

Neither did Devlin. It had "trap" written all over it.

But they were here, and they had a job to do. So they set the explosives quickly and retreated back into the protective capsule as the charges went off in a thunderous blast and a blaze of flames that quickly died down around the fire-retardant concrete and steel.

With an ominous groan, the heavy four-feet-thick door creaked open just slightly.

Maximus led the way and secured the perimeter, ushering Devlin and Grace inside the vault while he and Simca remained on guard by the door.

At a nod from Devlin, Grace immediately got down to business. She found the central mainframe almost at once; she recognized it from the blueprints. Taking her tech equipment out of her hard-cased brief, she plugged in the necessary wires and routers.

Mainframes were quite archaic in this day and age, and certainly strange to find in the hottest new tech startup in town. Most companies nowadays used server farms and Cloud services, no physical location for their technology infrastructure needed.

But Zenn was in a sense ingenious to still use a mainframe. Hacking into it would require an understanding of old programming languages that were all but extinct today, like Latin or even more obscure—Sumerian cuneiform.

Fortunately, where technology was concerned, Grace was fluent in all languages, dead or alive. Within minutes, she found the files she was searching for and began the decryption process.

"We have company."

It was the only warning Devlin gave.

As instructed, Grace merely gave a nod that she'd heard and didn't even look to see what was happening, continuing to concentrate on her hacking.

Dimly, she was aware that he'd left the vault to fight alongside Maximus and Simca. Distantly, she heard the sounds of battle, the clash of metal against metal, low grunts and muffled moans, mixed in occasionally with a panther's growl.

Grace single-mindedly focused on her task and successfully infiltrated the security gateways, breaking into the files and unlocking them.

The first file Devlin had flagged appeared to be some sort of list. It had hundreds of names, both anglicized and in their original language, many of which were symbols Grace didn't recognize. There were numbers next to the names, like serial numbers, but with a distinct logic to them.

Dates? Grace thought. Dates indicating when people were born or when they lived or died?

And finally there were locations. Not addresses but coordinates. Longitudes and latitudes that sometimes varied as she scanned through the information, indicating that these were live traces, updating with each person's movement.

After downloading the decrypted file, she moved on to the second of Devlin's flagged files, the one about her parents.

A loud thud crashed against the door of the vault. The fighting grew closer, as if one or more of their enemies had entered the chamber.

Grace paid them no mind. Some part of her understood that her life was very much at risk, that if their enemies had entered the vault, then her protectors were losing ground, possibly heavily injured. Some deeply buried part of her recognized that Devlin might have suffered grave wounds; she instinctively knew that he'd die before he let the attackers near her.

But Grace's cold logic and powerful processor of a brain quickly computed what Maximus had told her before. It was pointless to worry; there was nothing she could do to help the fight. She could only complete the task before her, a task none of the others had the skills to accomplish.

So she ignored the gruesome sounds and splatters of blood that flicked upon her person, one particularly long-traveling clot of gore hitting her directly on the side of the face.

Yes! She unlocked the second file and scanned the information as it downloaded into her disc.

Images and words flew past her eyes so fast she could barely absorb them, even with her almost inhuman speed in deciphering information.

Images like her parents going to work for Zenn's parent company. Their busy lives as cutting-edge IT professionals.

Her birth and their over-the-moon happiness. The family routine they settled into to accommodate her demand on their time and attention, especially since the private and public schools didn't work out.

Picnics at the park, rides on a carrousel, trips to the beach. Getting her a pair of goldfish and a chinchilla that they made a home for in their basement.

Grace involuntarily gasped. Someone had documented so many of her family's private moments with photographs. Snaps of moments in time she herself didn't recall.

Until now.

All the memories she'd submerged her whole adult life came rushing back. She was so overwhelmed by them she could barely continue scanning.

The battle drew ever closer. Something swooshed through the air inches above her head. A sword perhaps. She couldn't tell and didn't look.

A heel backed into her thigh as she knelt in front of the mainframe. A pained grunt overhead. And then the fighting was pushed back toward the entrance of the vault.

She continued absorbing the file's information as it downloaded to her disc.

Her parents being assigned to a special project. The initial foundations of Zenn that they developed. Their accidental discovery of the fact that they were being watched, along with unspecified information about the company's owner, A. Medusa.

The day her parents left for work and prepared her favorite breakfast on the kitchen table. Their return that evening at the usual time.

The shadow that descended upon them when they were upstairs changing out of their work suits. The shadow driving off in their car.

The police visit to the house the next day. Grace's brief incarceration with a top secret branch of the federal government.

Her aunt Maria picking her up to go live with her. Her first session with Dr. Weisman. A call from Zenn's HR to fill out an online application...

Just as the file finished downloading, Grace was gripped by the arm and jerked to her feet.

"Time to go."

Chapter Seventeen

It was Devlin.

He was dragging her out of the vault at a limp. He all but threw her into the capsule lift before making a dive for it himself.

The fiberglass doors shut just as two vampires pounded upon it with their fists and daggers, hissing and baring their fangs as the foursome descended rapidly down the tower.

For seventy-five seconds, there was only gusts of rapid breathing in the lift. Grace quickly saw that both Devlin and Maximus were injured. Even Simca had a few bloody streaks marring her sleek black coat.

"There must be more of them waiting," Maximus said grimly.

"Roger that," Devlin rasped, his chest still heaving.

"Simca, guard Grace," the Commander ordered his faithful feline.

A growl was all he got for reply. It didn't sound happy.

"Get back," Devlin bit out and pushed Grace behind them as they reached the lowest level and the capsule doors opened. He braced himself at the entrance.

But a battle was already taking place, Grace saw. A blur of black wielding a long, curved sword was at the center of the violent vortex. He moved so fast, Grace's wide eyes could barely track him.

"Would that be Ramses or another new friend you haven't told us about yet?" Devlin lobbed the question at Maximus, unsheathing two long daggers, readying to enter the fray.

"His timing is impeccable," the Commander replied, pulling a pair of sharp-pronged tridents from out of nowhere.

And with that, the three warriors (for Grace had started to think of Simca as a full member of her band of protectors) leapt into action, picking off their enemies one by one, though the newcomer called Ramses looked to be holding his own just fine even before they joined in.

With the odds reduced from more than eight-to-one to now much healthier numbers, the bloody battle didn't last long. Within minutes, piles of black ashes littered the tunnel while the victors remained standing, though in Devlin's case, just barely.

Ramses wordlessly led them to a black SUV with tinted windows. Maximus got behind the wheel and floored the accelerator after they all climbed inside, Simca riding shotgun, Ramses, Devlin and Grace in the back, taking up two rows of seats facing each other.

"I have a private jet waiting," were the first words out of Ramses' mouth, "Follow the GPS."

Grace noted his unique, lilting accent and smoky voice. Middle Eastern? Egyptian? She couldn't quite place it.

"Impeccable timing and brilliantly resourceful," Maximus complimented, driving out of the tunnel beneath Zenn's HQ like a bullet.

"Does this mean you've decided to join us?"

Ramses shrugged eloquently. "Perhaps. We shall see."

He slid his light-colored gaze toward Grace and tipped his chin at Devlin's sprawled form across the backseat of the SUV, his head in Grace's lap.

"Your lover needs blood, human," he said softly, almost gently, as if he regretted pointing out that Devlin might in fact be dying in her arms at this very moment.

Grace began to panic. She hadn't realized how severely hurt Devlin was with the dizzying pace of the last ten minutes. Surely they hadn't been here for even that long. Everything was a blur it happened so fast.

"Break the skin of your wrist across his fangs and hold your vein to his mouth," Ramses quietly instructed, pulling Grace out of her frozen terror.

She did just that and wetly breathed a sigh of relief when Devlin sealed his mouth to her wrist unconsciously and began to draw upon her vein, rhythmically swallowing, his eyes remaining closed.

His body had curved around her, his arms holding her tight.

But not in an embrace of affection. No. It was the embrace of a predator with his prey.

"I will tell you when to stop feeding him," Ramses said conversationally. "He will not know in his current state."

"Thank you," Grace felt obliged to say.

The Dark warrior didn't change his expression, but Grace thought he looked amused.

What he did was retrieve a thick, well-used cloth from the inside fold of his Asian-styled tunic and began to methodically wipe it across his curved sword, balanced across his knees.

"What is it called?" Grace asked, both because she was curious and to distract herself from Devlin's feeding upon her wrist.

A part of her wanted to take her arm away, the part that valued her life and sensed the imminent risk she faced. Another part of her wanted him to take every last drop, because that's what her purpose was. To provide this male the sustenance he needed to be well.

"Scimitar," Ramses answered. "Do you know what it is?"

"I think I've seen it wielded by mummies in... well... *The Mummy*," Grace said. "You know, the movie."

Ramses didn't respond, but she thought his amusement deepened.

"Why don't you—the lot of you—fight with guns?" The thought just occurred to Grace.

She'd been witness to two life-and-death battles now and none of the vampires or shadow assassins had fought with guns. They only used sharp objects and their own bodies as weapons.

"Bullets don't deter the older warriors," Ramses explained. "We're faster, stronger and more resistant to simple puncture wounds. The only way to kill a vampire is to sever his head or puncture his heart so deeply, cutting through the aorta, that it won't have time to heal."

"You'd have to shoot several rounds of bullets through the heart in the split second that a vampire will be still to receive them in the hopes of severing his aorta. Blades are far more precise, and you're close enough to your target to make sure you're doing the job right."

"Besides," he added, "gunshots are hard to disguise, especially with bullets powerful enough to explode the heart or head for quick kills. Whereas, blades are quiet. You could be decapitated and not ever hear it coming."

"Fascinating," Grace murmured and was thankful she wasn't squeamish about blood and gore.

"Your lover held his own admirably despite being newly made," Ramses commented.

"Why do you keep saying that?" Grace asked. "How do you know he's my lover?"

A low chuckle rumbled through Ramses' chest.

"I can scent it on your skin and his," he said. "A vampire marks his Mate when he Bonds."

"I'm not his 'Mate,'" Grace argued. "I mean, we're just together for the time being."

As if he heard her, Devlin's grip on her wrist tightened painfully and he deepened the penetration of his fangs.

Grace tried not to jerk at the burning sensation. Her arm was going to be black and blue when this was over.

"Are you sure about that?" Ramses countered. "Your lover seems to think differently."

Grace abruptly switched topics. "How can you say a two hundred thirty year-old vampire is 'newly made'?"

"My Kind has been around for tens of thousands of years. Perhaps even longer. There are some who have lived that long. By contrast, he is a veritable infant."

Ramses nodded toward Devlin.

"Like I said, he held his own remarkably."

"How old are you?" Grace inquired bluntly, never one for social diplomacy.

Ramses' lips quirked. "Old enough."

"You're quite remarkable yourself, human," this he said with a glint of respect in his eyes. "You don't seem phased by any of this."

"I'm not normal," she stated factually.

"Thank the Dark Goddess for that."

Then he said, "It's time to stop."

Grace tried to pull herself away gently, but Devlin only latched on stronger, curling his limbs around her, holding her tight despite his weakened state.

"He will take too much," Ramses warned and leaned forward as if getting ready to forcibly pry Devlin from her.

"Wait," Grace stayed him with a hand.

She dropped her head to Devlin's and whispered in his ear, "Devlin, it's time to let go. You can have more later. Right now, you're hurting me. Let go."

Ramses registered surprise as Devlin obeyed, gently disengaging his fangs from Grace's vein and licking the puncture wounds closed. Still passed out, he pulled Grace's torso close and nuzzled his face in her lap, exhaling deeply.

"He truly loves you," Ramses murmured, his voice thick with an unnamed emotion.

"I know," was all Grace said.

*** *** *** ***

They arrived back at the Cove by early morning the next day.

Devlin would probably wake up feeling chagrined again for having been carried by Maximus to and fro and finally settled in the healing chamber upon their return.

Her blood had been enough to pull him back from death's door, but not enough to accelerate his healing.

Grace learned on the plane ride over that only Blooded Mates of vampires could provide enough sustenance to recharge a severely wounded Dark One fully in a short period of time. And one could only become a Blooded Mate if one was of the same race.

Well, that ruled Grace out. She wasn't sure how she felt about that.

Something else she learned on the return trip was that only True Bloods, Dark Ones born, could turn a human into a vampire, and they'd lose a part of their soul in the process. Too many turnings would lead eventually to madness and death, for a splintered soul was never content, always striving to leave the body in search of wholeness once again.

The only exception was the sharing of souls between a Dark One and his Mate. Each would take a part of the other within them, and together, they remained whole, inextricably and eternally tied to one another. If ever one were to break the bond, death or madness could result, depending on the strength and depth of the union.

For this reason, vampires seldom chose to Mate. More often, they opted for a rogue's path—a solitary, lonely, selfish existence. On occasion a few vampires might form temporary hordes, like wolf packs. And rarely, large, sophisticated vampire hives were built, with a queen at its center.

One such powerful Hive belonged to the New England Dark Queen, Jade Cicada, the exquisite Asian beauty Grace had met briefly without even knowing who she was.

It was all terribly mind boggling for Grace, who could mentally grasp the concept of vampires, because stranger things occurred in the natural world. And she'd *seen* them with her own eyes. Touched, held and had scorching sex with one in particular. Aliens, too, definitely existed. It was just that humans hadn't found a way to either identify or make contact with them.

But things created by the human imagination to explain away that which were difficult to describe, like magic, destiny... souls—Grace didn't believe in the existence of souls. Even less than the notion that the heart was more than a muscle, a complex, blood-pumping organ that powered the body.

Therefore, she couldn't understand why anyone would ever choose to tie themselves irrevocably to a Mate. It wasn't logical, given the risks.

Not that it mattered where Devlin and herself were concerned. It was more than clear to her by now that they didn't belong together.

On the seven hour flight from London to New York she sat in a corner alone with Devlin, holding his head loosely in her lap, taking the entire rear of the private jet for themselves, while Maximus and Ramses sometimes conversed in low tones in front and Simca washed herself meticulously with her sandpaper tongue before stretching out for a cat nap on a row of buttery leather seats.

Grace used the time to mull over in detail everything she'd learned in the past few weeks, especially the past twenty-four hours.

Her mind flicked through the events she saw in her parents' file, triggering long-buried memories from her childhood. A knack for all things technology seemed to have run in the family, for both her parents had been just like her. Brilliant with codes, awkward with each other and their only child. But even so, they'd all fit together seamlessly. They'd understood one another and...

And loved one another.

Unconsciously, tears leaked from the corners of Grace's eyes.

Surprised, she wiped them away on her fingers and stared incomprehensibly at the wetness.

She never cried. The last time she felt tears was just the other night when she'd lived through Devlin's past. But that had to do with his pain, not hers.

Though some part of herself realized unwillingly that perhaps they were one and the same.

She hadn't cried when the police came to tell her that her parents had died. She hadn't cried or so much as rebelled when the government had come to take her into custody. She'd been dry-eyed and numb when her aunt Maria had taken her to visit her parents' graves.

Once humans died, there was nothing left. Their bodies decomposed into the earth again or turned to ashes if cremated. Why would she cry for something that would eventually happen to everyone?

Except.

Her parents had *loved* her. They'd lost a lot of time that could have been spent together had they lived to the end of their natural lives. Grace would have had two people who completely and unconditionally understood her, cared for her. It was somehow terribly important to be understood.

And she'd loved them in her own strange way. She couldn't explain it. She simply knew it.

She finally knew it.

Maximus had carried Devlin directly to the healing chamber and allowed Grace to remain with him, while he and Ramses went to debrief the New England Dark Queen.

She now sat beside Devlin's extremely comfortable-looking mechanical bed, holding one of his hands in hers.

It was like déjà vu. She wondered how many more of these exact same experiences she'd have if she stayed with him.

She'd had a lot of time to think. A lot of time to decide.

Just as she got up from her chair, releasing Devlin's hand, Anastasia entered the chamber.

"How is he?" the Chosen asked softly, concern for her comrade evident in her tone.

"He's still in his physical form and his body is intact, so he should make a full recovery," Grace echoed almost word for word what the other female had said to her before.

She realized now that the casual way Anastasia had spoken was intended to make Grace less afraid for Devlin, just as Grace did this time around.

A ghost of a smile appeared on Anastasia's curvaceous lips.

Looking at the warrior before her, Grace wondered why Devlin didn't choose to love someone like her. So fiercely beautiful and loyal. Obviously competent in martial arts, as everyone seemed to be in the so-called "Chosen" guard of the vampire queen.

"Why haven't you and Devlin ever gotten together?" Grace blurted out exactly what her mind currently chewed upon.

"Or have you?"

"No need to challenge me with that lethal stare, human," the vampire said, vastly amused.

Grace didn't know she was staring at the Chosen in any particular way, but at her words, she tried to force her expression into blankness.

"Just because we work and fight together doesn't mean we can't control ourselves from humping each other's bones. The same goes for all the other Chosen. Surely humans are not that different."

"But..." Grace tried to find the right words. "You're beautiful. He's beautiful. You probably respect and like each other. Don't you feel an attraction?"

Anastasia shrugged, leaning one hip against a table.

"Perhaps, when strangers first meet, and all you see is a healthy, red-blooded male or female in their prime. But very quickly you get a sense of what they're like on the inside."

She nodded toward Devlin, slumbering peacefully on his bed.

"This one is old-school. He is extremely private, even with those of us who've known him almost as long as he's been a vampire. He's closest to Takamura, whom you haven't met. But I'd wager none of us knows the full truth of his history. Not that we sit around divulging our deepest secrets, mind you. Devlin has always been the friendliest but also the most aloof within our group."

Grace knew his history. All of it. Did that somehow make her special? But he'd told her he loved her before her dream.

Why did he love her? She couldn't understand it.

Her parents' love, Aunt Maria's love, she could sort of comprehend. They were family. Devlin, on the other hand, he could be with anyone he wanted. Why would he choose her?

She walked to the chamber door and opened it to leave.

Anastasia stayed her with a hand on her arm.

"You're not waiting until he wakes?" The Chosen sounded surprised, and a disapproving frown lined her brow.

Grace shook her head. "I have things to do," she said without further explanation.

"Give this to him when he's up." She handed the Chosen her red notebook. "And tell him not to look for me."

Anastasia took it with now open consternation. "You're leaving him?"

"Yes," Grace replied without emotion. "A human can't remain with a vampire. It's against reason."

"But—"

Grace didn't wait for Anastasia to object further. She simply walked out of the healing chamber, down the long, unmarked corridor that took her to the private elevator tucked secretly within the core of the Chrysler building and stepped inside.

The elevator automatically descended, carrying her away from the Cove.

Grace didn't looked back.

*** *** *** ***

They have the list.

The Creature communicated telepathically with its Mistress, wondering whether she was very put out. She must have known already.

She always knew. Sometimes it wondered whether she planned it all. The setbacks they'd encountered over the past couple of years.

This recent one was mammoth-sized. Not only did the Pure and Dark Ones have the list of targets, they also destroyed Zenn's central mainframes, which brought the whole company to its knees.

One of Zenn's functions was to help spread the fight club networks through viral digital media using secured, untraceable data bundles. Now, not only was the technology backbone of Zenn broken, they'd also lost the ingenious architect behind it all—Grace Darling.

Moreover, Grace was more than just the digital architect. At times, the Mistress, through one of her minions, instructed Grace to work on "special projects," such as covering the fight club networks' tracks, hacking into secure government and other entities' databases, creating and falsifying records, finding the elusive whereabouts of the warriors on the list. They had other cyber geniuses at their disposal, but Grace was the best.

The Mistress remained silent over the brainwaves. Brooding? Plotting?

Probably plotting. She never seemed phased by setbacks and obstacles.

We failed to acquire Alend Ramses before he chose to join Jade Cicada's elite guard. He put up much more of a challenge than we anticipated.

You must anticipate better, child, she finally deigned to speak to him.

The Creature didn't mistake her reference to it as an endearment. She called it that to remind it its place. To remind it that it had a lot to learn. That it would never outgrow her reach and influence.

Ramses should never be underestimated, she continued. *He is very old and very powerful. One of the few remaining True Bloods.*

Older even than you, Mistress?

It was probably foolhardy to ask her such a private question, the Creature was aware. But sometimes, its curiosity got the better of it.

She ignored its inquiry, as she quite often did, saying instead, *He would make a formidable Consort for the Dark Queen.*

I doubt she has that role in mind for him, the Creature gently but firmly dissented. It had on good authority that Jade Cicada was enamored of another male entirely, none other than the Pure Ones' Consul Seth Tremaine.

Then she's a fool, the Mistress hissed. *And the advantage will be to us.*

She was fantastically brilliant whenever she plotted, but where the heart was involved, the Mistress had a tendency to miscalculate.

What should we do about the list? The Creature redirected their conversation to the original point.

Their enemies now knew who they were targeting to join their ranks. Its eyes and ears on the ground revealed that the Chosen Commander, Maximus, was already contacting every Dark One on the list and Seth Tremaine was doing the same with the Pure Ones.

The warriors both Pure and Dark that were on the list were already incredibly difficult to bring in when they didn't know they were being targeted. Now that they were forewarned...the Creature had its work cut out.

Get more creative, was all the Mistress said, her tone dismissive. She might as well have said instead, "Why do you bother me with such trifles."

The Creature decided to switch topics.

What do you want to do about the General?

Tal-Telal was never alone. His daughter or her Mate was always with him, else they were all within the unbreachable walls of the Shield, the Pure Ones' base. This did not mean that it was impossible to recapture him if it tried, but it would rather not make the attempt if the Mistress had other ideas.

Leave him, she issued the order, confirming its suspicions. *He will lead me straight to the one I truly desire. And then he will return to my bosom, where he belongs.*

The Creature gave a delicate shudder.

The Mistress's bosom might be one of the finest belonging to a female of any race, but the heart that beat within it was that of a monster.

*** *** *** ***

Devlin was groggy and weak when he first regained consciousness.

Damn.

Flat on his back in the healing chamber again. No recollection of how he got there. Must have been carried by Maximus, or worse, that newcomer Ramses. What a great way to establish oneself in the pecking order of the Chosen warriors.

Involuntarily, his hands felt around beside him for a familiar touch. When his seeking fingers found no mate, he forcibly peeled his eyelids apart and struggled to a sitting position.

Slowly, he scanned the interior of the healing chamber with a hazy gaze. Finally, it landed on a female form sitting cross-legged in a chaise lounge against one wall.

"She's not here," Anastasia greeted him with those inauspicious words.

"Where is she?" His voice was gravelly and it hurt his throat to speak. Guess that was what struggling out of the jaws of death did to a male.

"Gone," the Chosen said, not unsympathetically.

A blast of cold hurtled through him, freezing him from the inside out.

"She left this for you."

Anastasia got up lithely and came to Devlin's bedside. In her outstretched hand was some sort of a journal, bound by sturdy red leather.

Mission accomplished, Anastasia left the chamber without another word, though Devlin barely noticed her departure.

He rubbed his eyes and blinked hard, trying to dispel the last vestiges of slumber. With some trepidation, he turned the notebook to the first page.

Grace's handwriting reflected her personality quite accurately: neat, concise, minimalistic. It could have been typed it was so perfect.

A strange sort of panic welled inside of Devlin. It could mean anything that she wasn't here when he awoke, leaving instead her journal. She was never without her journal, he argued with himself; therefore, she must mean to come back soon to retrieve it.

But the almost pitying look Anastasia had given him warned him not to have high hopes.

The first few pages of the journal were mostly stream of consciousness, categorization of everyday things and activities. Mostly nouns and verbs, factual, to the point.

Then she started writing about the new pets she'd gotten for herself under his persuasion. She described the ever-changing colors of Antony and Cleopatra's scales, Miu-Miu's baby-soft fur and hypnotic black eyes. She wrote about Aunt Maria's hugs and her visits to the orphanage in Brooklyn where her aunt worked most days.

A third of the way through, she documented how they'd met for the first time and described in explicit, excruciating, triple-X-rated detail his smell, his scent, his voice, his body. With particular emphasis on the circumference, length, feel and taste of his reproductive organs.

And what she did with them, how they made her feel, and what she planned to do with them next.

Devlin jerked his head up and hastily looked around as if questioning the absoluteness of his privacy in the healing chamber.

The room was wired for sound and visual, and he feared he might have made a few gurgled noises as he read. Certainly his face was volcanic in its temperature and he didn't have to look in a mirror to know that it gave new definition to the color vermillion.

For the next fifty pages or so, the ant-like writing continued to march in orderly, almost cheerful fashion, from line to line, documenting in words everything he and Grace did in the two nights of marathon orgy. Devlin was so turned on, he was in danger of ejaculating right there in the mechanical bed, in the dirty, bloodied clothes he'd worn fighting ancient vampire assassins two nights ago.

She went on to describe from her point of view the life-changing events she experienced over the last few weeks. Though she used plenty of adjectives and adverbs as her writing grew more vivid, she still shied away from voicing her emotions.

As he began to grasp her thought process more intimately, he realized that she didn't lack for emotions. To the contrary, her factual, logical words all but thumped with feeling, like a raw heart beating, naked and vulnerable.

On the last page of the journal, she wrote:

"A human and a vampire cannot be together. It goes against reason. It would be conducive to my peace of mind to accept this truth."

Ruthlessly, in block letters she wrote next, "There. I accept. It's time to move on. The End."

Numb and barely breathing, Devlin closed the journal and lay back against the pillows. He felt like he'd been shot.

Again.

This time fatally through the heart.

Chapter Eighteen

The next night, Devlin left the healing chamber on his own two feet, spurning any assistance offered.

He'd been jacked up to countless bags of blood for two nights straight, but his body seemed to reject further attempts at healing. Some bones were still broken, and the internal bleeding still trickled, but this was as well as he was going to be until he got his head—and especially heart—screwed back in place.

The safe, frozen place before he met Grace Darling.

It seemed that Alend Ramses was making himself at home in the Cove. He'd conferred with the queen, pledged his allegiance and shared unstintingly everything he knew about the names on the list they'd retrieved from Zenn's HQ. Turned out, he knew quite a bit, having met many of the targeted Pure and Dark warriors over the millennia of his long existence.

Even Maximus was impressed.

Thus, he decided to join their small band of warriors, the New England Dark Queen's royal guard. The Chosen.

He'd already arranged for a total overhaul and remodel of Simone Lafayette's old quarters, making them his own.

Queen Jade bestowed the formal title of "the Sage" upon him, as wisest among the Chosen, probably because amongst the group of them, Ramses had lived the longest. Especially now that they no longer counted Inanna amongst their number, though they still considered her an ally.

Well, Devlin was certainly not a contender for that title. Maybe after another two-hundred and thirty years—make that double—he might have enough sense to love more wisely.

As in, never to fall in love again.

He entered his own chamber and tugged off his soiled clothes, moving by rote with little conscious thought. After a long hot shower, during which he was assaulted by memories of the last time he'd been here, who he'd been with, and what they'd done under the hot sprays, he determinedly dammed the flood of emotions before they could render him a bawling, demented mess on his mosaic tiled floor.

Nude, he absently rubbed a towel haphazardly through his hair and went to the carrier lift by his door to order something to eat.

Every convenience was delivered at the touch of a button or voice command within the Cove. It was so convenient, in fact, that Devlin decided to remain a rent-free tenant here rather than secure lodgings of his own elsewhere, despite his need for privacy.

Dirty laundry could be sent down the lift; clean, ironed and precisely folded clothes came back. Anything he wanted to watch on any channel on the planet or live stream through the Internet, he could throw up on the wall-sized screen that lowered in front of his bed.

And if he wanted to hone his cooking skills, there were three five-hundred-square-feet modern chef's kitchens on different levels within the Cove. Olympic-sized pools, massive martial arts training centers, a weapons hall large enough to outfit an entire army and countless private suites for "entertainment" were only a few of the perks that came with living at the Cove.

After all, vampires liked to live large.

Not Devlin though. Not tonight.

Or any night in the foreseeable future.

Whatever he ordered might taste like saw dust for all the appetite he had, but he wasn't going to lie down and die like he wanted to. He'd survived heartbreak and betrayal before. This was...

This was a lot worse. But he'd survive this too.

Before he entered his order in the touchscreen system, which gave him a complete menu of all the restaurants nearby, and farther away for that matter with a simple lookup display, the sliding door of the lift opened smoothly.

Inside was a large rectangular package wrapped in thick brown paper, tied with a string. Tucked within the confines of the string was a small sealed envelope.

Devlin regularly received deliveries through the mail, all sent up to him through the lift.

He was an avid online shopper, especially for men's fashion and tech gadgets. Once in a while he ordered a one-of-a-kind antique dagger or a specced out stiletto, his weapons of choice, but he was nowhere as prolific in the acquisition of those sorts of things as Anastasia.

Books, one of his guilty pleasures, he liked to pick up in person. He hadn't ordered anything in the past few weeks.

As he carefully unwrapped the package, he discovered that it was indeed a book that lay inside.

Could it be?

Devlin gingerly took the volume out and examined the outside from cover to spine to cover.

The *First Folio* of William Shakespeare's plays, compiled originally by John Heminges and Henry Condell, Shakespeare's fellow actors in the King's Men.

There were only a few copies left, most of which were held by various museums. Three were privately owned, and though Devlin had tried in the past to acquire one, their owners adamantly refused to sell. At a minimum, the book in his hands was worth several million dollars.

Setting the book gingerly on his built-in desk, he turned to the sealed envelope next. With much less care, he tore open the envelope and unfolded a small piece of quality stationery.

It was a letter. Written in a familiar ant-like regimented font.

Dear Devlin,

This is my first letter. I hope I'm doing it right. I hope you are healed.

I tried to see Dr. Weisman for an impromptu appointment. He was unavailable. But I did receive an email from him after I got home. He said that I am ready to graduate from writing to myself to writing to others. So here I am, writing to you.

Enclosed is my gift to you. Happy birthday.

I used almost all of my savings to procure it. (And I had to throw some other inducements in the bargain, not all of which are legal, so I won't be telling you about them. Suffice it to say my hacking skills came in handy). I hope it makes a good addition to your library, the upstairs one in the alcove.

Maybe one day you can read it out loud to me. I like listening to your voice. You could probably read an instruction manual and I'd still think it was sex wrapped in sin dipped in chocolate.

Look at that. I'm getting very proficient with my adjectives and descriptions.

Which reminds me—you can read it after we practice at least twelve chapters of the Kamasutra.

Sincerely,

Grace Darling

P.S. Don't come looking for me. I'm not ready yet.

What?!

Devlin rushed to his door and slammed it open, uncaring that he was still naked and wet from the shower, madly expecting to find Grace outside in the corridor, perhaps hiding against the wall, playing a prank on him.

No Grace to be found.

But Ramses and Maximus came into view as they strode around the corner. Both males paused mid-stride, their expressions equally blank, lips similarly twitching.

"Anything amiss, Devlin?" Maximus inquired solicitously.

Devlin slammed his door shut again and leaned against it, breathing rapidly.

What did this *mean*? Did she change her mind? Was she going to give them a chance after all? Why couldn't he go to her?

But she intended to see him again, surely. Her note implied as much. Was he supposed to wait idly until she was ready? How long would it take?

He was going insane with the endless questions buzzing like hornets in his head.

One thing was certain, however. Her words had reignited his appetite.

For food. For life. For just about anything.

With a whole lot of zest, he punched in the order for a medium-rare ribeye, a couple of lobster tails, roasted vegetables and chocolate lava cake for dessert.

It seemed that when he had hope to be reunited with the ultimate love of his life, his love of good food benefited as well.

*** *** *** ***

The next night, just as Devlin almost won the debate he had within himself to go after Grace, the lift door quietly opened again without ceremony.

Holding his breath with anticipation, Devlin approached the mechanical box like it was Aladdin's treasure trove.

Inside, another small envelope sat serenely, as if it weren't screaming the message "Open me! Open me!" to Devlin's certifiably giddy mind.

With none-too-steady fingers, he carefully tore the envelope open and retrieved the folded paper inside.

An Ode to Devlin Sinclair:
I tried to write a sonnet first,
But realized I lacked the skills,
So I tried instead to construct a verse,
That required a lot less frills.
It's actually not that difficult,
If you write a program with rhymes,
But making the words meaningful,
Was what stumped me many times.
What I feel is hard to say,
When I haven't the words to say them,
I think and dream about you everyday,
You'd blush at my thoughts to see them.
I don't know how to describe the feelings
That you stir within me with a look,
A touch, a whisper that sets me reeling
Emotions too infinite to confine in a book.
What I want to say, at last, is this:
My one, my only, my beating heart,
I may not know what love is,
But I know I never want to be apart—
For in your arms I taste true freedom,
My spirit, mind and heart unite,
Soaring through the heavens of our own private kingdom
Always with you, my love, my brightest light.
By Grace Darling
P.S. This is my first and likely only attempt at poetry, so don't laugh.

P.P.S. I'm still not ready. I'll come find you when I am.

Oh, Devlin was definitely laughing.

And then he was crying.

And then he was some strange combination of both, clutching the paper tight to his chest as he slid down against the door to his polished floors.

Oh God, she *loved* him! She truly loved him!

Maybe one day she'd actually say the words, but no male could possibly be as happy as he was right this moment, right now.

He took a shuddering breath and closed his eyes, leaning bonelessly against his chamber door. His heart beat so fast and so vigorously, he was surprised it hadn't pounded out of his chest by now.

So she wanted him to wait for her. Until she was ready to see him.

He'd wait as long as she required. But he wished and hoped and prayed she'd come to him soon.

He needed her so much. Loved her endlessly. And his patience was wearing threadbare thin. His body practically screamed to be inside of hers, his fangs quivering to penetrate her vein.

A loopy, drunken grin curled his lips from end to end.

She was *wooing* him.

Gifts. Letters. Love poems.

For a woman who claimed she didn't understand love, she was certainly doing a bang up job being meltingly romantic, as Devlin could attest from his sprawled position on the floor, too heady with joy to move.

Finally, he stood up and climbed the ladder to his alcove, letter in hand. There, settled comfortably in the plush pillows and thick sheepskin fleece, he read and reread the poem to his heart's content.

*** *** *** ***

Two nights later, Estelle Martin made her way slowly back from the Little Flower Orphanage.

She was weary to her bones and felt every bit as old as the false human body she wore.

She needed blood.

There had been several opportunities to take it over the past few weeks. Her shop, Dark Dreams, received all sorts of random visitors, including ones who stayed well into the night. Who perhaps felt a bit lonely, a bit lost.

They were perfect prey for a thirsty vampire under the guise of a non-threatening, comforting old lady. Each and every one of these vulnerable, needy humans would have Consented to give their blood. She could have taken her fill while enveloping them in warm, motherly hugs.

But the blood of humans, weak and diluted, would never satisfy her.

Not now, when she'd been reawakened by *him*.

Estelle stumbled in her stride, staggering from the sudden blast of raw lust and hunger that enflamed her. She leaned her shoulder against the wall of an office building to her right, taking deep breaths to calm herself.

Dark Goddess above, how she craved him again. Needed him. Wanted him.

And hated him anew for so effortlessly setting ablaze the serene, deadened pool of her psyche, the frozen tundra of her soul.

It had been thousands of years since she'd felt this way, overwhelmed and helpless, a slave to his every gesture and word, every look and touch.

He'd extended his hand to her that day. She would have lost all sense and control of herself if she had grasped it.

She squared her shoulders and continued walking, putting one foot in front of the other, willing her old lady's body to carry on.

He should be grateful that she'd controlled herself that day.

When she had been young, innocent and ignorant, she would have thrown herself at him, professed her undying love and passion and meant every word she said to the depth of her unblemished heart and soul.

Had she caught his hand this time, she would have dragged him into her lair no matter the onlookers and torn him apart.

She would have taken her fill of him—his blood, his body, his sex—until there was not a drop of him left. So thoroughly used, a wrung-out rag would have had more substance.

And then she would have discarded him without a care. Because he meant absolutely nothing to her. Just meat to devour, bones to spit out.

She told herself this great whale of a lie as she entered Dark Dreams from the back door, which led directly to her windowless private quarters.

And froze.

She scented it immediately, that familiar heady musk of sandalwood, sunlight, morning dew and warm, male skin.

Her old woman's knees almost buckled with the dizzying, immediate shot of lust that electrified her whole body.

No, she couldn't blame her human disguise for her reaction, for involuntarily, she'd already shifted into her true form, fangs extended and dripping with saliva.

"You should not have come here," she hissed into the darkness of the unlit room.

He did not reply, simply breathing evenly, seemingly unaffected by the sexual hunger that was all but eating her alive.

Just like the old days.

A fearsome dark rage surged through her blood, mingling with and polluting her lust. Dark Goddess help her, but she wanted to *hurt* him. Savage him. Drive him to his knees.

Make him feel even an ounce of the pain she'd carried inside of her for millennia.

Her vampire eyes quickly adjusted to the darkness and homed in on the motionless form sitting on her full-size bed tucked into a notch in the wall, encapsulated on three sides by brick.

His blind eyes were open and turned in her direction.

Even though she'd realized that day that he'd visited her shop that he couldn't see, right now it felt like he saw everything.

How badly she was shaking all over, like a leaf desperately clinging to its branch under the assault of gusty winter winds. How her body burned from the inside out, her blood clamoring for his, her fangs aching to penetrate him.

Anywhere. Everywhere. She would take *everything*.

"Last and final warning," she heard herself growl in an unrecognizable voice, deep and guttural.

"There will be no mercy."

His opaque turquoise eyes glistened with something bright and fragile. A sadness and pain so deep and consuming she felt her heart breaking all over again.

No, no, no, she berated herself. She would not fall into that old trap. She was far from innocent now, far wiser to the world. She would not be affected by him, not ever again.

As if he heard her unmitigated resolve, felt her steeling herself with icy indifference and vengeful intent, a shuddering breath left his chest in a long exhale.

"Then come and take me, *ana Ishtar*."

Oh Dark Goddess! His voice! His words!

My Star, he said.

Once upon a time she'd been his. Unreservedly and wholly his. She'd given him everything of herself; she'd wanted him for eternity.

But he had never been hers.

No, never hers.

She curled her lips back from her fangs and growled deep and low, the savagery of the sound resounding through the room.

And then she was upon him.

*** *** *** ***

That same night, Devlin pulled up a chair and sat in front of the magical, frustrating little lift, which hadn't produced any new notes for two whole days.

It might be childish to sit there staring at it as if doing so would make it pop out a letter or *something* from Grace, like a hen laid an egg, but Devlin couldn't concentrate on anything else anyway.

If she planned for him to wait years before she made an appearance, he feared he wasn't going to be a contributing member of society during that time.

The polite *beep* almost shot him to the ceiling he was so startled. He did manage to overturn his chair in his haste to leap to his feet. He dove for the lift and almost flung the door out of its rotating track to see what lay inside.

Nothing.

Disheartened and confused, Devlin shoved his fingers into his hair and pulled. He knew he didn't imagine that beep. Something definitely made a sound. What—

Beep.

There it was again. And he realized that it was the sound of his door bell.

His expectations effectively lowered by the disappointment of the lift, he pushed the button to unlock his door and put on a neutral demeanor, one he hoped projected equanimity and a full grasp of sanity.

"Hello, Devlin."

The slightly opened door revealed Inanna, known by her human alias as Nana Chastain, his old comrade in arms.

He tried to look glad to see her. And he was, really. He just wanted to see someone else more.

"How have you been, Inanna?" he asked with a smile, a little rusty on the charm, but it did curve his lips.

"I've been busy," she returned with a grin of her own, wide and blindingly bright.

"Shall we catch up over a nice bottle of wine?" Devlin suggested, getting ready to step out of his room. He never invited anyone into his chamber. Only Grace had ever been inside.

"Some other time," she said, her eyes twinkling at him, as if she was just bursting with a secret that wasn't hers to tell. "I have a more important engagement just now."

"Well," Devlin said, thinking it odd for her to suddenly appear and just as fast go, but he honestly didn't care enough to ponder the whys, "thanks for stopping by."

"I have a Blood Mate ritual to oversee," Inanna confided while continuing to eye him with a glint of conspiracy.

Devlin nodded. "Wouldn't want to keep you then."

"*Your* Blood Mate ritual, Devlin," she finally said, showing her exasperation.

"Pardon?"

And that was when his chamber door swung wider to reveal Grace Darling on the other side of it.

"Hello, Devlin."

Although, when she said it, it came out something like "Hewwo, Dewwin."

"Guh..." was all he could think to say as his eyes took in Grace's petite, typically disheveled form, her bushy eyebrows, curling eyelashes, wide mouth and clear, dark eyes.

"Will you marry—I mean—mate with me?"

She looked to Inanna to check if she'd said it right. Inanna merely smiled with encouragement.

She looked back at a still mute Devlin and took his hand in hers.

"Devlin Sinclair, I want to be with you forever. For richer or poorer, in sickness and in health."

She tilted her head a bit. "But vampires don't get sick, do they? Well, insert injuries in the place of sickness then. You lot seem to get injured plenty."

She straightened again and continued, "I vow here and now that there will only be you to sustain my life, nourish my soul, keep safe my heart. And I want to be that person for you too. So please be my Blooded Mate. I will have no other but you."

Inanna mouthed *good job* when Grace ended her little speech, filled with lisps that required concentration to interpret.

And that was when Devlin noticed.

"You have fangs."

Grace prodded the sharp edge of one with her finger.

"Neat, aren't they? I haven't figured out how to speak normally with them in my mouth yet. I asked Inanna to turn me into a vampire so that I could marry—I mean—mate with you. Now you have to say yes."

"For Goddess sake, Devlin," Inanna chided, "don't keep us in suspense."

But Devlin was still stuck on the part where Grace asked his ex-comrade to turn her into a vampire.

"You Turned her?" he asked her, stupefied. "You... you would do that?"

"I did do that," Inanna confirmed. "Your Grace is very convincing with her logic. She planned it all out meticulously. I don't know how she found me, but she just showed up on my doorstep the other day at our temporary lodgings. She explained who she was and why she was there and what she wanted from me in particular."

"Only a True Blood can turn a human into a vampire. A Mated True Blood could do so with diminished risk to their immortal soul since their Mate would replenish the part they'd have to inject into the human they Turn. Over time, their soul is whole again."

"I figured it out based on what Ramses told me on the plane ride back to New York," Grace chimed in.

"The list of names we got from Zenn had Inanna's name on it too. I noticed that a few names were italicized and figured out that those are True Bloods, Inanna and Ramses among them. The names with asterisks, I still don't know what they represent, but we can sort that out later."

"I then hacked into the Cove's archives and retrieved information on Inanna, discovered that she was recently Mated, and then I formally asked Queen Jade's permission, because it's illegal to Turn humans, right? I explained that I was doing it so I could Mate you; I had a whole monologue prepared. She said since Inanna is no longer part of her Hive, and only half vampire, there's no need to ask her permission and... well, here we are."

"Guh," was all Devlin managed to eek out.

"You *are* mating me, aren't you?" Grace asked, a little less certain. "I don't think I'd enjoy being a vampire if I had to hunt humans every few days for blood. And even souls."

She gave a full-bodied shudder at the prospect.

"With my lack of charm, I'll probably never get their Consent. And then I'd either starve to death or break the Dark laws and have you hunt me down and put me out of my misery."

"Yes, I'll marry—I mean—mate with you," he finally blurted, roughly pulling her into his embrace, all but crushing her to him in his desperation to hold her, to make sense of what was happening, to, *please, God!* not wake up from this incredible, glorious dream.

"Well, walk this way children," Inanna said, for the first time inviting herself into Devlin's private quarters, not that he seemed to notice or care.

"Since you're both relatively newly made vampires, I doubt you know the technicalities of performing the rite that will form the Blooded Bond between you. This is where I come in. But be forewarned."

She shut the door and locked it, looking from one to the other.

"It's going to hurt. A lot."

Chapter Nineteen

It did hurt.

A lot.

Grace would rather not ever have to do that again.

Apparently, a similar procedure would be required to forcibly break the Blooded Bond in the event that one or both parties changed their minds about the whole mating thing. Though breaking the Bond did not necessarily result in freedom from the other half. Death or madness typically occurred.

Vampires were apparently not made for divorce.

But the pain was so worth it (except she really wished she'd asked for general anesthesia before it began). Because for the past twenty-four hours, Grace had been gorging on the blood, body and sex of her Mate.

She'd used him so well, he could barely move. His body was covered in blue and black bruises where she'd sank her sharp new fangs into thick, sweet veins and drank and licked and kissed and sucked to her little vampire heart's delight.

This was awesome!

She'd never felt so alive before. If she was a sensualist before, now she was a...*hedonist*. And her sole purpose in life was to make Devlin come inside her again and again and again.

Despite his wasted state, he seemed ridiculously happy and contented. In the first few hours, he'd murmured words of encouragement to take more of him, to drink her fill and milk him dry. Now he had no words. She feared he even struggled to breathe.

But his long-fingered hand still cradled her head gently as she moved down his torso to nuzzle his steel-ridged belly, dip her tongue into his shallow navel and inhale deeply the muskiest, heavenliest part of him.

"I love having fangs," she said through a slighter lisp. "My pleasure combinations just increased exponentially and the permutations we have together require a super computer to process, the number is so large."

His fingers lightly massaged her scalp in response.

"I've always wanted to do this," she whispered, staring cross-eyed at his glistening cock, so enthralled was she by the most gorgeous, masculine part of him.

Taking his aching, swollen staff in hand, she snuck an impish look at Devlin to gage how he was holding up.

He regarded her through slitted eyes, his lips peeled back to reveal his fangs. He might not have the strength for words, but that slumberous, heated look was enough.

It said: *Go ahead. Do what you will with me. I'm yours to take as you please. My body will keep giving as long as you want. Nothing is forbidden within our Bond.*

So she licked her lips with anticipation and focused on the thick, long, fabulously hard, pulsing erection in her hands.

Slowly, she licked just around the crown of him, where he was most sensitive and raw. She squeezed the turgid column rhythmically, in time with her lapping tongue, and a thin stream of pre-cum seeped out of its eye, adding to the wetness of her saliva, making her tight grip on him slick and hot, teasing her tongue for a fuller taste of him.

Mindlessly, he moaned, his brilliant blue eyes glittering through his slitted lids, another flush spreading across his chest and up his long, strong throat.

So she took the head of him in her mouth and suckled with perfect pressure, her hands continuing to squeeze up and down the pulsing column, as if his very heart beat here in the core of him.

His hand in her hair clawed into a fist, his hips beginning to grind and lift.

Still, she was in no hurry with her hard-won feast, peppering his sex with small kisses and bites, alternating with deep draws into her mouth and tight strokes with her fists.

"Please," he begged her, his voice deep and gravelly, filled with tortured pleasure and blissful pain.

Holding his glittering gaze, her own unblinking and victorious, she bared her fangs and slowly, painstakingly, agonizingly sank them into the thickest vein in his cock, making him feel her penetration one millimeter at a time— her absolute, total possession of him.

The flush exploded across his face as his blood and semen simultaneously erupted into her mouth. The flavor combination could only be described to Grace as ambrosia. Now that she'd tasted it, she knew she would be having this cocktail often and inexhaustibly.

Endlessly he came, and endlessly she suckled him, swallowing everything he gave her, milking him for more.

And then her empty core clamored for him too, so she disengaged her fangs and licked his wounds closed, then crawled up his body to straddle his hips, seating herself down upon his magnificent erection with one unerring undulation.

She laid her body upon his, chest to chest, and held his gaze as she moved slowly, voluptuously upon him, taking them both closer and closer to another climax, yet holding them there at the peak, drawing out their pleasure, making their release infinite and endless.

"I'm making love to you," she told him sleepily, drugged by the essence, feel and taste of him.

"Yes," he said, as if he were enslaved by her, as if it was the only answer he could give to any and every question she'd ever ask.

"I am claiming you as my very own," she stated with more strength in her voice, lest he mistook this act for just another marathon orgy with just another partner.

"Yes," he answered, his hands moving up to cup her face, his thumb stroking across her swollen lips.

She savagely bit that thumb and sucked it into her mouth, drawing on his blood.

Her hips moved faster and faster, taking him deeper and deeper, harder and harder, and he arched up to move with her, his buttocks clenching, his muscles tensing, his teeth bared as she hurled them over the edge.

She grasped his face in her hands too, as the shockwaves of their release coursed like lightning through their bodies, their blood, the throbbing, aching heat of their sex. She kissed him deeply as they came, greedily swallowing his tortured groan.

In the aftermath, they lay tangled together, still intimately joined.

"You slay me," he rasped, his beautiful smile at odds with the violence of his words.

"I love you," she said, staring unblinkingly into his eyes. "This is how I love."

His breath hitched and his smile spread wider, his sapphire blue eyes incandescent with joy.

"Then slay me again, my darling Grace," he entreated, nuzzling her throat, scratching the tender skin there with his fangs.

And she did.

Always.

Epilogue

Just when things are looking up—the fight club networks are under control, we've gotten a hold of an important list that might give us an edge over our enemies (or at least no longer two steps behind them), old friends pop up where you least expect them (I'm still waiting for Ere to contact me for that trip to Dark Dreams), loved ones are reunited—

Disaster strikes.

We left for the Shield in the pitch of night.

I'm not sure what happened. Someone, probably Inanna, roused me awake, told me to pack only essentials and be ready to leave immediately.

A violent thunderstorm raged outside. Rain was being hurled from the sky like liquid javelins. Lighting streaked in fiery veins and the thunder was so deafening and ominous, even I, who love thunderstorms, felt my heart restart a couple of times.

It was only when I got in their SUV that I saw Tal lying across the backseat, his whole body contorted as if in a seizure, his face etched in agony, his jaw all but breaking from how hard he was clenching his teeth.

The dark, long-sleeved shirt he wore was torn from the neck halfway down his chest, the gaping material showing raw wounds still oozing blood, claw marks, bite marks, as if he'd been attacked by a bear or a tiger.

Everywhere his skin was exposed, his veins stood out like tree roots, black and blue. His throat was tightly bandaged by several layers of gauze, but even so, I could see the dark red of his blood saturating the cloth, still seeping from unclosed puncture wounds.

Dear Goddess! I've never seen anyone so savaged before.

I couldn't help the tears that flowed down my face when I saw him—his pain and anguish were so tangible they were a living thing, shrouding him in darkness, almost as if he weren't here with us, as if he were trapped in his personal hell.

Before I could ask questions, Inanna said that she'd found him this way close to our apartment just as she was returning from an errand at the Cove. She didn't know any more than I did beyond that.

So the five of us set out for Boston at a furious speed, Gabriel driving without lights in the inky blackness of night. He must be gunning the engine to one hundred and twenty miles per hour on longer stretches of road.

We'll be back at the Shield very soon.

Perhaps Rain, our most experienced healer, can work some magic, though she no longer has the Gift she used to.

I understand, now, why it was so difficult for her to choose Valerius, her Eternal Mate: she's had to give up her powers of healing. Powers unique only to her, only one such Pure Healer since the beginning of our race it seems.

In times like these, still having her Gift might mean the difference between life and death for a valued friend, a beloved father, a noble warrior.

Inanna and Gabriel are speaking in low tones in an ancient language I've never heard before (and I'd recognize plenty given my field of interest). Benji is blessedly sleeping beside me, hugging his lamby blanket fiercely, his head in my lap.

At first I wanted to sit with Tal, to see if I could do anything for him, anything at all. But Inanna said that nothing could ease him, not in his current state. And he might lash out at me unconsciously through his pain.

I prayed to the Goddess, if she indeed exists, to comfort him, watch over him, at least lessen his torment if...

Well, I will not think of ifs. He will recover. He has to.

But…

Sometimes I wish I didn't have these natural linguistic skills. Because as I listen more to Inanna and Gabriel conversing, I'm starting to pick up the logic of their words.

I heard "accelerate," "a couple of days, maybe less," and the most dreaded word of all for the Pure race:

Decline.

Where a Pure One dies within thirty days for giving him or herself to the wrong person.

Sex, that is. Having sex with someone he loves but who doesn't love him, or love him enough, in return.

The Decline is irreversible and indescribably agonizing. And if I heard her right, Inanna said that Tal's condition is accelerated, that he doesn't even have thirty days, but two or less. Even if Rain were at her full power and still retained her Gift, I doubt she can save him if it's truly the Decline.

But I know who can.

The person to whom Tal gave himself.

If we could just find her… If she loves him back…

But even I, having only lived nineteen-going-on-twenty years, know that love cannot be pleaded with, nor wished for, nor forced.

Love can only be given of free will.

For Tal-Telal, I fear, the one he loves has given heartless, vengeful pain.

But please Goddess, please, please, *please*—not death.

I guess we'll find out within the next two days.

Author's Note

The history of many of my characters, despite being in a paranormal-fantasy contemporary series, are in fact real.

Part of my inspiration comes from making legendary figures in ancient and more recent history take on new lives and personas. While taking copious liberty with the facts, of course.

Devlin's history is based partly on the life of a real spy in Wellington's army during the Peninsula Wars. The Duke of Devonshire is a real duke, and Devonshire House sat right on Piccadilly and was famous for hosting elaborate social events and for being the center of London's political life. Unfortunately, after the 8th duke's death in 1908, Devonshire House passed to his nephew, who abandoned his expensive, unnecessary London mansion and consigned it for demolition.

So I moved my fictional Devonshire House into another currently standing grand mansion—the Apsley House, which belonged to the Duke of Wellington, who purchased it in 1817 and took over a decade to renovate it. Apsley House is open for visitors as an English Heritage Museum.

Excerpt from Book #5 *Pure Rapture*

Chapter One

"You should not have come here," she hissed into the darkness of the unlit room.

Tal turned his blind eyes in the direction of that soul-deep familiar voice, now filled not with love and warmth but icy vengeance and blazing fury.

Outside, a deafening crash of thunder harkened the onslaught of a deluge.

The rain came down so hard, like sheets of arrows from the heavens, that he heard it pound the roof, the sides of the building, the streets outside, even from within the thick concrete walls of her private quarters behind their brick façade. It appeared that the skies agreed with her mood.

No, it was not wise to have come here.

It was suicide to appear before her, when he knew, deep inside, that she had no love for him.

Not now. Not anymore.

A sharp, splintering pain seized his heart at this truth. For he had never ceased, not for one moment, to love her with his entire self, body and soul.

It hurt just to breathe the same air as her, sitting on her bed not three feet away from her, when all she pushed back at him with her very aura was hatred, bitterness and fury.

And now that he was here, only two things would happen if he stayed: she'd gorge her fill of his blood—he could sense her desperation and starvation before she even entered the door.

And she'd slake her lust upon his sex.

While he gave all of himself in return.

After all, when a vampire Mistress beckoned through her blood, calling for his, which even now was roiling through his veins to Serve her, feed her, quench her thirst, a Blood Slave had no choice but to obey her command.

A Blood Slave who loved his Mistress.

"Last and final warning," she growled, deep and guttural. "There will be no mercy."

He stared intensely in her direction, willing his sight to return.

There was so much he wanted to say, so much he wished he could communicate. But he knew that she could see none of his feelings, desires and dreams, just as he could see only endless darkness and pain.

A shuddering breath left his chest on a long exhale.

If this was all he could give her—the strength of his blood and seed, the vengeance she would wreck upon his flesh and bones—if this was what it took to obliterate her hatred, pull her back into the light, erase the stains he'd spilled upon her soul, then so be it.

He'd endured millennia of anguish and torment, ever hovering on the edge of death. If this was to be his end, at least he chose it.

Just as he'd chosen her so very long ago.

"Then come and take me, ana Ishtar," he invited, his voice deep with regret and sorrow, his heart open and bleeding.

She would hurt him, he knew. More than all the punishment he'd endured at the hands of the vampire who'd held him prisoner for thousands of years.

She would rip him apart.

Physically. Emotionally.

He would not survive it.

This would be his ultimate price for loving a Dark One. For daring to embrace the heavens' brightest star.

She curled her lips back from her fangs and growled deep and low, the savagery of the sound resounding through the room.

And then she was upon him.

*** *** *** ***

Other Books in the *Pure/ Dark Ones* series:

Book 1, *Pure Healing*

Book 2, *Dark Longing*

Book 3, *Dark Desires*

Book 5, *Pure Rapture*

Book 6, *Dark Redemption*

Book 6.5, *Pure Awakening*

Dear reader:

Thank you for reading *Dark Pleasures*. I hope you enjoyed reading it as much as I enjoyed writing it!

Please be sure to leave a review on Amazon, Goodreads and any other social book sharing site of your choice (a short one sentence of what you enjoyed about it will do, but feel free to expound!) I read every single one of my reader's reviews, and I endeavor to take your feedback to heart as I continue developing the series.

Would you like to join my trusted reader list? Read my next book before it publishes for Free! All you have to do is Mail to Aja James (megami771@yahoo.com), and I'll add you to the list of readers who are notified about upcoming books, excerpts, giveaways and promotions! And if you have burning questions about the Pure/ Dark Ones series, well, I just might answer them :)

Give me a shout! And happy reading!

Aja James

Glossary of Characters

Jade Cicada: Reigning Queen of the New England vampire hive. Known Gift(s): unclear.

The Chosen: Jade Cicada's personal guards and advisors.

> **Maximus Justus Copernicus:** The Commander. Leader of the Chosen. Known Gift(s): anticipating opponents' moves two or three steps in advance, the ability to see through the eyes of his familiar. Weapon of choice: varies, but often fights with familiar Simca.
>
> **Simca:** Maximus' familiar. A black panther that is an extension of Maxiums, who can see through her eyes wherever she goes, and feel what she feels.
>
> **Ryu Takamura:** The Assassin. Executes special, often covert missions for the Queen. Known Gift(s): to be seen. Weapon of choice: Ninja blade or *ninjaken*.
>
> **Devlin Sinclair:** The Hunter. Hunts down and eliminates vampire rogues. Ensure security of the New England hive's borders. Known Gift(s): photographic memory. Weapon of choice: varies, but usually a saber or gun.
>
> **Anastasia Zima:** The Phoenix. Jade's head of security, ensures safety of the Queen and assists Maximus with affairs of state. Known Gift(s): telekinesis. Weapon of choice: varies, as a lover and expert in all manner of weapons. Soft spot for daggers.

Inanna: The ex-Angel of Death or Angel of the New England vampire hive under Jade Cicada, used to be member of the Chosen. After discovering her Pure Soul as the daughter of a Pure and Dark One and having her Awakening, she is known as the Light Bringer. Human alias: Nana Chastain. Known Gift(s): the ability to see through any material and zoom in and out like a telescope or microscope. Weapon of choice: chained whip.

Gabriel D'Angelo: Inanna's Blooded Mate. Used to be known as Alad Da-an-nim, born a Pure One, died and reincarnated as a human. Turned into a vampire by Inanna but retains his Pure Soul. Gift(s): unknown, but is a skilled martial artist as a human and was one of the fiercest Pure warriors in ancient Akkad.

Benjamin Larkin D'Angelo: Inanna and Gabriel's adopted son.

Ava Monroe Takamura: Ryu's human wife and mate. Brilliant geneticist who developed and took a serum that makes her uniquely super-human, with the Pure Ones' ability to heal, the source of their eternal youth and apparent immortality.

Kane Takamura: Ryu and Ava's son.

Medusa: An unknown entity, presumably female, that appears to be the arch nemesis of the Pure and Dark Ones, as well as humans.

The Creature: an enemy of both the Pure and Dark Ones. Seems to be working with Medusa. Known Gift(s): the ability to transform into different humanoid shapes, some form of telepathy.

Sophia Victoria St. James: Queen of the Pure Ones. Known Gift(s): the ability to see Pure souls and the true intentions of all beings.

The Circlet: The Pure Queen's royal advisors. Part of the Dozen or Royal Zodiac.

> **Seth Tremaine:** The Consul. Handles the Pure Ones' diplomatic affairs. Talented negotiator. Known Gift(s): the ability to project a spiritual version of his physical self anytime, anywhere.

> **Ayelet Baltazar:** The Guardian. Main responsibility is to guide and educate the Pure Queen, caretaker and mother figure. Known Gift(s): the ability to feel and experience what others feel using a physical artifact of the individual; deep empathy.

> **Eveline Marceau:** The Seer: Records and interprets Pure Ones' potential future in the Zodiac Prophesies. Known Gift(s): spells.

> **Rain:** The Healer: Ensures the health and vitality of Pure Ones, especially members of the Royal Zodiac. Known Gift(s): ability to absorb pain and poison from severe wounds using the needles of her hair, called *zhen*.

The Elite: The Pure Queen's personal guards. Part of the Dozen or Royal Zodiac.

Valerius Marcus Ambrosius: The Protector. Hunt down rogue vampires who hurt humans. De facto Leader of the Elite given that the previous leader was killed. Known Gift(s): fast healing, beyond even the typical Pure Ones' ability to heal. Weapon of choice: Chained scythe.

Dalair Abd Amirah: The Paladin. Recruit humans and Pure Ones to their cause. Known Gift(s): hyper-developed senses. Weapon of choice: Twin Dragon Blades or two half-moon crescent blades that can be combined into a disc.

Tristan du Lac: The Champion. Historically, he is the first warrior to be dispatched against enemies in one-on-one combat. In modern times, he helps train human Chevaliers. Known Gift(s): none. Weapon of choice: Excalibur or long sword.

Aella: The Strategist. Plan all manner of defense and attack vs. enemies and threats. Known Gift(s): speed. Weapon of choice: three chakrams, which can link together and stiffen into a longer-range hand-to-hand weapon or be thrown individually.

Cloud Drako: The Valiant. Train Pure Ones and humans in combat. Known Gift(s): ability to exert strong compulsion on anyone who stares into his eyes. Weapon of choice: long spear.

Ere: Sophia's ex-teaching assistant.